Yu, Jennifer

Grief in the fourth dimension

GRIEF IN THE
FOURTH
DIMENSION

GRIEF IN THE FOURTH DIMENSION

JENNIFER YU

AMULET BOOKS • NEW YORK

Cataloging-in-Publication Data has been applied for and may be obtained from the Library of Congress.

ISBN 978-1-4197-6727-2

Text © 2024 Jennifer Yu
Book design by Micah Fleming

Published in 2024 by Amulet Books, an imprint of ABRAMS. All rights reserved. No portion of this book may be reproduced, stored in a retrieval system, or transmitted in any form or by any means, mechanical, electronic, photocopying, recording, or otherwise, without written permission from the publisher.

Printed and bound in U.S.A.
10 9 8 7 6 5 4 3 2 1

Amulet Books are available at special discounts when purchased in quantity for premiums and promotions as well as fundraising or educational use. Special editions can also be created to specification. For details, contact specialsales@abramsbooks.com or the address below.

Amulet Books® is a registered
trademark of Harry N. Abrams, Inc.

ABRAMS The Art of Books
195 Broadway, New York, NY 10007
abramsbooks.com

This book is dedicated to the many teachers who have indulged and encouraged my writing over the years. You all have shaped every word I write.

PART I / II

KENNY

1 | mom and dad

My mother doesn't cry at my funeral.

My father . . . well, he's crying enough for the both of them. His eyes are red; his face swelling. He keeps taking his handkerchief out of his jacket pocket, wiping his face, and then refolding it, as if he's not about to need it again in thirty seconds. The crowd warbles its way through "Amazing Grace," their voices echoing in unison off the walls of the half-empty community center, and neither of my parents sings a single note.

At the front of the room is a casket. Surrounding the casket are two sticks of incense and a photograph of a boy, ten years old, smiling up at the camera from behind a birthday cake. His lips are blue with frosting.

The boy, of course, is me.

Once, as research for a history paper, I spent half a day watching video footage from the funerals of various world leaders: crowded, elaborate affairs with hours of speeches and processionals thronged with people. The videos always made me feel bad for their families—standing huddled together in the maelstrom of grief, surrounded by strangers all claiming a piece of the deceased as their own.

It makes me grateful for the fact that the people here today are the people who matter, and not many more besides them. There's Iris, standing with Casey and

Filippo and the other Science Olympiad upperclassmen; Jianyu, clustered together in the front row with the rest of his family; and a few of the teachers that I had been close with, looking unmoored and uncertain outside of the classroom.

Afterward, at the reception, the attendees mill around my parents, radiating sympathy, saying things like "sorry for your loss" and "please let us know if there's anything we can do" and "we brought a pasta—we hope that's all right." My mom always manages a small smile, then she says, so many times I lose count:

"Thank you. We really appreciate your support. Kenny would have been glad to know you came."

Sometimes my dad nods. Sometimes he reaches for his handkerchief. Sometimes he doesn't react at all.

I want to tell him that everything is going to be OK. That he and my mom survived thirty-two years without me before I existed, and they can definitely survive another thirty-two years without me now that I'm gone. I want to tell him that there's going to come a time when he has to be strong for my mom the way she's being strong for him right now, offering up their thanks to strangers bringing condolences and casseroles like either could lessen their grief. I want to tell him that I'm sorry.

But I guess it's a little late for all that now.

2 | the room

The room has white walls and white floors and a high, sloping ceiling lined with skylights. I'd think of the skylights as a potential escape route if the room contained a ladder, or a table, or any furniture at all. But there's nothing except for the seventy-two-inch high-definition television recessed into one of the walls—the television currently playing my funeral.

Whoever put this room together really should have included a chair, I think, and I've barely had the thought before there's a little *pop* and a wooden stool, real basic, materializes in front of me. On the stool is a small piece of paper that's been folded into a tent, like the name tags we used to make out of notebook paper in middle school, and on the piece of paper, in big blocky letters that look hand-written, are the words:

ANY SPECIFICATIONS?

OK, cool. So I'm dead *and* I've gone crazy.

I want a sofa, I think, because if I'm going to be dead, and crazy, and trapped here forever, I might as well be comfortable, and then there's another popping noise and the stool turns into a sofa, centered perfectly in front of the television.

The sofa is an enormous L-shaped sectional, with tapered wooden legs and dark-blue upholstery. It's the kind of fancy that makes me think of the furniture catalogs my parents used to get in the mail when we were first opening the restaurant, which all had titles like *Amsterdam Showroom* and *Antique Galleria* and were filled with prices several digits away from being something we could afford. It's the kind of fancy that makes me feel like I shouldn't even be looking at this sofa, much less sitting on it.

I want something a little less pretentious, I think, because *pretentious* is the only word I can think of that makes expensive and classy sound like something you wouldn't want. Another *pop*. The piece of paper flutters to the floor, displaced by the transfiguration, and the enormous blue sectional is replaced with an equally enormous leather couch that looks ancient, with cracks running down the cushions and arms so worn that in places the leather is almost white.

Not leather, I think—the sofa is reupholstered in black fabric—*and maybe something smaller?* The *pop* this time is louder—more insistent, almost—like the room is getting annoyed with me.

Now I'm looking at a plain black recliner: big puffy cushions, no frills. It reminds me of the recliner in Iris's living room, which her dad used to sit in every night while watching the evening news. Except a couple of months ago, one of their cats decided the recliner belonged to her, and it wasn't long before the entire thing was covered in a thick layer of cat hair that never seemed to go away no matter how many times her dad tried to clean it. We used to call the cat Princess Moonlight because of the way she sat on that chair: like it was her throne, like the whole living room was her kingdom.

I can feel the lump rising in my throat as I picture Princess Moonlight, as I picture Iris. I can't believe I made it all the way through the funeral and now I'm going to lose my composure because of a *cat sitting on a recliner*, and then there's the loudest *pop* yet, and every inch of the chair is covered in a rash of tiny yellow smiley faces.

"You've got to be kidding me," I say, out loud, and then—*pop*—a piece of paper lands on my head.

PLEASE DON'T BE SAD, it says.

Then, almost immediately, there's another *pop*. This time I look up in anticipation, which turns out to be a mistake: The note hits me in the face. When I unfold it, it says:

PLEASE. LIFE REALLY ISN'T THAT SERIOUS.

Another *pop*.

OR DEATH, FOR THAT MATTER.

Pop.

OH, WELL, WHO AM I TO SAY. I SUPPOSE EVERYTHING IS EXACTLY AS SERIOUS AS YOU FEEL IT IS.

Pop. I'm starting to think that this is how I'm *actually* going to die, because clearly the first time didn't take: buried alive by hundreds of pounds of notebook paper. Which, come to think of it, is not unlike how I lived.

I'M SORRY. I DON'T MEAN TO TRIVIALIZE YOUR FEELINGS.

Pop.

BUT I KIND OF LIKE THE RECLINER DECORATED THIS WAY. DON'T YOU?

Pop.

IT'S ZANY.

"Where is this all *coming* from?" I say. I look up again, scanning the ceiling for a vent or chimney. But there's just the skylights and the haze beyond. Then I look around, scanning for—what, exactly? It's the same white floors, the same white walls, the same wide-screen television—though it seems someone has turned the TV off, because its screen is now black and lifeless. My gaze lands back where it started: the recliner, its legion of smiley faces, the pile of notebook paper starting to form at its feet.

Pop.

PLEASE SIT IN THE CHAIR. IT'S COMFORTABLE, LIKE YOU WANTED. AND IT'S CHEERFUL, LIKE YOU NEEDED. AND I SOURCED IT FROM ONE OF YELP'S MOST HIGHLY RATED BOUTIQUE FURNITURE STORES. SOMETIMES THIS SPECIFIC RECLINER HAS A WAIT LIST SEVERAL MONTHS LONG. WE'RE LUCKY THAT THE HOUSING MARKET HAS BEEN IN SUCH A SLUMP LATELY—THE HOOPS I USED TO HAVE TO JUMP THROUGH TO GET A CHAIR LIKE THIS; YOU CAN'T EVEN IMAGINE.

I sit in the chair, because it's the normal, polite thing to do, and being normal and polite feels like my only available defense against the insanity of the situation. The recliner is, in fact, quite comfortable. "Thank you," I say out loud. I'm expecting another note, but instead a heavy fleece blanket materializes on the left arm of the recliner. "Er, thanks again," I say. I am, come to think of it, very tired, and I'm just about to close my eyes and try to go to sleep—maybe for good this time, should I be so lucky—when Caroline Davison appears out of thin air in front of me.

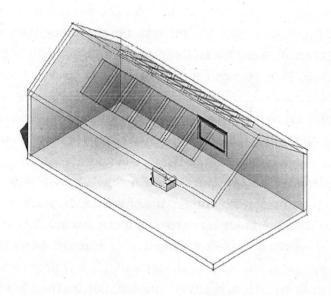

CAROLINE

3 | this is not how I thought I'd wake up this morning

Mrs. Macmillan, my art teacher, always says that in order to paint a scene, you need to understand the scene, and to understand the scene, you need to see the scene. Not just look at it—but really *see* it.

So here's the scene:

Empty room. Weirdly rectangular—maybe twenty-five by fifty feet, though it's hard to get a sense of the scale because it's so empty. Vaulted ceiling with rows of skylights on both sides of the center beam, beyond which there's a wash of white, like the blurry film of slowly moving clouds. No other light sources or fixtures. White drywall. Vinyl flooring. Big TV mounted onto one of the walls.

Oh, and then there's Kenny Zhou, lying in a recliner that's emblazoned with hundreds of tiny yellow smiley faces, underneath a blanket emblazoned with one very large yellow smiley face. Kenny is looking at me like *he's* the one who can't believe what *he's* seeing, which feels unfair, given 1) his choice of décor, and 2) the fact that he's been dead since winter break.

"Kenny?" I say.

Kenny blinks, doesn't respond. I guess I can't blame him, on account of the #2 of it all. Also, I figure that Kenny is a figment of my imagination, and I don't think we had interacted enough before his death for my imagination to be conjuring up realistic responses. I'm not sure I even remember what Kenny's voice sounded like. Mostly I knew Kenny because he appeared in the school newspaper every couple of weeks for winning some regional science competition or another, and also because sometimes the softball team wound up at his parents' restaurant after games.

"Principal Meyers did tell us everyone processes grief differently," I say. "Though this is oddly peaceful for a stress-induced fever dream."

"That's what you think this is?" Kenny says. His voice is deeper than I'd have guessed. "A stress-induced fever dream?"

"Either that or a really intense acid trip," I say, looking once more at the emoji chair. "But I'm not really in that crowd, so I'm going to go with fever dream."

"What's the last thing you remember?" Kenny asks.

"Well, yesterday I had softball practice," I say. "A bit of a disaster, really. We started late because Becca was flirting with Tyler at the lockers after last period instead of changing into her uniform, and then we finished late because Coach Navarro made the whole team run extra laps as punishment. And then in the locker room after practice, Maddie got into it with Becca because she had plans to meet up with Logan before dinner to 'work on their AP history project together,' which I'm pretty sure was code for—"

"What about after practice?" Kenny interrupts.

"I don't know, I must have gone home. What's the last thing *you* remember?"

Kenny takes a long time to think before he responds, like he's surprised I've turned the question around on him. Eventually, he says: "I was in my room. I had just finished my math homework."

"Oh, that's *right*," I say. "On my way home I called my parents to tell them I wasn't going to be home until after six, so they could go ahead and start dinner without me. That got me a lecture, even though it wasn't remotely my fault practice ran late."

"Did that have something to do with math homework?" Kenny asks.

"There wasn't a lot of traffic on Route 9, so I figured there was a chance I'd actually make it home on time and then they'd feel bad about giving me a hard time over the phone. But it was raining, and you know how drivers get when it's raining."

"I don't, actually," Kenny says. "I don't have my license."

"I was listening to this playlist Dom made me in an attempt to convince me that Yung Werther is the best musician of the twenty-first century, though frankly, I think I am less convinced now than I was when he started. Have you heard his latest album? It's just *noise*, I mean honestly. Anyway, by the time I got home, my parents—"

I frown.

"They must've been upset, because I had missed grace. Or maybe I managed to get home on time after all?"

"Caroline," Kenny says, and all of a sudden he goes very, very still.

I go back to softball practice, to walking to the parking lot with Maddie, to getting into my car and turning the key in the ignition. I try to retrace my way home: Route 9, a left on to Hengrove, a right on to Walden, the road ends in a cul-de-sac and we're in the brick house with a maple tree out front. Fourteen and a half minutes from start to finish. A drive I've done hundreds, maybe thousands of times.

"I don't think you got home on time," Kenny says, quietly, and then he slumps into the chair, and then, and I kid you not, the smiley face on his blanket turns upside down into a frown.

"No, I don't think so either," I say. "I spent like fifteen minutes stuck behind a Honda Odyssey."

"That's not what I meant," Kenny says. "I don't think—"

"Hengrove, Walden, Cottonwood Circle," I say. "So then I got home, and my parents were like—"

But I don't know what my parents were like. I can't remember.

I give it another shot, this time with my brother. "Cooper was probably a real jerk about it," I say, "because he'll take any opportunity to show me up. I remember the week after he made varsity as a freshman. Insufferable. And last night—last night—"

Kenny stands up out of his chair, looking panicked. His blanket falls to the floor. A bunch of scrap paper floats up into the air and then resettles, scattering around his feet.

"I don't think you got home, Caroline," Kenny says.

"Of course I got home," I say. But I'm back on Route 9 now, and this time I feel like I'm really remembering it: the steady patter of the rain, growing heavier and heavier; the steady pulse of the windshield wipers, drowning out Dom's playlist; somewhere, distantly, the screech of tires.

"There must have been an accident after Lake Street," I murmur. "You know how tricky that turn can be." My voice sounds distant, even to my own ears. I'm in the car, I'm squinting through the rain, I'm starving from practice, and I'm annoyed with whoever is driving this Honda Odyssey for going twenty miles per hour on a forty-five-mile-per-hour street.

"I don't drive," Kenny mumbles.

"It must have been bad," I say. "There were a lot of sirens . . ."

I trace the memory back one more time. This time, the Odyssey is washed in blue and red. The windshield wipers are still running, back and forth, back and forth, back and forth across my field of vision. I can see the wheel, but my hands aren't on it. I can hear the engine, but the car's not moving. Then—

"Oh my God," I say, and it's hitting me now, really hitting me: "Oh my God, Kenny, I think I'm *dead*."

And Kenny sinks back down into his insane recliner and says, "Yes, Caroline, that was the conclusion I had come to as well."

4 | dom

When Dom steps into Principal Meyers's office, Mom, Dad, and Cooper are already there, huddled around the desk in the center of the room. I used to go there all the time to drop things off for Principal Meyers from my mom—cookies, dinner invitations, one time a bunch of old stuffed animals that she thought his dog might like.

"What is this?" I say. I spin around, searching for some kind of explanation, but there's still just Kenny, reclining in his chair. "This can't be real."

Part of me can't believe I'm seeing them. Part of me will do anything so I never have to take my eyes off them again.

"Sometimes the TV shows us things," Kenny says.

"What things?" I say.

"I haven't figured that part out yet," Kenny says.

"But—" I start, and then fall silent as Dom's voice cuts through the room.

"What's going on?" Dom demands. "Where's Meyers?"

Dom doesn't have the same fond memories of the principal's office that I do.

"Elliot just wanted to give us some privacy," my mom says.

If this were any other situation, on any other day, hearing my mom call Principal Meyers "Elliot" would be by far the most bizarre thing happening right now. But it's not any other situation, and it's not any other day, and instead the most bizarre thing is how my mom looks: how exhausted, how frazzled, how unlike herself. My mom is the type of person who hosts the PTA's book club every month and always manages to procure tiny sandwiches and a fruit platter, even if they've switched the dates around at the last minute. She doesn't ever leave the house without putting on a high-SPF moisturizer, and I don't think she even owns a pair of sweatpants.

"Dominik," my dad says. "You might want to—"

"Please don't tell me to sit down," Dom says. "No one ever gets good news after they sit down."

That gets a laugh out of Cooper, though it doesn't sound very much like any other time I've heard my brother laugh.

"Dom," my mother says. "There was an accident two nights ago. As Caroline was driving home from softball practice. She was running late, and it was raining."

"Yeah, she texted me," Dom says. "After she finished practice, I mean—not while she was in the car. Caroline would never—she's one of the safest drivers I know. If there was an accident, if she's in trouble, it definitely wasn't her fault."

Dom's always been like this: quick to the trigger, especially when people he cares about are involved. One time word got out that Ian Miller called me a puck bunny and Cooper and I had to talk Dom out of starting a physical fight. Those types of reactions weren't fair or healthy, I told him, and it was insulting that he didn't think I could take care of myself. But right now his protectiveness makes me want to reach out through the screen and touch him. It makes me adore him so much that it hurts.

"It wasn't her fault," my mom says. "But yes, Dominik, there was an accident. We don't know all the details yet, but there should be a police report soon."

"A-police-report-Jesus-*Christ*," Dom says, all one breath. "Is she in the hospital? Can I see her?"

"She was taken to Bridgeport after the accident," my mom says. "But they transferred her to General Memorial last night because Bridgeport doesn't conduct—"

She cuts off, pressing her lips together so tightly that they start to go white. She's not wearing a trace of lipstick, not even the tinted balm I got her for her birthday, which she always keeps in her purse. Next to her, Cooper is crying. I haven't seen Cooper cry since he was eight years old. It's the kind of thing I would make fun of him for, if only I were around to make him feel better first. That's the sibling code, after all: You can tease each other all you want, but it has to come from a place of love.

"Bridgeport doesn't conduct autopsies," my dad finishes. His voice is totally flat, like he can strip the words of their meaning by saying them like they have none. "So Caroline is currently at a medical examiner's office. There will be a service next week."

"We wanted you to hear it from us, Dom," my dad says. "We know Caroline cared about you very much."

Dom sits down.

5 | eight, but none like that one

After the meeting, Dom goes to the hockey rink.

He runs through a routine I've watched him do hundreds of times: forward laps, backward laps, S steps, hockey stops. Eight months ago I wouldn't have been able to name a single one of these drills. Now I know which ones are done on the inside edge and which ones are done on the outside edge. I know Dom lets his weight fall to his heels when he turns too fast, and I can tell how winded he is by the shape of his stance.

Between practices and scrimmages and games, I had always thought that I spent a lot of time at the softball field—but it was nowhere near the amount of time Dom spent at the rink. Sometimes he'd head there after last period and run through drills for hours instead of going home, for no reason other than to "clear his head." Sometimes on the weekends he'd take his backpack and write his history papers or read English assignments while sitting in the stands, his class notes spread out on the bleachers around him. The rink was where he took me for our first date; it was where I found him after our first fight; it was where, four weeks and five dates later, he said, "Caroline, I want this to be a real thing," and I said, "Isn't it?"

Maddie and Becca had winced when I had told them we were official the next day, some combination of embarrassed at our cheesiness and disappointed in my taste in boys. "It's just," Maddie had said, eventually, "the whole good girl–bad boy thing never works out in real life the way it does in the movies. You do know that, right?"

Becca had tried to kick her under the table and kicked me instead. "Ouch," I said, and Maddie must have taken it as a response to her comment, because she added: "I'm sorry, Caroline. Everyone is saying it. But I'm your best friend, so I'm the one who's going to say it to your face."

Personally, I thought calling Dom a "bad boy" was both 1) a stretch, and 2) pretty generous. In the movies, bad boys were cool and charismatic. They wore leather jackets and always had impeccable hair, which was miraculous considering all the crazy debauchery they were supposedly getting up to in their free time. Dom, on the other hand, alternated between five T-shirts and pretty much lived in his letterman. He could be brusque, sure, and he wasn't one for small talk. But none of that was personal. "Army kid habits," he told me once: "No point making nice with people you aren't going to see again."

But in a town like Winterton, where everyone knew everyone else, outsiders didn't generally get the benefit of the doubt, especially if they weren't making nice. When Dom asked me out, what I was supposed to say was, "Oh my God, wow—I'm flattered, but I'm just not interested in dating anyone right now." Something courteous and tasteful and girly enough to be sort of cute but not so girly that it seemed ditzy, and something that definitely meant "no."

Instead what I said was, "You want to take me on a date to the skating rink? Novak, do you have any idea how many ice skating dates I've been on?"

"This'll be different," Dom said, and when I asked why, he smiled and said: "Because they can't skate the way I can."

He was right. No one could skate like Dom could. I remember sitting down in the middle of the face-off circle after about thirty minutes on the ice had worn me out and just watching him do laps around the rink: easy, effortless. I remember thinking that for once in my life I could be anyone I wanted to be, and Dom wouldn't even know that I wasn't being the right person.

"Skate the other way," I told him, "I'm getting dizzy."

Dom did a few laps in the other direction and then skated over to center ice. "We can do something else," he said. "I made a couple of backup plans, so—"

I stood up and kissed him. Then I lost my balance and brought both of us down to the ice.

"You're leaning too far in on your ankles," he said. "A lot of beginners do it. You have to learn to trust your legs."

"Shut up," I said. It was not the kind of thing you were supposed to say to a boy on a first date, but I said it, and then kept saying it: "Shut up, shut up, shut up," and he was laughing, but he did.

Then there's a sudden burst of static on the TV screen, cutting through the reverie of the memory, ending the video feed. Dom is gone as quickly as he appeared.

"Where'd he go?" I say. *"Bring him back,"* and I don't mean for it to be a shout but my desperation gets the best of me.

"I don't control it, Caroline," Kenny says, helplessly. "The television has a mind of its own. Well, not literally, because we haven't even achieved preliminary robotic sentience. But—"

Then, before Kenny can finish his sentence, the screen clears and the video resumes. Only it's not Dom we're looking at anymore.

6 | the television

In death, the stuff of life all starts to feel pretty insubstantial.

I had always thought that I didn't own very many things. I rarely went to the mall, I never had pets, and we didn't travel enough for me to come back to Winterton every summer with piles of souvenirs from far-flung corners of Earth. But now that I'm watching Iris and Jianyu comb through my bedroom, the detritus seems endless: old notebooks, tournament medals, books I've forgotten I'd bought and papers I've forgotten I'd written.

Iris is wearing a black T-shirt and jeans so distressed I can see most of her legs through the denim. Jianyu is wearing a sweater that has become about two sizes too small over the last year, his shoulders straining the cotton. The two of them are arguing, just like old times.

"This feels wrong," Iris says. "Kenny would have felt weird about us going through his stuff."

"His mom said he would've wanted us to put it to good use," Jianyu says. "And besides, Kenny's not around anymore to feel weird about it."

"I don't know why you have to say it like that," Iris says. "Like—like—"

"Like what?" Jianyu says.

"Like it's something I don't already *know*," Iris snaps.

A tear tracks down Iris's face, and Jianyu looks regretful. It's a familiar sight. For most of high school, the constant arguments between Iris and Jianyu had seemed harmless—just good-natured back-and-forth between friends—but they had started to feel oddly personal after junior year, when Jianyu had quit the Science Olympiad team to join Model UN, and then had started ditching our hangouts to hit the gym instead.

"I'm sorry," Jianyu says. "I didn't mean . . ."

He trails off, apparently having exhausted his capacity for emotional engagement.

"It's fine," Iris says. She pulls her long box braids into a bun piled on top of her head, which is what she always does when she's stressed, and then closes her eyes and takes a deep breath. When she opens her eyes again, her expression is contained, her voice matter-of-fact. "Let's just get this done. Three piles: leave, take, donate. We can start with the bookshelf."

"A whole section of books about string theory," Jianyu sighs, "and yet somehow the copy of *A People's History of the United States* I bought him last year was 'too dense to get through.'"

This was another familiar argument. Jianyu's headfirst plunge into the world of international politics via Model UN had led him to the conclusion that I had forsaken my civic duty by being largely uninterested in discussing anything remotely political—as if LARPing as an ambassador from an obscure Asian country four times a week made him some sort of expert on being a citizen of the world. I told him that I got far more than my desired allotment of global citizenry during the twenty hours a week I put in at the restaurant, and if he wanted to switch off so he could experience globalism firsthand via Eastern Wind's "authentic Chinese cuisine," I was more than happy to accommodate him.

"Kenny did get through *A People's History*," Iris says. "He just didn't want to talk about it. 'This thing's broken. That thing's screwed. Death, taxes, gridlock in Congress.' He found it all very morbid."

"The point of politics is to change the broken things," Jianyu says. "Is that really so morbid?"

"You know I'm on your side," Iris says. Ironically, politics was one of the few topics where she and Jianyu mostly agreed. The two of them both had grand plans to spend the next ten years of their lives racking up eyestrain and student loan debt in order to become lawyers; the only difference was that Iris wasn't constantly trying to convince me to livestream C-SPAN town halls during our free time together. Mostly, she was content to send me articles about socially responsible science and pretend she believed me when I said I had read them. Sometimes I wondered how I ended up befriending the only two members of the Science Olympiad team who didn't actually want to be scientists.

"Really?" Iris had said, the first time I had expressed the thought. "Is it really such a mystery?"

We had been eating lunch, sitting at our usual table in the cafeteria. She had gestured pointedly at Jianyu, and then gestured pointedly at me, and then gestured pointedly at her hair, and then looked around at the rest of the senior class, which was entirely white.

"Oh, don't be so cynical, Iris," Jianyu had said. "Don't worry, Kenny—it's not about race. It's mostly about your dad's cooking."

"Isn't that kind of about race, though?" I had said.

On-screen, the two of them have moved down the bookshelf, past the coffee-table books of NASA's space missions to a stack of yearbooks sitting underneath a thin film of dust. Iris picks up the one on top and riffles through the class photos, the student clubs, the senior portraits, until she gets to the signatures. She reads a few out loud while Jianyu continues to sort books: "'Three years down, one year to go. From, Filippo.' 'See you on the flip side—Casey Carter.' 'Keep on cruising, you big brainiac.' That one's Ian, obviously."

Iris flips a page; keeps reading.

"'See you at Eastern Wind!' 'The big K-Z! Gonna miss you in stat class, buddy.' And then like seventeen million versions of *Have a great summer.*"

Iris turns the page again—except the following pages are all blank. I had gone home after that, running out of people I knew and hating the idea of asking random classmates to sign my yearbook solely for the sake of appearances.

Iris stares at the blank page in front of her for a moment longer and then snaps the yearbook shut.

"Iris?" Jianyu says, warily.

"All of this is so *shallow*," Iris says. "I just—I wish people would remember Kenny the way *we* remember Kenny. The way Kenny deserves to be remembered."

Jianyu shoots a regretful look at the bookshelf, which is still half full, and then sits down on the floor next to Iris, puts a consoling arm around her shoulders.

"'See you at Eastern Wind?'" Iris quotes. "'Gonna miss you in stat class?' I mean sure, Kenny was smart and—and the restaurant was great, of course, everyone loved the restaurant—but Kenny was also nice, and funny, and an incorrigible romantic. He liked Carl Sagan because he was a great writer, not just because he was a great scientist, and he's the only person outside of my family that Princess Moonlight ever let pet her, and I just . . ."

By the time Iris trails off, Jianyu has gone from looking uncomfortable to looking thoughtful to looking *inspired,* which is never a good sign. "And you want people to know," he murmurs. "You want to tell them. Of course you do. Of course we should. Some kind of memorial event, maybe . . . ?"

"Oh, no," I say.

"Why 'oh, no'?" Caroline asks. "Personally, I think they're being very sweet."

I don't know how to explain to Caroline that Iris and Jianyu's many "big ideas" have generally backfired in equal proportion to the nobility of their intentions. First there was the Great Lunch Lady Unionization Fiasco, which had nearly led to Iris's expulsion in freshman year. And then, just last year, the Underclassman Empowerment Movement, which the vast majority of underclassmen found neither empowering nor moving.

"It's just," I tell Caroline, "they've gotten into their head that I'm some kind of tragic cause, you know? But

I'm not. I'm not an exploited laborer or an abandoned animal. I don't—"

"But you *died*," Caroline says. Everything about her softens: her voice, her eyes, the corners of her mouth. "That's tragic. Everything about it is tragic. God, this sucks."

She looks at me expectantly.

The problem is, I don't know what to say. I hate talking about my feelings, and even if I didn't hate talking about my feelings, I wouldn't know where to start. This was one of the best parts of my friendship with Jianyu: I didn't try to make him go into anything too deep, and he didn't try to make me go into anything too deep, and if for whatever reason one of us was feeling more than, say, 2.5 emotions at any given time, we picked something random to complain about until the feelings went away.

Caroline must mistake my silence for misery, because she takes a deep breath and declares: "But it's going to be all right. Because we're getting out of here."

So much happens in my head in the next split second that for a few moments I really can't even respond. First of all, there's the suggestion in and of itself, which is absurd. And then there's the fact that she says it like it's supposed to reassure me somehow, which is not only absurd but deeply concerning.

"Getting out of here?" I say. "What are you talking about?"

"The room is magic," Caroline says. "And we're obviously not *really* dead—otherwise we wouldn't be having this conversation—"

"You think we're not actually dead just because we're here talking to each other?" I say. "What if this is the afterlife?"

"I am pretty certain there is nothing in the Bible about magic TVs," Caroline says. "Therefore, this isn't the afterlife, we're not dead, and there must be a way back."

"What about the Quran?" I say. "Or the Bhagavad Gita? Or the weird scrolls they found off the coast of Egypt?"

"Don't think any of those have magic TVs either," Caroline says.

"Well, no, they don't," I say. "But that's not the point. The point is—"

"The point is that we're getting out of here, Kenny!" Caroline says, as if *I'm* the one being unreasonable for not going along with her crackpot plan to escape from a room with no windows and no doors that defies at least eighty laws of physics. Actually, there isn't even a crackpot plan for me to go along with!

"I have confidence in us," Caroline adds.

"You have confidence in us," I say. "Caroline, you don't even know me."

"I know you're the captain of the Science Olympiad team," Caroline says. "I read about it in the newspaper a few months ago."

"People actually read the school newspaper?" I say. Then I throw my hands up. "I can't believe I'm even entertaining this idea. This isn't science! This—all of this—isn't remotely within the realm of scientific inquiry!"

I wave my hands at the television, which, apparently sensing that both of us have stopped paying it any attention, has once more shut itself off.

"So, what?" Caroline says. "You're just going to give up? You're just going to let everyone you love think you're dead?"

"I *am* dead!" I say. "And the sooner everyone accepts that—"

I think of Iris, staring tearfully at my bookshelf, riffling through yearbook pages, declaring my love of Sagan so ardently that it might as well have been her own, and I feel a lump rising in my throat—

"—the easier it's going to be."

"Well, I don't accept it," Caroline says. She stares at me, defiant, and I stare at her, genuinely at a loss, and then there's a loud popping noise and an even louder thud as an enormous hardback textbook materializes out of thin air and lands in front of the television.

Caroline looks at me, and then at the book, and then back at me, and then back at the book.

Oh, right, I think. *She's new here.*

Caroline walks over to the TV and picks the book up from the floor. "*The Handbook of Conflict Resolution,*" she says. "*Theory and Practice,* Third Edition."

Then there's another *pop* and a piece of paper flutters onto her shoulder. She unfolds it and reads it out loud, too:

PLEASE DON'T FIGHT. EVERYTHING IS GOING TO BE OK.

"Oh, yeah," I say. "That happens sometimes, too."

7 | the room, part ii

"So let me get this straight," Caroline says. "The room just—gives you stuff? With little anonymous notes attached, like a secret valentine?"

"Generally you have to ask," I say. "Except sometimes I think it sees—hears—senses?—what's going on and tries to be proactive." I look ruefully at the monstrously cheerful recliner in the center of the room, and three hundred smiling faces look back at me, unblinking. The blanket has disappeared.

"It can be hit or miss," I say.

Caroline looks thoughtful for a moment. Then she says: "Thank you for the textbook and for the note. I was wondering if I might be able to get a box of tissues?"

A box of Kleenex appears on the floor in front of her. "Wow," Caroline says. "It actually worked!"

She blows her nose and then tosses the Kleenex into a trash can that materializes in front of her the moment before the tissue hits the ground. Then she does a slow turn in place, looking around the room, and furniture starts appearing around me: a coffee table, a writing desk, the same blue sectional I swapped out for the recliner before she got here. "Ooh, I love color," she says.

"How are you doing that?" I say.

"I just asked," Caroline says, and a potted plant springs into existence on the coffee table.

"Yes," she continues. "More plants, I think," and before I can even respond, half a dozen plants of varying sizes appear around the room, including one hangs down from the ceiling in a graceful arc to the floor. Now she's summoning stuff so quickly I can barely keep up: a mirror that runs along the length of the wall opposite the television, a dark-green throw blanket that drapes itself over the couch, a cabinet with tiers of glass trinkets on top, two nature photographs that flank the television.

"What's the sleep situation?" Caroline says, at the same time a shag rug materializes under my feet. "Do we get tired?"

"I haven't," I say.

"Hmm," Caroline says. "Well, just in case we want some privacy," and then a glass partition appears that divides a fourth of the room into two separate sections, with thick green curtains on both sides of the glass.

"What's the food situation?" Caroline says. "Do we get hungry?"

"I haven't," I repeat.

"Yeah, me neither," Caroline says. "And yet . . ."

A coffee station appears in a corner of the room opposite the bedrooms, with a French press, a grinder, and a kettle of water that's already boiling. "Can't shake that particular craving, even in limbo. And now I think we just need . . ."

There's a beat of silence while I try to figure out what on Earth we could possibly still "just need" on top of furniture, bedrooms, eighty plants, and caffeine. Then a bulky-looking CD player materializes on the coffee table.

"Huh," Caroline says. "I wasn't sure that would actually work."

"You asked for a CD player?" I ask. I don't know the last time I encountered an actual CD, much less a CD player.

"I asked for music," Caroline said. "And this is what we got. I guess the room's kind of retro."

She walks up to the coffee table, where a tower of CDs is materializing one disc at a time, and feeds one into the machine. There's a whimsical-sounding organ melody, and then we're listening to Frank Sinatra's "That's Life," which feels to me like a choice of song so ironic given our current predicament that it verges on cruelty.

Caroline must clock the look on my face because her smile fades a little and she says: "You can ask the room for something else if you're not into this. I just thought of Sinatra because he's, you know, classic. And his voice is so soothing, don't you think? But Dom always tells me I have the taste in music of a seventy-year-old woman. And then I always tell Dom he has the taste in music of a fourteen-year-old boy. And then—"

"This is fine," I say, before Caroline can get any further into the musicology of her relationship. I'll take anything over Dom's penchant for Yung Werther.

"Oh," Caroline says. "Well, OK then. Any other necessities, Kenny?"

The room around me is completely unrecognizable—except for, of course, the recliner and its many smiles, which will probably outlast us all. But other than that, it's beautiful. It's stunning. It looks like a hybrid between an antiques store and a college admissions office. It looks like Jianyu's house; like all the houses on the other side of Wisteria Park.

"It's really nice, Caroline," I say, and she beams. Then I look up at the ceiling and say, "Any chance we could get a clock in here? It's sort of hard to tell how much—"

But before I can even finish the thought, a piece of paper lands on my shoulder.

UNABLE TO FULFILL REQUEST. ERROR CODE #204.

"Seriously?" I say. "We can get half of West Elm delivered via ten-second air but we can't get a clock?"

Pop.

I DO APOLOGIZE. BUT ANY CLOCK I COULD PROVIDE WOULDN'T BE VERY HELPFUL, ANYWAY.

"What does that even mean?" I say.

"There's no point in getting annoyed with the room," Caroline says, which mostly makes me annoyed with her in addition to being annoyed with the room. "It's clearly doing its best."

"There just isn't any internal *logic* to this place," I say. "Furniture and food, no problem. But no clocks?"

"You'll figure it out, Kenny," Caroline says.

"Will I?" I say.

"We'll figure it out," she amends. "That's Life" comes to a close and transitions into "My Way"; Caroline sprawls out on the sectional with a cup of coffee in her hand, steam curling into the air. She looks happy, peaceful—above all else, hopeful. "And then we'll go back," she says, and this time I don't even have the heart to argue with her.

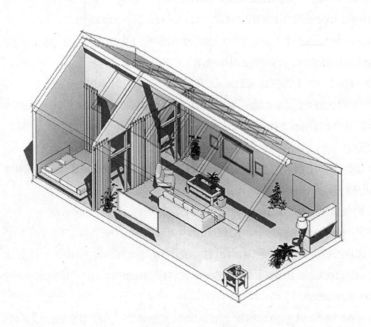

8 | the phone call

By the time a new video begins, Caroline has gone on another decorating spree, converting the remaining corner of the room into a miniature library one piece of expensive-looking furniture at a time. She's just added a glass whiteboard next to the mahogany bookshelf on top of the antique writing desk when the music cuts out and there's a familiar buzz of static.

My breath catches as the image clears; at the exact same time, Caroline says, "Are those . . . ?"

"My parents," I say. I can feel Caroline looking at me, but my eyes are glued to the screen, my feet moving toward the television as if drawn by magnetism.

It's the first time I've seen them since the funeral.

My parents are huddled together in the office of Eastern Wind. The office is a mess, which is mostly because the office is a pantry, with not nearly enough space to contain the register, the shift schedules, the telephone, dozens of binders full of paperwork, and a desktop computer. The office is also, for some reason, where we keep our entire supply of fortune cookies, which we buy in truly absurd bulk quantities once every three months, and which now sit in cardboard boxes stacked almost up to the ceiling.

My parents are poring over the computer monitor— my mom scrolling through a spreadsheet, my dad jotting down numbers on a sheet of scrap paper next to the keyboard. I've done this with them enough times at the end of the month to know the kind of math they're doing: Do the receipts match up with what we have in the register? Did our suppliers raise their prices? And then, with increasing anxiety as the numbers add up and the zeroes accumulate: How much is the gas bill? The electric bill? Rent? Income tax, sales tax, the armada of small business fees?

Then, in Mandarin, the forecasting starts.

"If next month isn't better," my mom starts.

"It will be better," my dad says.

"Zhou Jun," my mom says. "People don't want to be reminded of what happened while they're eating; tragedy makes people lose their appetite. If next month isn't better—"

"If next month isn't better, then March will be better," my dad says. "We just have to find a way to make it work for a few months longer. Eventually, our customers will come back."

"A few months longer?" my mom says. "We could barely make it work when the restaurant was full every night, and now the restaurant is empty even on weekends. Zhou Jun, I know you want to keep the restaurant open, and I don't know what we'd do if we had to close it. But we just don't have the money!"

The thing about growing up poor is that you become very good at distinguishing minor and manageable cases of we-don't-have-the-money from more serious instances of financial distress, in which you capital D, capital H, capital M really just Don't Have the Money. Mostly you figure if you can stave off the apocalyptic Don't Have the Money situations, it's more or less fine to go from minor case to minor case, skipping a dental cleaning here and there and patching up the soles of your shoes with duct tape. But you also kind of live in constant paranoia that it's only a matter of time until you hit the big one, until one day you wake up and it's the thirty-first and rent is due and even though you've spent the last month only buying pantry staples and sleeping in sweaters instead of running the heater, you still really, really Don't Have the Money.

"We have Kenny's college fund," my dad says, quietly, and that's how I know this is really bad.

I don't actually know how much money is in my college fund, because my parents would never tell me. "It's our job to worry about the money," my dad always said, "and your job to get good grades, get into a good school, marry a good girl, and then all of our worrying will be worth it." But it was hard not to worry about the money when it was so incredibly obvious the insane lengths that they were going to in order to get it. Every household necessity that my mom scrounged up from local garage sales or eBay or friends of friends instead of just buying off Amazon. Every trip back to China that my parents wanted to take but didn't, forgoing the opportunity to see their own parents just so they could stash away the airfare. "We can't afford to be wasteful when college is so expensive in America," they'd say, or, "We'll all take a trip back together after Kenny graduates college."

Sometimes I resented it. Sometimes it felt like I had been conscripted into an exchange that I had never wanted to be a part of in the first place, and I was now doomed to spend the rest of my life living out one very long never-ending guilt trip while I tried (and often failed) to deliver on my end of the bargain.

"What are they saying?" Caroline says, but how am I supposed to explain this? Any of this? The restaurant is losing customers and it's my fault. As a result of the restaurant losing customers, they're running out of money, which is then, transitively speaking, also my fault. I did not get good grades. I did not get into a good school. I certainly did not marry a good Chinese girl and make their seventeen years of worrying all worth it.

My mom starts crying. "Kenny's college fund was supposed to be for Kenny," she says.

My dad says: "All of this was supposed to be for Kenny."

I've spent a good portion of the last who-knows-how-many days watching people cry. My dad at my funeral. Iris in my bedroom. Caroline watching Dom skate. You'd think that I'd be numb to it by now, or at least that I'd have come to terms with the fact that there's nothing I can do about it other than bear witness and move on. But instead I can feel the accumulated grief coiling around my shoulders, my torso, growing tighter and tighter with the weight of all that my parents have lost.

"Kenny, what's happening?" Caroline says, looking increasingly anxious.

"They're talking about closing the restaurant," I say. "Business is down. My dad says they should liquidate my college fund, but my mom doesn't want to, because— because—"

I can't get the words out.

I understand how much the restaurant means to my dad because I understand how much the restaurant means to *me*. I remember standing three feet back from the stove as one of our cooks tried to teach me how to heat hot oil in a wok, flinching in terror with every pop and sizzle; I rememember laughing with the other servers about which shifts brought the worst customers. The restaurant: a gold thread stitched through the quilt of my childhood memories, and through the often-patchy tapestry of my relationship with my father. Other kids in Winterton watched sports games with their dads or went down to the river to fly-fish. Mostly, my dad and I sat in the kitchen and folded dumplings together by the hundreds. Sometimes I'd get a misshapen wrapper or add too much filling and botch the whole thing; when that happened, my dad would always look down at the problem dumpling, amused, and say, "That's not so bad—just do it like this, see?" before plucking it out of my hands and sealing it effortlessly.

"I just wish we had a phone or something," I say. "Some way I could *reach* them—"

And then a phone booth appears. Not just a phone—an entire bright-red phone booth, like something out of the 1900s, like something out of Great Britain. Next to the coffee station in the back of the room.

"Holy shit," I say.

"Oh my gosh," Caroline says.

"What do I do?" I say. "I didn't mean it literally, I just—"

"Call them," Caroline says.

"I can't just *call them*," I say.

"Call them!" Caroline says.

"What am I supposed to say, Caroline? *Oh, hi, Mom, it's Kenny. I know you were just at my funeral, and that I am one hundo percent definitely deceased, but I just wanted to call and say hi from this insane extra-dimensional space my corporeal form is currently trapped in. Hope that doesn't freak you out!* Do you really think that's a good idea?"

"Look," Caroline says. "What it comes down to is this: Don't you want to try? Don't you want them to know you're thinking of them? Isn't there anything you wish you had told them?"

The truth is that there are lots of things I wish I had told them. The last time my parents and I said that we loved each other was probably before I started high school. Which wasn't to say that we didn't love each other, or even that we didn't know we loved each other—it just seemed so embarrassing and unnecessary to say the actual words. Instead, they said things like, "Kenny, how could you even think about leaving the house without a jacket on when it's fifty degrees outside," and I said things like, "Dad, this eggplant might be the best eggplant in the entire world."

"OK," I say. "OK, you're right. I want to try."

Caroline clambers up so that she's sitting on one of the arms of the sectional, her legs swung over the side. I walk into the booth and pick the phone receiver off its cradle.

"There's a dial tone," I tell her. "There must be some way that this phone is wired into the television network. Old-timey pay phones like this don't have microchips to convert the audio waves into—"

"Science later," Caroline says. "Emotional reunion now."

"Right," I say, and then, before I can stop myself, I punch in the phone number for the restaurant.

For a few seconds, nothing happens. "Is it working?" Caroline asks, looking from the phone booth to the television screen to the phone booth to the television screen. Then I hear two sets of ringing start at once—the first, coming through the phone receiver, and the second, exactly in sync, emanating from the television speakers.

"There's no delay at all," I say. "It's instantaneous. How is that possible?"

"It's working," Caroline breathes.

It's difficult to see what's happening on-screen, because the phone booth has iron bars latticed across all four glass walls. But I can make out my mom pushing her chair back and standing up to walk over to the phone, and I can hear her say, in Mandarin, "Who would be calling us right now?" And then, still in Mandarin—

"Hello?"

I can't talk. I can't think. I can't even breathe.

It's one thing to hear my mom talking through the television speakers, thanking guests at the funeral for coming or talking to my father about their finances. But this—this is something else entirely. This is her, talking directly to me; this is sound so close and so clear that I can hear the slight raspiness of her voice, the uncertainty in her greeting, and I want to drink it up, I want to tape it, I want to record every tiny decibel fluctuation so I never have to forget the sound of my mother's voice.

A softball hits the outer wall of the telephone booth, and then bounces neatly back into Caroline's hands. "Say something!" she mouths.

"Hello?" I say.

"Hello?" my mom responds, almost immediately, the word just as much of a revelation the second time around, and I think, *It's working*; I think, *She can hear me*; I say, all reservations about how she'll react to hearing the voice of her dead son eclipsed by my desperation to keep her on the line: "Mom? Mom, it's me, Kenny—Mom, can you hear me?"

"Hello?" she says again, and then: "Hello? Is anyone there?"

She holds the receiver away from her ear, turns the volume up.

"Mom, it's me," I repeat, and now I can hear the problem—my voice is completely distorted on her end, the words garbled.

At first I don't believe it. It seems unfathomable that *this* is where things would break down—after the dial tone, the ringing, the connection. All the other impossible things were real—so why not this impossible thing, too? "Mom, it's Kenny," I say again, even though I can hear as I say them that the words are incomprehensible. "Use my college tuition. Please. Use my college tuition, keep the restaurant open with Dad, I'm sorry I never—"

My mom switches to English: "Hi, this is Eastern Wind Dumpling and Noodles, can I help you?"

"Mom," I say again, "it's Kenny, I don't know where I am but—"

There's a click, and then the long hum of the dial tone.

I put the phone back in its cradle and look up. Caroline meets my eyes, her face stricken, and I feel—

I feel nothing. It's like all the panic, all the desperation, all the fierce, fierce hope from the previous moments have flooded out of my body in one big rush, and now there's just this vacuum where my feelings used to be.

"It didn't work," I say, flatly. "And why would it have worked? It would have been categorically, scientifically impossible for it to have worked. I know you've got some bizarre idea that all of this is happening for a reason, but—"

"Just because they couldn't hear you doesn't mean it didn't work," Caroline says, quietly, and when I look up through the bars of the phone booth again, the screen is dark. But it's not dark because the television has shut itself off. It's dark because all the lights in the restaurant have gone out.

CAROLINE

9 | I would die all over again for one of those croissants

Fifteen seconds after his parents' restaurant goes dark, the video cuts out entirely. Fifteen seconds is enough time for Kenny to scramble out of the phone booth. For us to hear his parents' immediate reactions to the power outage, which I can only assume are various Chinese versions of "What the hell is going on?"

Fifteen seconds is *not* enough time for anyone—not Kenny, not me, certainly not his parents—to actually figure out what the hell is going on.

"What did I do?" Kenny says. He's gone pale.

A buzz of static, and the desperation on Kenny's face is replaced with relief so powerful it almost looks like joy. But when the static resolves, we're not looking at the inside of Kenny's parents' restaurant anymore.

"Oh," I say. "But this is my house."

"You live here?" Kenny says.

"Yes," I say.

"You have a taxidermied deer in your house?" Kenny says. "In your house, where you live?"

"The only reason my dad leaves it up is to scare my boyfriends," I say. "Everyone else hates it. Cooper says it's creepy. My mom says it's gauche."

Kenny looks like he doesn't know what to do with this information. He would not pass the boyfriend test.

"Well, did it work?" he asks. "Did it scare Dom?"

I snort. "Dom grew up on army bases. The china cabinet in the dining room scared him more than the deer; he was sure he was going to break something."

The camera tracks through the foyer and into the kitchen, where almost every inch of counter space is covered in boxes of food. It looks like we've gotten a delivery from every restaurant in town over the last few days. There are casseroles, pastas, fruit baskets, tea sets, at least five bottles of liquor, not to mention a collection of baked goods and desserts that could fill several display cases.

"A pastry basket from Arcetta's," I moan. "And I'm not even there to eat it! Purgatory sucks."

"That's a lot more than a pastry basket from Arcetta's," Kenny says.

Then we're weaving through the kitchen and into the living room, where there's no food—my mother would never allow it—but instead vases and vases of flowers. Orchids on the coffee table, a riot of purples and yellows and pinks. Lilies clustered atop the end tables, crowded so tightly their petals are unfurling into each other. Carnations dotted sweetly in between.

Finally, spread out around the room, each sitting on a different item of furniture, are my family members. My mom is alone on the sectional, even though there's more than enough room on it for everyone—*especially*, I think, my chest tightening, *now that I'm not there*. My dad is on the love seat, gazing vacantly into the darkened television screen. Cooper is on an ottoman in front of the coffee table, shredding the petals of a carnation one by one onto the rug.

No one speaks. The silence is so heavy and loaded I can feel it coming through the speakers and coalescing in the air between me and Kenny like thick fog.

"They should be talking," I tell him. I'm feeling defensive, almost—I want him to know this isn't usually what my house is like. It's usually lively and bright, full of movement, full of easy conversation. Full of love.

"They should be watching the baseball game," I say. "My dad should be shouting in Cooper's general direction about how the lineups are all wrong and how our coach should have been fired two seasons ago, and Cooper should be pretending to listen while actually texting his friends about something else entirely. And my mom—"

My mom's cell phone rings. The shrill peal of the default ringtone, which Cooper and I have been trying to get her to change for ages.

At first, no one moves. The only indication that anyone has even heard the sound is the slight stutter of Cooper's fingers, which pause for a split second around a petal. Then my mom clears her throat, picks her phone up off the couch, and says, "Hello?"

The conversation takes all of thirty seconds, and my mom's end is nothing more than a string of affirmations: "Yes, it is . . . Of course, thanks . . . Thanks for letting us know . . . Yes, of course. Bye now"—so vague that it could be about anything. But we're not left wondering for long, because as soon as she hangs up, my mom says:

"It was Kriminsky. They've set a date for the driver's sentencing hearing."

The news settles over the room without so much as a hitched breath.

"Cooper," my mom continues, "if you could give me and your father some privacy—"

"I want to know," Cooper says, so instantly defensive that it must be an argument they've had before. "I want to know what's going on. Kriminsky—that's our lawyer, right? Is the other driver going to go to jail? Is he *already* in jail? And who—"

"Of course you have questions, honey," my mom says. "But first, your dad and I have some legal matters to discuss, and we don't want you getting caught up in them, not when you have so much else going on. We'll fill you in when the time is right—won't we, Roy?"

She looks over at my dad, who doesn't seem remotely prepared for "some legal matters to discuss." He's still looking at the TV, his body still and his expression blank, like there isn't a conversation around him happening at all.

"Roy?" my mother prompts, and my dad flinches in a way I suppose could be interpreted as a nod.

"Thank you," my mom says, smoothly. "Cooper, if you wouldn't mind . . . ?"

"Fine," Cooper snaps. "I'm going to Dom's."

"That's fine, honey," my mom says. She looks, once more, exhausted, and when she tells Cooper that he should bring Dom one of the lasagnas, there's something in the sudden softness of her voice that almost sounds like an apology.

"Fine," Cooper repeats. He grabs his car keys out of the drawer and the lasagna out of the refrigerator, and then the video follows him as he walks out of the house and the front door shuts with a heavy thud behind him.

10 | I probably should have just said it

Outside, the colors of suburbia are growing dark and rich in the fading light of dusk: the indigo of the sky, the orange of the porch lights, the muddied white of the snow slicking the streets.

The scene is so familiar I could sketch it from memory. Not just the look of it but also the *feeling*: the air growing cool as the heat of the day dissipates, the sudden windlessness of nightfall, the sentimentality that often accompanies dusk and dawn. But it feels like something out of another world. It's been days—a week, maybe; who knows how time is passing inside the room—since I've seen the outdoors.

We follow Cooper as he backs out of the driveway and heads down Cottonwood, as if we're in a car trailing behind him. The whole thing is eerie, and only gets eerier as the shadows lengthen and the streets darken.

"Someone killed me," I say.

Kenny turns away from the screen; looks at me.

"I thought we knew that already," he says.

"Well, yeah, I guess I *technically* knew that already, but now that I've actually processed the information, I find that I'm really angry!"

"I'm sorry, Caroline," Kenny says.

"I thought I just got hit by a car and died. But I didn't just get hit by a car and die. Someone *hit me with their car and killed me!*"

Kenny says, "I'm sorry, Caroline" again.

I guess there's not much else he can say.

"The good news," I say. "Is that this whole purgatory situation is starting to make sense now."

"Is it?" Kenny says.

"We're not *supposed* to be dead, Kenny," I say. "It wasn't our time to go. And God—the universe—whatever it is you believe in—knew it wasn't our time to go, not really, and so now we're here until things topside can be put right and we can go back."

"Caroline," Kenny says, "I know you want to go back." Which is a weird thing to say, because, like, doesn't he also want to go back? It seems like between Option A, which is spending the rest of forever in this room where there's nothing and no one; and Option B, which is going back to the real world where we can be with our families, with our friends, with the people who love us, with the people whom we love; where we can go on runs at dusk awash in primary colors and cheat on our diets with croissants from Arcetta's, the better option is pretty clear.

"It's just," Kenny is saying, "how does that work, exactly? Everyone already knows we're dead. Our physical bodies are in literal graves, and—"

"Cremated," I say, and pull a face, because—graves, rotting bodies, all that dirt, ick. "I hope, at least."

"My point is," Kenny says, "do you really think everything will just go back to normal, even if we do somehow make it 'topside'?"

Cooper is taking the long way to Dom's, which means he's winding his way through Wisteria Park instead of just driving around it. Dom and I spent a lot of winter break there, walking around wrapped head to toe in wool; marveling at the intricate configurations of the branches, which would soon be obscured by curtains of the park's namesake purple flowers. One last blissful week of uncomplicated happiness before we got back to school after break ended in January and news of Kenny's death turned everything upside down.

"I kind of prefer it in the winter," Dom had said, one afternoon. "It's peaceful. And you don't have to worry about stumbling into people groping each other in the groves."

"You're a real romantic," I told him, because the two of us had spent no shortage of our first couple months of dating doing just that.

I had realized that I loved him that afternoon, which sounds very dramatic, but in the moment it just felt like another fact about Dom, like: His lips were chapped from the cold, he was in desperate need of a haircut, this was a person that I loved.

"I don't know how it'll work," I say. "But this—all of this—this is *magic*, Kenny. Maybe, when we go back, we'll go all the way back—not just to the real world, but to the real world on the days that we died, so that we can do things differently this time. I could skip practice or take a different way home. You could see a doctor."

When we first got back from winter break, no one actually knew how Kenny had died—whether there was some medical condition his family had been keeping under wraps, or if he'd contracted some rare disease while on vacation or something. In the end, word got out that it had been a freak accident—his heart had just stopped one night, no warning signs, no preexisting conditions. I remember people commenting about how the randomness of it made it feel more unfair—and also scarier, because if it could happen to Kenny, a perfectly healthy seventeen-year-old boy, couldn't it happen to anyone?

"All right, Caroline," Kenny says. "In a world in which we are capable of both resurrection and time travel, maybe it's not so hard to believe we could alter the course of history once we got back." He laughs a little, and in the sound I hear an echo of my brother's laugh from Principal Meyers's office: more resigned than amused, more sad than happy.

"Everything alters the course of history," I say. "Isn't that the butterfly effect?"

"No one should learn science from movies," Kenny says, sadly.

"You can explain it to me later," I say, because on the television Cooper is turning on to Dom's street, then reversing into an open parking spot along the curb. "That, and the time dilation stuff."

"You really want to know?" Kenny asks.

"Of course I want to know!" I say. "How else are we supposed to get out of here?"

"I thought we were chalking it all up to magic," Kenny says. He's smirking a little, which suits him more than the sorrow, at least.

Cooper climbs out of his car, locks it, and heads up the street toward Dom's house. When he gets there, Dom is already sitting out on the front porch of the duplex, dribbling a basketball from one hand into the other. There's an old-timey portable radio next to him, which is tuned to the local hip-hop station and playing a song I don't recognize.

"I got your text," Dom says.

"I had to get out of the house," Cooper says. In one hand he's still holding the lasagna dish. In the other he's swinging his keys around his index finger: a nervous habit.

"Yeah," Dom says. "I get that."

Cooper walks up to the porch steps and places the lasagna down. "Compliments of the Bertells," he says.

"That's nice of them," Dom says.

"Mom wanted me to bring it over. We have an insane amount of food right now, so . . ."

Cooper trails off. I wonder if he's thinking the same things I'm thinking: Is anyone sending Dom food? Lasagnas and fruit baskets and potato salad and croissants? What about flowers—carnations for grief, orchids for healing, lilies for remembrance? I can feel the questions echoing between my head and Cooper's; an invisible string that connects the two of us across the dimensions, maybe even across worlds. He'll never ask them out loud, though, and neither would I: Both of us already know the answer.

"Well," Dom says, and bounces the basketball neatly into Cooper's hands. "Shall we play a game?"

11 | I definitely should have just said it

They had started playing one-on-one in the fall, after Dom and I had been dating for a few months. One pickup game had turned into two, which had turned into a standing weekly tradition—Thursday nights, the only weeknight when neither Cooper nor Dom had practice, at four P.M. sharp.

Tonight they're just shooting around, which is what they do when the basketball is really just an elaborate pretense for wanting to talk. The sky grows darker around them, wide swatches of dark blue drowning out the pink and yellow streaks in the west until it's all just a sweep of indigo, horizon to horizon. The two of them settle into a steady rhythm of bounce passes, layups, and shots from the arc, silent until Cooper says, "You holding up OK?"

Dom grimaces; misses a layup. "Everyone keeps asking me that," he says. "Do I look like I've been crying all night or something?"

"No," Cooper says. "But I'm sure no one would find it weird if you did."

"Well, I'm glad that I don't," Dom says, and sinks a three.

They move along the three-point line, alternating shots without speaking so the only noises Kenny and I can hear are the sound of the basketball hitting the gravel, the occasional clang off the backboard, and the music playing from the radio, which Dom has moved to the top of the driveway. Then Cooper says, quietly, "Sometimes I've been."

Dom catches the chest pass from Cooper and holds the ball instead of shooting it. "What, crying all night?"

Cooper nods, sits down on the driveway. Dom takes one last shot, which misses, and lets the basketball roll into the snow before also sitting down.

"Maybe not *all night*," Cooper says. "But sometimes it's two A.M. and I can't get to sleep and it all comes rushing toward me at once, like—*Holy shit, I'm never going to see her again. I'm an only child now.*"

"You're never going to be an only child," Dom says.

Cooper lies back onto the driveway and crosses his forearms over his eyes.

"I'm really sorry, Cooper," Dom says.

Cooper doesn't respond.

"I wish I knew what to say," Dom says.

"And that's the other thing," Cooper says. "No one knows what to say. I definitely don't know what to say. My friends don't know what to say. My mom doesn't even know what to say, and have you met her?"

"Your parents must be taking it pretty hard," Dom says.

"I have no idea how they're taking it," Cooper says, "because they won't tell me anything that's going on. It seems like my mom is sort of keeping it together—she's handling everything with the lawyers and the journalists and the hospital. But Dad . . ."

Cooper sits up and looks at Dom, fidgeting with his keys again. Nervous, though I don't know why. But then he says, stuttering through the discomfort: "Was it similar—I mean—when your dad passed away—"

"You had to go there," Dom says.

Bringing up Dom's father is a good way to shut him down. I had learned that the hard way after our first couple months of dating, when any attempt to ask about his father or, God forbid, how he *felt* about his father, inevitably led to an afternoon of tense silence. But Cooper doesn't know that. Cooper says, like he's reaching out for a lifeline: "I mean, maybe it wasn't exactly the same for you, obviously, but do you think it was maybe similar for your mom? Maybe you could talk to her about things, ask her how she felt after—"

"Drop it," Dom says, sharply, and Cooper looks at him, surprised by the sudden anger in his voice.

"Just let it go, Cooper," Dom says.

"All right," Cooper says. He gets up off the asphalt and collects the basketball. "You want to shoot around some more?" he says.

Dom picks himself up, too, but he heads away from the hoop, toward his front door, and switches the radio off. "Kinda late," he says. "Kinda tired."

"Yeah, I feel that," Cooper says.

"Thanks for coming over, though," Dom says. A flash of guilt, like he's only now realizing he shouldn't have snapped at Cooper. "And thanks for the lasagna. I, um—I appreciate that you guys are thinking of me."

"Anytime," Cooper says. He stands there for a moment longer—wanting to say something more, unsure of what to say—before turning around and walking back toward his car. But our video doesn't follow him back—instead, we stay with Dom, hearing but not seeing the car being unlocked, the door opening and then shutting, the engine being turned on and then growing fainter and fainter as Cooper drives away.

There's a click as the streetlights turn on, and all of a sudden Dom is bathed in fluorescent orange light.

"Are you OK?" Kenny asks, and I shush him even though it's rude because all I want is to look at Dom while I still can: the basketball tucked into the crook of his elbow, the radio at his feet, his hair tousled from the game, his cheeks red from the cold. His face underneath the streetlights, defensive and guilty at once, aglow like that of a fallen angel.

"Caroline," Dom says, and I think I must have imagined it until he says it again.

"I feel like an idiot," Dom says, and I laugh, which comes out watery and stifled because at some point in the last ten seconds I've started crying. Then Dom laughs, too, and *that* comes out watery and stifled, because at some point in the last ten seconds *Dom* has started crying. "I also feel like an asshole," Dom says, "which might be worse than feeling like an idiot. But I just—"

He cuts off. Dribbles the basketball a few times, takes a deep breath.

"Dom never gets like this," I tell Kenny, at the same time that Dom says, "I just miss you," and all three of us exhale at once, in sync.

"People keep trying to talk to me about you, and whenever they try to talk to me about you, they try to talk to me about my dad, and it just—it makes me so angry, it makes me *furious*, because I don't want to think about him when I think about you."

Next to me, Kenny asks: "When did his dad . . . ?"

"Dom was eight," I say.

"I had no idea," Kenny says.

"He never talks about it," I say.

"And it's like everyone expects me to know what I'm doing, because they think I've done this before," Dom is saying. "But I have no goddamn idea what I'm doing."

"Oh, Dom," I say, even though he can't hear me, even though I know he may never be able to hear me again. Because this is the thing: *No one* thinks Dom knows what he's doing. The only person who thinks Dom is supposed to have any idea what he's doing right now is Dom.

"And I keep thinking that if you were here, then maybe it'd be all right," Dom continues. "Maybe you'd know what to do."

And that makes me really laugh, half choked, because it's just so untrue. I've never met anyone more competent, more independent, more *good at things* than Dom. One time while we were out driving I ran a flat tire and was three rings into a phone call to Triple A when Dom said, "Wait, what? We don't need Triple A for this, Caroline," and climbed out of the car to change it. Dom got the radio he's been playing out of a junkyard, for God's sake, and then was annoyed when it took him longer than three weeks to fix it because that meant he couldn't give it to me for Christmas—"you know, because you love oldies and all that boring stuff"—never mind the fact that most people wouldn't have been able to fix it at all.

"That is such a joke," I say out loud to Kenny, and then I turn to the screen and say it to Dom: "That is such a joke." He's still standing at the top of the driveway, staring out over the street; looking, as he rarely ever looks and as I've rarely ever seen him, lost. And I so desperately want to be there with him—not because I think I'd know what to do if I were there, but because I'm feeling just as lost as he is, and because I miss him, too, with a fierceness I didn't know I was capable of, and because I wish I could talk to him, that's all, and that when I did that he could actually hear me.

Pop, and I almost jump into Kenny: It's been a while since we've heard from the room. Kenny grabs the note out of the air before it lands and unfolds it so we can both read the message.

USE WHAT YOU HAVE, it says.

"Did you ask for something?" Kenny says.

It takes me a minute to retrace my thoughts. "Not anything specific. I was just thinking about how badly I want to talk to Dom. About how I wish he could actually hear me—*oh.*"

I look over at the phone booth mounted to the floor in the back of the room, excitement building as it hits me, as I realize what I need to do. "The telephone. It wants me to use the telephone to call Dom, just like you called your parents."

"Except that didn't work," Kenny says. "They couldn't understand me. It must be referring to something else."

Kenny looks around the room and starts listing out items: "Television, phone booth, plants, coffee machine, coffee table, CD player, *The Complete Reprise Studio Recordings*—wait, hold on a second. Caroline, the CD player."

Kenny turns to look at me, his eyes wide.

"I don't understand," I say. "I don't even really know how to use that thing. I just put the CDs in and hope I've got the right—"

"It's also got a radio," Kenny says. "My parents have one of these in the kitchen of the restaurant."

He pulls the CD player toward us and starts hitting buttons: EJECT, POWER, AM/FM.

There's an answering blitz of static. Kenny starts flipping through stations, hitting the NEXT TRACK button over and over again—but it's all just feedback. "Guess reception's not so great out here in purgatory," Kenny mutters.

"Maybe I should try the phone booth," I murmur. "Just in case . . ."

Kenny turns the volume up even louder and hits a button labeled SCAN.

And then Dom's radio turns on.

We both hear it before we see it: static coming through the television speakers, on top of the noise already emanating from the CD player. Then it clears and we're listening to a country song—something about pickup trucks and bonfires and denim shorts—playing, in perfect sync, on both Dom's radio and ours.

"Holy shit," Kenny says.

The country song dissolves back into static. Then there's a few seconds of Christian rock. A blast of pop, then static again—longer this time and fuzzier in some moments than others. Some kind of infomercial, more pop music, more static, a burst of jazz.

"It's channel surfing," Kenny says. "Is this you? Are you doing this?"

"I have no idea!" I say. "I'm not trying to!"

Dom crouches down and punches some of the buttons on the radio, but it doesn't seem to have much of an effect: We're still cycling through stations, buffeted by static. He hits the ON/OFF switch, which doesn't work—if anything, we start to cycle through the channels more quickly. Then Kenny tries shutting the radios off from our end, which doesn't do anything at all.

"I can't get it to stop," Kenny says. "I think we're locked in."

Pop, and I unfold the note so quickly I almost rip it. I read the words out loud:

WHAT DO YOU WANT TO SAY?

I look up at Kenny, who shrugs a little, as if to say: *Well?*

I look over at Dom, huddled over the radio, the night darkening around him.

What do I want to say?

I want to say that it's OK to be sad, that it's OK to be confused, that it's even OK to be angry, but that people like his teachers and his teammates and Cooper are talking to him because they're trying to help, not because they expect something from of him. I want to say that I remember him in the same way he remembers me—capable and confident, an anchor and a compass and a hero. Teaching me how to pitch a tent on our first camping trip. Bending over the trunk of my car to pull out a spare tire I didn't even know existed. Putting that radio back together for Christmas—for me.

The two radios have been picking up, in speed and in volume. We're getting more static than we are music now, interrupted by little clicks as the radios flip from channel to channel. Dom puts the basketball down so he can use both hands to fiddle with the radio, but then there's one last click, and suddenly the cycling stops.

The static disappears. For a moment it's totally silent.

And then: a piano riff. A series of broken chords I know like the back of my hand. Clear as day: every word, every note, every tremor in Elvis's voice as he makes his way through the opening verse and into the first chorus of "Can't Help Falling in Love."

"That has to be you," Kenny whispers.

Dom looks stunned. He hits a button on the radio. Nothing happens. He hits another button on the radio. Nothing happens. He stares at it, dumbfounded.

Then Dom sits down. He leans back onto his hands, and he looks once more out at the street. We're still facing him, the house and the hoop in the background, but I've been there enough times to know what he's looking at, and, in a way, to look at it with him: the row of duplexes opposite his, all painted in different bright pastels; the long stretch of his street, vanishing into a point on the horizon in a case study in perspective; the streetlights lining the edge of Wisteria Park in the distance, like a row of faraway flares.

If we're stuck here long enough, I decide, I'll paint this. All this, everything I never want to forget: Dom's house and my house and the park, a whole series.

There's one last chorus—and that final held note, voices layered in harmony—and then the song is over. Almost immediately, the static returns, loud and jarring and dissonant in the aftermath of the song. Dom flips the ON/OFF switch. This time, both our radios shut off.

Dom looks at the radio, his expression some mixture of confusion and disbelief and wonder; his expression something that I want to memorize, to paint. But there's so much detail there—the light from the street catching in his eyes and hair, the crease between his eyebrows, the stubble starting to emerge on his jaw—and I've barely had time to look at him, to see him, the way Mrs. Macmillan talks about, when our television shuts off, too.

I turn to Kenny.

"That was—" he says, at the same time that I start, "What even—"

We both cut off. In the ensuing silence, there's a *pop*, and another note lands on my shoulder, light as a feather.

IT WAS A LITTLE SCHMALTZY, it says. BUT ALL IN ALL, NOT A BAD CHOICE.

KENNY

12 | Faith

I didn't think about God very much growing up.

My parents weren't religious—a legacy of the oppressively atheist Mao years—and most of my friends weren't either. The one exception was Iris, who offered to bring me to Christmas Mass with her family every year without exception, and also without success. Honestly, it seemed difficult enough to contend with the corporeal challenges of existence—puberty, acne, homecoming—without adding a whole set of spiritual concerns to the list, too. I figured if there was a God to believe in, it was the God of science, which made itself visible in the laws of physics that governed the many natural miracles around us, from the lives and deaths of human beings to the intricacies of plant photosynthesis to Saturn's rings.

Now I don't know what to believe. Caroline keeps calling the room purgatory, and to her point, our little zaps into the real world feel as close to divine intervention as I'll ever experience. How could I think otherwise, after watching the moment Caroline and Dom just shared? After seeing the look on his face, like he was standing before a miracle—and the look on hers now, knowing that the miracle was her?

"I don't even know how I did that," Caroline says. "I was just looking at Dom, and—"

Then she stops, overwhelmed, and summons another box of tissues.

The truth is I want that for myself. That moment of epiphany, that undeniable connection. I want to be with my parents again, even if it's just through a radio, a song, a shared memory. And I was so close with the phone booth. If I could do it again—if I could figure out how the transmission works and why—then maybe I could communicate more clearly. Maybe I could get it right this time.

There's an answering *pop*, and a note flutters out of the ceiling and lands on my shoulder.

YOU WISH FOR SOMETHING DIVINE, it says. BUT YOU FIND YOUR SELF LACKING IN FAITH.

"The whole mind reading thing gets a little creepy, you know that?" I say. "Maybe you just don't inspire a lot of faith."

Caroline looks up at me.

"I was just talking to the room," I explain.

"Right, of course," Caroline says. Still teary but now bemusedly so. "Just talking to the room, nothing to see here."

Pop.

THERE ISN'T OFTEN A BURNING BUSH.

Pop.

OR A FLATTENED MOUNTAIN. OR A BATTLEFIELD AVATAR. I'M NOT PARTICULAR ABOUT THE PARTICULARS. BUT THERE ARE OPPORTUNITIES, it says.

"Opportunities to what?" Caroline says, and then startles as the television turns on with a loud burst of noise.

Light floods into the picture all at once, whiting the whole screen out; pixels dissolve and reconstitute until we're looking at the inside of Iris's car. Iris is in the driver's seat, Jianyu is on the passenger's side, and the speakers are blaring a song Alice has made me listen to so many times that I know it's the first track of a playlist she titled "smooth jazz for smooth girlies."

The clock on the dashboard reads 4:13 P.M. Caroline must notice it at the same time that I do, because she says: "But that's not possible. There's no way it's been a whole day since we saw Dom and Cooper—"

"I think time is passing differently out there than it is in here," I say. "I've been noticing for a while, haven't you? It never feels like longer than a few hours between different videos."

"But that's—" Caroline says.

"It is possible," I say. "Scientifically speaking, at least. According to Einstein's theory of special relativity, time passes differently for objects traveling at different speeds. So if the room we're in happens to be inside, say, a spaceship moving at close to the speed of light, that could explain the difference in how time is elapsing inside the room versus in the real world. It's called time dilation. Of course, the closest humans have gotten to speed-of-light travel is—well, not very close. So, I guess that while scientifically speaking it might be possible, practically speaking, it is not very likely."

Caroline blinks at me. "I think Dom and I watched a movie about this, too," she says again, and I repeat, even wearier this time: "No one should learn science from movies."

Then Jianyu and Iris start talking, and I forget all about Einstein's theory of time dilation.

"It's almost quarter past," Jianyu says.

"I'm already going five over," Iris says. "I'm not risking my license just because you're late for a soccer game."

"Iris," Jianyu says, rolling his eyes.

"And even when we get there, I am not letting you out of the car until we're done planning. It's been two weeks and we don't even know who we're inviting—"

"I still have access to the student body email list from running for class board last semester," Jianyu says. "We can send out an Evite."

"To the entire school?" Iris says. She wrinkles her nose, the idea of memorial-as-mass-spectacle clearly as distasteful to her as it is to me.

Sometimes it hurts how well Iris knows me.

"Maybe just the junior and senior classes," Jianyu says. "And then underclassmen he liked."

"That's still three hundred people," Iris says. "Where are we going to put three hundred people?"

"It's not like everyone we invite is going to come," Jianyu says. "Honestly we'll be lucky if our invite-to-attendance ratio is more than thirty-three percent."

"Invite-to-attendance ratio," Iris repeats, drily. "Is that something you think frequently about?"

"We need some way of getting people interested in the event," Jianyu continues. "A hook. Like a charity cause or something—'Come to our barbecue in honor of beloved WHS senior Kenny Zhou. All proceeds will go to impoverished African children.'"

"That kind of comment should get you kicked out of Model UN," Iris says.

"I'm always China," Jianyu says, as if that has anything to do with anything. "But that's a good point—it should have some kind of Asian connection. Or some kind of Kenny connection, I guess, one of which could be that Kenny is Asian."

"OK," Iris says. "An event with a connection to Kenny. Some kind of Kenny-related theme or issue. What kind of issues did Kenny care about?"

"Kenny didn't care about any issues," Jianyu says. "Or much of anything at all, by the end. That was kind of the problem, wasn't it?"

Jianyu says the words like they're a foregone conclusion, like my unsatisfactory attitude was something he'd resigned himself to long ago, and there's nothing that Iris can say in response, because he's right. If I had to boil down the last year of my life to a single emotion, it would be apathy. It was as if the way I had always felt about politics had gradually consumed every facet of my life, until extracurriculars and college applications and grinding at the restaurant to stave off Just Don't Have the Money for another few weeks all felt just as morbid and futile and stagnant as watching senators have legislative dick-measuring contests on the nightly news.

By Thanksgiving break, I was making it to Science Olympiad meetings and not much else, and the only reason why I made it to those was because Iris and I had last period together and she'd steer me straight from our history classroom to the Science Olympiad classroom, bypassing lockers and the parking lot and all other potential opportunities for escape. Sometimes I still didn't make it, and Iris would show up at my house after covering for me at practice, angry but trying not to show it, disappointed but trying not to show it, worried but trying not to show it, and then I'd spend ten minutes standing at the front door making dumb excuses for why I hadn't shown up that we both knew weren't true, and then making dumb excuses for why I had to go that we also both knew weren't true.

I hated seeing Iris hurt, but I knew that the more time she spent with me, the worse she was going to feel about not being able to cheer me up, and the worse *I* was going to feel about not being *able* to cheer up. It was much easier with Jianyu, who sent me a text one evening that said, "hey Kenny seems like you've been down lately let me know if you ever wanna talk," and then disappeared back into his circle of newfound Model UN friends. Sure, both he and I knew that was an offer I was never going to take him up on. But it wasn't like it was an offer he genuinely wanted me to take him up on, anyway.

On-screen, Iris is listing off various fundraising causes while Jianyu provides commentary:

"Cancer research."

"Raises too many questions. Everyone'll think he died of cancer."

"Habitat for Humanity."

"Don't we already have a student group for that?"

"Animals. Abandoned animals. *Endangered* animals."

"Kenny didn't even like animals," Jianyu says.

"What are you talking about?" Iris says. "Kenny liked my cats."

"He liked you, and you liked your cats," Jianyu said. "There's a difference."

"You liked her?" Caroline interjects. "Or you *liked* her?" But before Caroline can take me down the same line of questioning I'd gone down with my mother hundreds of times, the epiphany hits me. Clear as a burning bush, despite what the room had said.

I jump up off the couch.

"All right," Caroline says. "We don't have to talk about it."

"The restaurant," I say. "If they host this memorial event as a fundraiser for my parents' restaurant, then that buys some time for my mom to come around, and if my mom comes around, then *that* buys some time for the customers to come back . . . That's all they need, right? Some time?"

"That's brilliant, Kenny!" Caroline says. "But how . . ."

I pace toward the telephone booth—no, that won't work; it needs to be more precise than just garbled audio—and then to the CD player. Iris isn't using a radio, but if the logic is the same . . .

I hit SCAN. Immediately I know it's worked: Iris's song cuts out as the audio system switches from her cell phone over to the radio. Her eyebrows furrow in confusion and then in disgust as she registers the cheery synthesizer melody of a pop hit.

"Leave it," Jianyu says, but Iris is already restarting Bluetooth, trying to get her playlist back.

"What did you do to get the Elvis song to start playing?" I ask Caroline.

"I don't know!" Caroline says. "I mean at first I was just so frazzled, you know, and the radio was all staticky, which was making me more frazzled, and then the radio was even more staticky, which was—"

"OK, but then what?" I say.

"And then, I don't know!" Caroline says. "I just—I was watching Dom, and then the music started playing!"

Caroline looks upward.

"No, don't—" I start, because it feels like cheating to ask for help. But it's too late: Caroline has already said, "Look, we're trying, but we're kind of stuck. Could you throw us a bone, please?"

"—ask the room," I finish, and sigh as Caroline catches the note in midair, a pleased expression on her face.

"Why do you always look *up* when you talk to the room?" I grumble. "Maybe whoever is running the circus is in the walls. Maybe they're underneath our giant expensive sectional. Maybe they have no corporeal form at all."

Caroline ignores my complaints and reads:

WHAT IS YOUR INTENTION?

"My intention for *what*?" I say.

Caroline thinks for a moment. "I think you need to really *know* what you're trying to communicate to them," she says. "That's basically what the room was asking me when I was watching Dom, right? 'What do you want to say?' And I thought that meant I had to come up with some kind of speech in my head, or actually say something out loud. But maybe it was enough just to know."

"What did you know?" I say.

"It's hard to put it in words," Caroline says, looking uncharacteristically embarrassed. "I was just thinking about things we had done together—our first camping trip, a Christmas gift he had gotten me. And I knew—well, I don't know, the room figured it out, I guess," she finishes, and flushes red.

"You knew you loved him," I say.

"Well, we never used that word, exactly," Caroline whispers. Who'd have thought: Caroline Davison, embarrassed to talk about being in love with her hockey star boyfriend. Then she pulls a pillow over her face, and says, muffled, "Ugh, let's talk about something else."

"OK," I say. "Sorry."

"This isn't about me, anyway," Caroline continues. She removes the pillow and tries to look composed, which would be more successful if the residual static wasn't causing her hair to fly in a million different directions. "This is about you, and your friends, and your parents, and their restaurant."

"So what you're telling me," I say, "is that I just need to *know* what I want to say to them, and it'll happen. Somehow."

"I'm telling you, that's how it worked for me," Caroline says. "Who knows what'll happen for you."

I look back at the television screen, where Iris and Jianyu are midconversation about raising money for a local science museum.

"Tell me about the restaurant," Caroline says.

That's the whole point of all this, isn't it? The restaurant.

"What people don't always understand," I say, "is how much of yourself you put into a small business like a restaurant. How much more it is than a regular job. Not that people don't work hard at regular jobs," I add, hastily, but Caroline just snickers and says, "My parents made Cooper and I work at an ice cream shop one summer for our pocket money, and we definitely did not work hard at our regular jobs."

"Right," I say. "Because when you clocked in, you were just trying to get through your hours so you could get paid, and when you clocked out, you stopped thinking about the ice cream shop until the next time you clocked in. But working at the restaurant isn't like that for my parents, because it's *their* restaurant. They came up with the name; they chose every dish on the menu. Every dish on the menu means something to them."

Iris's sound system switches over to the radio again, now scanning through stations—country, indie rock, her ever-detested Top 40.

I feel oddly calm now—not because I'm certain this is going to work, because I'm certainly not, but because this is something I want Caroline to understand regardless of whether or not it works. Something that feels worth it to tell her even if my memorial ends up being a fundraiser for some tiny downtown museum and not Eastern Wind Dumpling & Noodle House.

It's ironic, in a way. Now that I'm dead, I find that I'm more invested in what's happening over in the real world than I ever was in my last year of living. If you had told me six months ago that there was a chance the restaurant was on its way out, I would've said, "That's going to be pretty tough for my parents," and then gone back to sleep. Now I'm sending coded messages across time and space, trying to convince my mother that a few more months of fighting is worth it; trying to get Jianyu and Iris to buy them those months.

"If we close the restaurant," I say, "all of that will just be—gone. Every person we've met. Every meal we've served. Every hour of our lives we've put into it. It all just becomes—a memory, I guess, lost in the past. Wouldn't you want to save it, if it were you? Wouldn't you want to do something?"

"Of course I would," Caroline says.

And then there's one more burst of static and the radio is playing "Jin Tian Bu Hui Jia"—a staple of the restaurant playlist; the song my mother liked to end each night with because of it reminded her of growing up in Hunan.

You can never go home, Kenny, my mom used to say. *The only thing you can do is create a new one.*

"Is this playing from your phone?" Jianyu says, delighted. "My mom loves this song." He starts to sing along, badly, while Iris pulls into the parking lot of the local soccer field.

"*Is* this playing from my phone?" Iris says. "I don't remember saving this song, but . . ."

The clock on the dash reads 4:28. The blast of nostalgia seems to have alleviated Jianyu's need to get to the soccer match on time, because he sits back and says: "Kenny's mom loves this song, too. I think it's like the equivalent of a Beatles song but for old Chinese people."

"The Beatles were very popular internationally," Iris says.

"I feel bad for his parents," Jianyu says. "My parents said they've been to the restaurant a few times since the funeral, and there's hardly been anyone else there."

"Really?" Iris says. "But people love the restaurant. It's the only good Chinese place within fifty miles. Unless you count Panda Express. Which I expressly do not."

"They think it's something to do with . . ." Jianyu starts, and then trails off.

"Come on, guys," I say. "You're so close. Iris, I know you can get there."

"They think it's something to do with Kenny," Iris finishes.

"Well, it's not the most hospitable feeling in the world, you know? Thinking about death while you eat your noodles. Even if your noodles are delicious."

"I guess we haven't been back since December either," Iris says, quietly.

"Yeah," Jianyu says. "Though that might be because—"

Then he breaks off. The unspoken words hang in the air: *Because we never hang out anymore. Because even when we do, it ends in a fight.*

"We should go sometime," Jianyu says, offhand, and Iris looks touched: It's a reminder that Jianyu can be accidentally sweet just as easily as he can be accidentally cruel.

"I'd like that," Iris says.

"Next Friday? Actually—" Jianyu says, and then stops dead, right in the middle of lacing up his sneakers.

"Actually . . . ?" Iris says.

"Actually," Jianyu says, "What if we did it at the restaurant?"

"Oh, wow," I say. "I really wasn't expecting it to be him."

"I thought that's what we were saying," Iris says.

"No," Jianyu says. "What I mean is: What if we did the memorial at the restaurant? The fundraiser. And then people would have a memory to associate with the place that isn't sadness and grief, which would help business, and obviously we can donate whatever we raise to his parents, since they're p—"

Jianyu stops himself from saying the word on the tip of his tongue, which is *poor*. Instead, he swallows, pauses, and says: "Well, I'm sure they could use the money."

Iris is welling up. "I think Kenny would have liked that," she says. Jianyu looks around for tissues, but there aren't any. If only they, too, existed in a dimension where a mysterious invisible entity dropped the things you wished for out of the sky.

"I think this is the best idea I've ever had," Jianyu says, and Iris looks so immediately exasperated I think the tears may actually flow *up* her face and back into her eyes.

"This isn't like Model UN," Iris says, "we have to actually pull it off, not just talk about it. We'll have to pitch the idea to his parents. And we'll have to figure out who to invite—I think the restaurant can only seat, like, one hundred and fifty people."

"We'll be fine," Jianyu says. "Kenny didn't have one hundred and fifty friends."

"He was being so nice a minute ago," Caroline says, frowning.

"Jianyu is like that," I say. "Jianyu giveth, Jianyu taketh away. It's why he'll be alone forever."

"Well, I don't know about *that*," Caroline says, and then blushes a little.

"And we'll have to pick a date," Iris continues. I don't think Jianyu's last comment even registered; she's in her own head now. "And we'll have to serve food. Lots of food. Good food. To tip the balance of remembrance, to make the restaurant a place of joy again."

"That's basically what I said," Jianyu says.

"Kenny loved that restaurant," Iris says. She smiles: fond, nostalgic. "He wrote his college application essay about it—did you know that?"

"I didn't," Jianyu says, looking like he's surprised himself with the truth.

"About how working at the restaurant was how he learned to cook, and learning to cook was how he learned Chinese. And how learning how to cook and learning Chinese was how he learned about his parents, and about himself. And also how now the only things he can talk about in Chinese are food, family, and how to give directions to the bathroom."

"Wow," Jianyu says. "I wrote my college application essay about volunteering at the soup kitchen."

"That's very original of you," Iris says.

"I really have to go," Jianyu says. "I'm late to the game. Everyone's probably talking shit about me right now."

"Go," Iris says. "I'll text you tonight about the event. We can go over to his house after school later this week and talk to his parents."

Jianyu swings his backpack over his shoulders and starts to head out. Then: "Oh, Iris," he says, pausing in the open car door.

Iris turns on the car. "Yeah?"

"I would still like to have dinner at the restaurant next Friday," Jianyu says. "If you're still down."

Iris smiles at him—a little gooey, actually, and I'd be worried that this is the beginning of the most tumultuous romance ever if it weren't for the fact that they're basically brother and sister. "Of course I'm down," she says.

"Cool," he says, and jumps out of the car. We stay in the parking lot while Iris pulls away, hovering behind a fleet of minivans. A few seconds later, the television switches off.

"Good job," Caroline says. She's beaming.

"I can't believe that actually happened," I say, but the words come out all wrong, all warbled. For the first time since arriving in the room, for the first time in the last year, even through all the bedridden afternoons and futile interventions, I've started crying.

13 | the pitch

We watch the scene from the entryway, as if we're standing just inside the front door—close enough to make out their expressions; not close enough to hear the words.

My father's jaw is stubbled with the beginnings of a beard that matches his hair: everything now graying, now salt-and-pepper. How long has it been like that? He looks different, older, tired—but perhaps it's just the gaps between our visits to the real world making even the most minute physical changes seem exaggerated. Jianyu and Iris sit at the kitchen table with him, each with a steaming mug of tea in front of them.

The house looks—normal, mostly. Clean, uncluttered. No pastry baskets lined up on the kitchen counter; no fresh flowers from well-wishers. Then again, I hadn't really expected there to be. Mom and Dad mostly kept to themselves, other than occasional Sunday nights when the restaurant closed early enough for them to meet up with the only other two Chinese couples in Winterton to play cards over baijiu and fried peanuts. But even on those nights, they were usually too tired from the week to do much socializing.

Jianyu does most of the talking. My parents like Iris—in recent years, they'd started to like her a little too much, actually, asking offhand questions about when the two of us would start dating with increasing frequency—but they've always had a special fondness for Jianyu. He's the closest thing they have to a nephew on this side of the

Pacific; in some ways, he's the second child they always wanted but never found time to have after the restaurant took off. We'd have him over for dinner all the time, growing up: my mom showing off her cooking, Jianyu showing off his Mandarin, me trying to sneak sips of baijiu out of the bottle without anyone noticing.

Jianyu came around a lot less after his family moved across town, but who could blame him? "Busy with homework, such a good student," my mom always said. Sometimes my dad would send me to school with entire portions of kou shui ji to give to him at lunch—"His mom is not as good a cook as me, one time I remember he said he eats sandwiches for dinner, how can that be OK for growing boy to only eat sandwiches?"—which got more and more awkward as Jianyu started spending all his lunches with the Model UN kids. I always felt out of place dropping off those lunches: like me and my dad's cooking were both relics of his former life, intruding into his new one.

Jianyu gesticulates while he talks—something else he picked up after starting Model UN—and even from a distance I can tell when he's done speaking based on when his hands fall back to his sides. There's a brief moment when Jianyu isn't talking and Iris isn't talking and my dad isn't talking and I think maybe he'll be too proud to accept the help; insist on standing tall but alone at the helm of his ship while it sinks.

Then my dad pulls Jianyu into a hug. A real hug: the kind you only really see between dudes when someone has just won a sports championship or shot their first deer on the range or something. Honestly, I don't know if my dad has ever hugged *me* like that—not since I was a kid, anyway. None of us have ever been particularly big on PDA. Like declarations of love and expensive Christmas gifts, it's always seemed so embarrassingly gratuitous.

My dad takes a stuttered half step in Iris's direction like he's going to hug her, too, but then I think self-consciousness gets the best of him and he clasps her hands in his instead, shaking them while smiling, while nodding, while saying, *Iris, thank you, thank you.*

I can't make out Iris's response, but the look of charmed mortification on her face—and the one of bemusement on Jianyu's as he slides his phone out of his pocket to take a picture—is clear as day.

My dad invites them to stay for dinner, I'm sure, but they backpedal their way down the hall and through the front door with familiar rueful excuses: homework, time with family, now they've got an actual event to plan. He stands on the front porch while the two of them teeter down the driveway, Iris clutching Jianyu's arm for balance. There's been three or four more feet of snow since I was last home, which blankets the frostbitten ground in glistening white sheets, studded with their footprints.

My dad stays outside long after Iris and Jianyu have driven away, presiding over the desolate front yard, the dead grass, the bare trees. Twenty, perhaps thirty minutes later, when the television turns off, my dad is still standing there: his hair still gray, his beard still uneven, still looking different, older, and tired, but also, in that final, lingering image, looking hopeful.

CAROLINE

14 | etta james's "at last" is a close second

For a split second after the television turns off, Kenny and I just stare at each other. Then, our voices rising in unison:

"I can't believe all of that actually worked. I mean you *have* to believe it's magic now—"

"There's *gotta* be some explanation for this in a physics textbook somewhere—"

We both cut off. There's a loud *thwump* and a physics textbook lands at Kenny's feet.

"Oh, great," Kenny says, a bit faintly. "Just some light reading."

Then another noise from behind me—something like the dry rustle of wind through the leaves in the fall—and I spin around in time to watch the CD player vanish. Into the same thin air from which it had appeared, not a single CD left behind.

"But our tunes," I say, at the same time Kenny says, "I think I'm going to need a bigger textbook."

Pop.

TICKET #39,842,430, it says. CONDUIT 1 OF 3: CLOSED.

"Ticket number *what*?" I say, indignant. "We're not a ticket."

"Conduit one of three," Kenny says. He looks thoughtfully at the empty space where the CD player has just dematerialized. "It's closed—because we both used it, maybe? And the telephone booth is still here because you *haven't* used it?"

Then he frowns. "But how?"

"The how is more your department," I say.

"Why does the how always end up being my department?" Kenny says. Then he adds, sounding considerably more cheerful, "I guess I'll hit the textbook."

"I think you just answered your own question," I say, but Kenny is already carrying the book over to the library. He sits down without responding, starts leafing through the index, a pen caught between two fingers of his left hand.

I leave Kenny alone in the library with his textbook and his big ideas, and I walk to the back of the room, where there's a long corridor between the sectional and the mirror that runs along the wall. I'm thinking about Winterton at dusk again: Cooper walking to his car while the sun sets behind him, Dom's features set in shadow and light under the streetlamps. I ask the room for an easel, oil paints, brushes, my favorite brand of canvas paper. *Winterton, Evening Hours,* I title the series. And then I paint.

15 | the muffins were terrible, but everyone always said it was the thought that counts

My dad is in the kitchen when my mom gets home, sitting at the island with a white three-ring binder laid open in front of him. The binder holds twenty-five sheets of canvas paper, each thick with oil paint and sheathed in plastic. It's been years since I flipped through these paintings, which were all done over the course of a three-week summer camp I attended after freshman year. But the one that my dad is currently looking at is familiar, even after all this time. It's the first self-portrait I ever tried to paint.

"Roy, are you around?" my mom calls, and a few moments later, she appears, her purse slung over her shoulder, a cardboard box in her arms.

"It's all of Caroline's things from school," she says, setting the cardboard box on the floor. "Elliot has been holding on to them for us."

Then her eyes catch on the binder. "I remember this one," she murmurs. "Caroline stayed up all night to finish it, and then refused to look at it when it was done."

When people meet my parents for the first time, they usually assume my mom is the beauty of the family, and my dad is the brains. But actually my mom is probably both the brains and the beauty of the Davison household, and my dad is something else entirely—the one who volunteered at all our Little League games; the one who never misses a cousin's birthday even though we have upward of thirty. Dad has always been the first person I show a painting to when I'm finished—sometimes even before I'm finished, when all my thoughts are still as messy on the page as they are in my mind, hurt and joy and confusion spilling onto the canvas in ribbons of color.

My mom slides into a chair next to my dad and turns the page, the plastic slipping smoothly between her fingers. The next painting is a portrait of Cooper, in which I had deliberately painted his nose to be twice its actual size.

"I remember this one, too," she says, and the corners of her mouth curve into a soft smile. "She spent the next week trying to convince him that this was actually what he looked like."

Her gaze lingers on the page for a moment longer, and then she looks back up at my dad.

"I was on the phone with Kriminsky earlier," she says. "He wanted to know if we'd made a decision about giving victim impact statements at the sentencing hearing."

My mom looks better than she did the last time we saw her—her skin brighter, her voice clearer, not as grainy from exhaustion. It's hard to say the same for Dad.

"I don't want to do it," he says. His voice is quiet, unfamiliar. Hoarse from disuse, as if this really is the first time he's spoken in weeks.

"Roy . . ." my mom says.

"I don't want to do it," my dad repeats.

"Why not?" my mom says. She's trying to be delicate here—trying not to push too hard when my dad is so fragile, so obviously not himself—but I can hear frustration creeping into her voice.

"All we've done since the funeral is go from meeting to meeting, answer question after question about the accident," my dad says. "What year was the automobile purchased? When was the last time you went in for servicing? Which hospital declared time of death? And now all this time in court, endless meetings with the lawyers. We need to be moving on, Amy. We need to be moving forward."

My dad picks the keys of my mom's car up from the kitchen island and pitches them from one hand into the other, like a baseball, and in the wringing of his hands I can see the genealogy of Cooper's nervous tics, and of mine.

"Is this moving on, Roy?" my mom says. She looks pointedly at the photo album on the countertop then around the kitchen, where dishes have started to pile up in the sink, where dozens of unopened boxes of food have turned into dozens of half-eaten boxes of food, their contents spilling out onto the tabletops and the floor in trails of crumbs and crumpled wrappers.

"I don't want to spend the next month in meetings with Kriminsky, fighting for a sentence we may never get. We got a conviction—isn't that enough? What does it matter if the sentence is longer or shorter, if the fine is a few hundred or a few thousand dollars? And Cooper . . ." my dad continues, his voice suddenly rising, energy bursting through the dam of grief. "Cooper has to know that things are going to go back to normal! That he's going to finish the semester, that he's going to go to college in a year, that he's not going to spend the rest of his life in mourning!"

"Things are never going to go back to normal," my mom snaps. "It never will for us, it never will for Cooper, and it never should for Caroline's killer either. Driving drunk, Roy, through *our neighborhood,* where *our kids* live, where *Caroline—*"

My dad drops the keys. He starts crying.

"Oh, Roy," my mom says. "I'm sorry."

She places one hand on his knee, the other on his forehead. Tender.

"It's just," my mom says, "This is our chance. Our chance to make sure the judge knows just what we lost—what we *all* lost, every single one of us, the whole town—when we lost Caroline."

"What does it matter?" my dad says. "None of this is going to get her back."

"It's not about getting her back," my mom says. She sweeps her right hand across my father's face; tucks a lock of his hair, which has grown long since the accident, behind his ears.

16 | why twenty-six?

For a long moment after the television shuts off, I continue to stare at the screen, unable to look away even though the video is over.

I can see Kenny and myself reflected in the dark glass, our appearances unchanged from when we first arrived in the room. I haven't slept, but I don't feel tired. I haven't showered, but I still have perfect first-day hair. It's like time isn't passing at all.

"I'm sorry," Kenny says. "That couldn't have been easy to watch."

"It is what it is," I say. I'm trying to project a sense of calm, but even as I say the words, I can feel the emotions roiling underneath my composed façade: some awful combination of shock, sadness, frustration. And with the emotions come the memories, which are even harder to beat back. The feeling of cold rain, seeping through my shirt; the sound of the sirens; the smell of burning rubber.

I'm definitely going to be late to dinner now, I had thought, one split second of lucidity before it had all gone dark.

Suddenly I can't breathe. It's like I'm back in the car again, boxed in on all sides, trapped in sensory overload. I take shorter, harder breaths, but it's like trying to fill my lungs underwater—the more I gasp, the less air I have.

"Caroline?" Kenny says, and vaguely I register the note of alarm in his voice. He summons a mug out of thin air, which fills from the bottom up as he hands it to me.

It's tea—something dark and woodsy, nothing like the chais and lattes I'm used to ordering at the coffee shop. I drink in small sips until I feel like I can breathe again, and then I sit up, realizing as I do so that at some point I've doubled over.

"Someone *killed* me," I say, and now, along with the shock, sadness, and frustration, there's fresh anger surging through my veins as the truth of the words sink in, and as I process the fact of my death all over again.

"He *should* go to jail," I say, fiercely. "Whoever hit me, I don't know why my dad isn't supporting my mom in this."

"I understand," Kenny says, but he doesn't look completely convinced.

"Do you?" I say.

"I mean, your dad said the driver has already been convicted, right? So it's already going to be on his permanent record, even if he doesn't get sentenced to jail time . . . I don't know, Caroline, justice is complicated. It probably doesn't even matter what I think."

"Of course it matters what you think," I say, and at the same time, there's a sharp *pop* of noise from right above my head. I flinch, thinking once more of screeching tires, of scorching metal, but it's just the room, sending another one of its little notes.

THE TIME MAY COME WHEN IT MATTERS MORE THAN YOU THINK, it says.

"Well that's . . ." Kenny starts, and then finishes: ". . . ominous."

Another note.

NOT OMINOUS, it says. BUT PERHAPS INEVITABLE. SURELY YOU'VE NOTICED YOUR INFLUENCE OVER THE EVENTS ON THE OTHER SIDE OF THE MIRROR.

"What mirror?" Kenny says.

"I think he's talking about our superpowers," I say.

"I think calling them 'superpowers' is generous," Kenny says. "It implies that we're superheroes."

I read the end of the second note again, out loud: "*Surely you've noticed your influence over the events on the other side of the mirror*," repeating the words over and over again until they start to make some semblance of sense.

"We're not in purgatory so that we can go back after things are set right," I say. "We're in purgatory to set things right *ourselves*. On your end, that means saving your parents' restaurant. And on my end—on my end it must mean helping my parents through the court case. Making sure that driver isn't able to hurt anyone else."

There's something else, too—something that I don't say out loud because I can already picture the face Kenny would make if I did. But I can't help but have the thought: *Maybe, after we fix things, after Kenny's friends pull off the fundraiser and my family gets the sentence they want, there'll be some cosmic realignment that brings me and him and everyone else back to the morning of Saturday, March 12. Like—everyone's learned their lesson, and now we can run it back, and start over, and do it better this time.*

I wait for the next note—for some kind of correction or confirmation—but none appears. Instead, the television turns back on, the sudden burst of noise making both Kenny and me jump.

"This is way more television than my parents let me watch when I was alive," Kenny says. And for the first time in what feels like weeks, we're looking at Dom.

17 | it took us two months to make those shelves

The last time I saw Dom was when we were listening to Elvis Presley together, his eyes turned toward the sky and mine turned, as always, to him.

This time, he's in the kitchen, setting the table while his mom cooks. He takes the time to fold each napkin before setting it down, then arranges the silverware carefully on top.

It always meant a lot to Dom when he and his mother ate dinner together. Sometimes he'd go weeks at a time without even seeing her.

"Entire weeks?" I had said when he'd told me. "But where does she go? And what do you do?" It had been unfathomable, the idea of not seeing your family for weeks at a time. If I went two days without being on the receiving end of an idiotic prank from Cooper, I'd be worried that he'd been kidnapped. Sometimes I thought about using my entire savings account to send the rest of my family on a vacation to some remote island, just to get some alone time. But when I actually got alone time—when my parents went to the movies on date night and Cooper went to a party at a friend's place and I was stuck at home writing essays by myself—the house felt too big, too quiet, too lonely.

"She doesn't go anywhere," Dom had said. "We haven't had a working car in months. I think she just stays in her room."

"But what does she eat?" I had asked.

Dom had made the kind of face that suggested he was tired of talking about it. "I don't know, Caroline," he had said. "Maybe she has dinner while I'm at school."

"But if she eats while you're at school, why doesn't she just wait for you to get home, so you can eat together?"

"Caroline," Dom had said, "not all families are your family, OK?"

"But," I had said, "but—couldn't you just knock on her door? Couldn't you just—"

Dom had made some snarky remark and then stormed off and walked home by himself. The next day after school we had sat together at the rink, in the bleachers, trading long, drawn-out apologies: *I'm sorry for pushing. I'm sorry for running away. I'm sorry I don't understand. I'm sorry I don't know how to explain.*

"You'll see it for yourself soon enough," Dom had said.

When she was around, Mrs. Novak was warm, expressive, quick to laugh. It never seemed to bother her when Dom and I baked and left all the kitchen utensils out, dripping batter onto the counters. Nor, surprisingly, did it ever seem to get in the way of our conversations that I didn't speak a word of Polish and her English was elementary at best. Whenever she'd get stuck on a phrase or a word, she'd turn to Dom, saying: "Domek, kochanie, help me, how is it that we say—" before launching into a string of Polish that Dom would dutifully translate.

Oftentimes, though, she just disappeared. She'd spend more and more time staring at the far wall of the living room—where all of Dom's father's military awards were hung up, the only part of the house that seemed to get dusted regularly—growing less responsive by the day. When she did speak, it was always in Polish, and it was always addressed to Dom, excusing herself from the meal we were having or the movie we were watching or the board game we were playing, and then one day I'd come over after school and she wouldn't be around at all.

Tonight, Mrs. Novak looks fully present, bright behind the eyes in a way that makes me long to be there. She's chopping up peppers, cucumbers, cherry tomatoes, and lettuce for a salad. "Domek," she says, and then asks him a question in Polish.

"I'm pretty hungry," Dom says.

More Polish.

"No, I think we still have leftovers from that soup you made the other day, remember?"

More Polish.

"Let's just throw the chicken in the salad. Otherwise it'll start to go bad."

Mrs. Novak says, "OK"—which even I can understand—and then starts digging through the fridge, pulling out random Tupperware containers and Ziploc bags and stacking them on the only available surface, which is the microwave.

Probably the reason why Mrs. Novak was never upset about Dom and my rather lax approach to post-baking cleanup was because you could never see the countertops, anyway—or, for that matter, the vast majority of the surfaces in the house. Dom and I had made shelves together and mounted them to the wall to try to create more space, but after a few months of being rigorously organized they, too, had devolved into miscellaneous clutter. For Christmas I had gotten them one of those robot vacuum cleaners, but it backfired when Mrs. Novak named it robaczku—Polish for "little bug"—and started feeling guilty about putting something so cute to work.

By now all the food is on the table—chicken tossed into the salad, steam curling over the soup, a loaf of potato bread set aside next to the dishes. Mrs. Novak ladles soup into two bowls and Dom slices and butters the bread. The two converse intermittently, though I only understand Dom's half of the conversation:

"It's this Thursday at Exeter. We never beat them, but I don't think we'll lose as badly as we did last time."

"I haven't really thought about it."

"It's just one year. Lots of people don't go to college at all."

"I'm not saying *I'm* not going to go to college at all; I'm just saying lots of *other* people don't go to college at all. So even if I *did* decide that I didn't want to go to college at all, it still—"

Mrs. Novak has been growing increasingly agitated, and by the time she interrupts Dom she's only a few decibels short of a shout. She goes on for a few minutes, gesturing animatedly, and when she finishes her thought it's on two words that I recognize: *your Karolina.*

Dom's mother always called me *your Karolina* when she spoke to Dom about me, despite the fact that I had never really transitioned from *Mrs. Novak* to *Jola* no matter how many times she said *Please, Karolina, you are family*. The familiarity never felt quite right, even after all those dinners together, even after six months of dating—not with Dom still "Mrs. Davison" and "Mr. Davison"-ing all over the place when he was over at our house, terrified of walking within five feet of the china cabinet.

"It's ridiculous," I had said once. "You spend two hours a day on literal skates, on literal ice."

"The most valuable thing I could break in the rink is one of my bones," Dom had said, totally without irony. "My bones are a lot less valuable than your china."

Present-day Dom sits back in his chair, evidently unsure how to respond. Mrs. Novak adds a sentence, this time at regular speaking volume.

"That's not fair, Mom," Dom says.

"I wish I could understand what she's saying," I say, frustrated, and then a note appears:

YOUR WISH.

When I look back at the television, there are subtitles translating Mrs. Novak's words as she says them.

"Are you kidding me?" I say. "That's it? It's that easy? We should've had these when we were watching your parents, Kenny—then I would've known what was going on."

"I don't know about that," Kenny says. "I speak Chinese and sometimes still don't understand what's going on."

Mrs. Novak's latest sentence has been rendered in typewriter font across the bottom of the screen:

I liked Caroline, it says. **She helped you see sense. And now that she's gone, it seems your sense is gone, too.**

"Thanks, Mom," Dom says. "That's very comforting."

I'm sorry, Mrs. Novak says. **I'm sorry, kochanie, that was thoughtless of me. I just get so worried about your future. I don't want the grief to cloud your vision.**

"I'm not grieving," Dom says.

Domek, Mrs. Novak says—a little sad, a little knowing. **You're going to spend the rest of your life grieving. And that's OK. It won't be every day. But it will always be there.**

Dom cuts another slice of bread and offers it to his mom. When she shakes her head, he butters it for himself and dips it into the soup. When she doesn't break the silence—not even after he's finished his bread and his soup and eaten all the chicken out of his salad, leaving a bed of lettuce behind on his place—he says:

"It's been nice," Dom says, "Eating dinner like this. We never used to do it very much."

I've spent enough time at the house to know how rare this is—not just the homemade dinner, not just the actual place settings, but the way the two of them are looking at each other right now: with equal parts hope and hesitation, like the conversation is approaching uncharted territory they've decided to breach together.

I wish that wasn't the case, Mrs. Novak says. **But yes, I'm very glad also.**

"Caroline always thought it was strange how we didn't eat together every night," Dom says. "They were big on family dinners."

Of course, Mrs. Novak says, looking faintly amused.

The one time our parents had met was before homecoming last fall, when my parents had insisted on dropping me off at Dom's beforehand. They had greeted

Dom's mother with the kind of sparkly enthusiasm that, as Dom had explained to me afterward, "people outside of America generally find kind of creepy," and then tried to ameliorate Mrs. Novak's obvious increasing discomfort with a barrage of vigorous compliments.

"I don't think that went very well," Dom had remarked, afterward. "But it was nice of them to bring cookies."

On-screen, the levity has faded from Mrs. Novak's face. **But your Karolina's parents are right, Dominik**, she says. **I wish that we hadn't—that I hadn't—that it had been more like this before. I know that after your father passed, we were not—I was not . . .**

Her eyes flick over to the far wall, landing briefly on the portrait of Dom's father smiling thinly in a perfectly pressed military uniform, before returning to Dom's face.

But anyway, she says, as if scuttling the thought altogether, **we're going to do it differently this time. You must know that. You must know I'm trying.**

Dom *mms* a little in acknowledgment and then gets really interested in chasing around the dregs of his soup with his spoon. Eventually all that's left at the bottom of his bowl is a little cluster of parsley, and then Dom says: "Mom—why don't you ever talk about what happened with Dad?"

I talk about your dad, Mrs. Novak says, but the look of uneasy surprise on her face suggests otherwise.

"You talk about him as a person," Dom acknowledges. "'Great man, humble man, died serving the country he loved.' 'Gave you your eyes, your hair, and your stubborn attitude.' But you never talk about what happened."

Do you want to talk about what happened? Mrs. Novak says. **You've never asked.**

"I don't think I knew how to," Dom says.

It's very difficult, Mrs. Novak says. The words appear more slowly as she considers them. **For me, still, too. I don't . . .**

A cursor blinks in place at the end of her sentence. She looks over at Mr. Novak's wall again—all the colored ribbons, the medals, the plaques. Shiny pieces of paper framed in shiny pieces of wood. A folded American flag.

I don't like to remember how things ended.

"What about it don't you like to remember?" Dom says.

Oh, Domek, Mrs. Novak says. **It was just a terrible time. It was so unexpected, and suddenly we were all alone, and I used to think— I used to think—**

She blinks a few times, her entire expression shuttering with her eyes. **But we're finally having family dinner**, she says. **Now, after all these years. Let's not spoil our appetites.**

"I thought you said we were going to do things differently this time," Dom says. "I thought you said you were going to try."

Domek, Mrs. Novak starts.

"It's fine," Dom says, with the bitterness of years and years of accumulated hurt. "Forget about it. Whatever."

Domek, Mrs. Novak says again, and this time it sounds like she might start crying. It occurs to me that I've never actually seen Dom's mother look sad, look *hurt* in this way. *It's the vulnerability that's so unfamiliar*, I think, which was so absent from both the easy cheer of her better moments and the vacantness that preceded her disappearances.

"I'm sorry," Dom says. "I didn't mean to get upset. I mean, I know it's hard. I just wanted to ask. I wanted to know."

He pauses. Drags his spoon around the bottom of his bowl even though it's now quite empty.

"It's just—" Dom starts. "Sometimes I feel like Caroline is still here. Even though I know she's gone."

His eyes are dry, his voice steady, but I can see his fist clenched under the table, his nails digging into his palm.

"And I just wanted to know if you ever feel like that with Dad," Dom says. "But you don't like to talk about it, so—"

He laughs: dry, awful. "So—don't worry about it. Dinner was great. I mean that."

Mrs. Novak considers him for a moment. Then her response unfurls across the screen word by word, letter by letter.

I always felt like he was still here. He was in the bed where we slept, the car that we drove, the house that he built. I sold all of it—the car, the bed, and I burned everything he had ever touched—and I came here, far away from the cruel sunshine of California, where I had moved for him so many years ago. But even here, thousands of kilometers away, he was in the highways, so much bigger than anything I had seen growing up. He was in the chain restaurants where we used to eat, when we were too poor to go to the grocery store. He was in the wide smiles of all our new neighbors, the kind of smiles for no reason would make people in Poland think you are simple. This whole country, he was everywhere in it. And that was when I realized I would never be free of his ghost for as long as I remained in America. The country that he had taken me to. The country that had taken him from me.

Dom looks stunned. "You should have said something," he says. "And I could have—we could have moved. We could've moved to another country; we could've moved back to Poland."

Oh, darling, Mrs. Novak says. **My sweet boy. How could I have asked that of you? Here was your home, your motherland, your mother tongue. No, it was the right thing to stay. But I should have said something. I should have let you in earlier on. We could have helped each other, and maybe now it would not be like this still. Maybe now I would not be like this still.**

"Why didn't you?" Dom says.

Mrs. Novak starts crying. **I'm sorry, I'm sorry**, the screen says. Przepraszam. Przepraszam. **But those days— you have to understand. Seeing him everywhere was not the hardest thing.**

"What was the hardest thing?" Dom asks.

Oh, darling, Mrs. Novak says again. She reaches out across the table; she touches his face, his hair, his shoulders. **I wanted to say something. I wanted to share my grief and take some of yours. But I can't lie, I couldn't have lied. The hardest thing was seeing him in you.**

18 | right before the screen goes black

After dinner, Dom goes up to his room and makes a phone call.

"Hey," he says. "This is Dom Novak—I got your number from the school directory. Is this Iris Mutisya?"

KENNY

19 | Friday night

And then the scene changes, and there she is, sitting alone at a table for two in my parents' restaurant.

"Iris," I say.

The setting, the whole scene is intoxicating in its familiarity. I feel like I should be watching myself walk through the doors of the restaurant. Like I should be taking my place across from her and pouring out tea—first filling her cup, then mine—like I've done so many times before.

"Well," Caroline says. "This will make a very beautiful story, won't it? 'Two WHS seniors find healing in each other's arms after tragically losing their high school sweethearts within the span of—'"

"Wait, hold on," I say, wondering if I'm misreading her tone, or if Caroline Davison is actually—"Hold on, are you jealous?"

"Of course I'm not jealous," Caroline says. "I'm dead. Dom should be out getting dinner with other people."

"It's not like this is a date," I say. "They don't even know each other! Plus, Iris—"

I stop, thinking better of the rest of the sentence. Now is probably not a very good time to say, "Iris would never date a jock, just on principle alone," even if she's proclaimed as much to Jianyu and me on numerous occasions.

Fortunately, my dad saves me from having to finish my sentence. He's just walked up to Iris's table, a bowl of steamed rice in one hand and a platter of mapo tofu in the other.

"Oh. Oh, Mr. Zhou," Iris says, drawing Caroline's attention back to the screen. "You didn't have to. I was just waiting for Jianyu to get here to order."

"See?" I say. "Dom has nothing to do with this."

"Jianyu will order more when he arrives," my dad says. "Not good to sit so long without eating. Eat, eat," my dad continues, when Iris looks like she's going to argue. "I bring more rice if you finish. And dumpling, like always."

Iris doesn't have the heart to tell my dad that it had always been my request to order the dumplings. Her go-to was the tofu, and Jianyu had always preferred noodle dishes. But dumplings were one of the few menu items at the restaurant that I actually made—even if I made them imperfectly—and it felt like a waste somehow to not enjoy a single one after spending hours every weekend folding them.

"Thank you," she says, her voice catching slightly on the words, and my dad heads off to check on the only other party seated in the dining area: a middle-aged white couple that I don't recognize. Other than Iris, the couple, and one guy standing at the front waiting for a takeout order, the restaurant is totally empty.

The last time I had worked a Friday evening shift, we had to seat multiple parties at the eight- and ten-person tables because it had been so busy. It had been so loud that it was difficult to hear people's orders, with one set of toddlers chasing each other up and down the restaurant and another set wailing periodically at the top of their lungs for no apparent reason other than to make their presence known.

Personally, I had always found families with young children to be the worst customers: noisy, impatient, more often grumpy than not. But their business was what kept the restaurant thriving, my mom reminded me, time and time again—parents who were too busy or too frazzled or just too tired to cook dinner, but who wanted something a little nicer than the Pizza Hut on Main.

I hadn't even been scheduled to work a shift that night, but my parents had called me at seven P.M. after one of the other servers had begged off, claiming he had the stomach flu. "Is there no one else?" I had asked, even though I already knew the answer.

Over the course of the last two years, the number of times I had been called in to work last-minute shifts when my parents found themselves unexpectedly understaffed had been steadily increasing, and the pace of the average shift had gone from quiet to manageable to frantic. "You guys really need to hire more people," I had said one evening after closing, so tired it seemed like the height of injustice that I still had to sweep the floors. But sometimes my exhaustion and my exasperation would evolve into something closer to pride: *We did this*, I would think, looking at the stack of receipts toppling over at the register, the paper napkins strewn across the floor, the bits of sweet-and-sour glaze hardening on the tables with each passing second, all of which had somehow become endearing.

Watching the television screen tonight feels like I'm looking at the wrong restaurant, a different restaurant entirely, like all of Winterton has been thrown into an alternate dimension and not just me and Caroline. Everything looks darker, mustier without the liveliness of a crowd—the wallpaper cheap instead of charming, the carpet drab instead of homey. My dad has still taken the time to lay out menus on each table, perfectly clean, perfectly straight, waiting for guests that aren't ever going to arrive. And there's a banner hanging over the register that proclaims a ☺NEW DINNER SPECIAL!!!☺ for $14.99, clearly designed in Microsoft Paint by an amateur. I picture my dad hunched over his computer, changing the font colors of the smiley faces, pasting in photos of spring rolls and crab rangoons. It feels like an ice pick to the chest.

"It's not usually like this," I tell Caroline.

She looks at me, a little too much sympathy in her eyes. "I know, Kenny," she says. "I used to eat there all the time."

"Oh," I say. "Right." I had always tried to avoid the shifts after big sports games, petrified of the awkwardness of waiting on my classmates. We didn't have to wear embarrassing uniforms, like some of the kids who worked at other restaurants in town, but somehow it still seemed like the height of indignity to have to ask someone like Caroline Davison if she'd like more water, or if I could get her anything else before the check.

On-screen, Iris is getting frustrated: I can see it in the way she's pushing around her tofu, the crease that's appeared between her eyebrows.

"Jianyu bailed," I say. It's the only explanation for the look on her face.

"Maybe he's just late," Caroline says.

"Nah," I say. "He bailed."

Iris slides her phone out of her pocket, taps the screens. Scrolls. Scrolls. And then her face falls.

"He actually bailed," Caroline says. "Dang. I was just starting to like him."

"Jianyu giveth, Jianyu taketh away," I say. My personal motto when it comes to all things Jianyu.

There was a time when Jianyu's flakiness hurt my feelings the way it hurts Iris's—right around when he was first beginning his ascent up the social ladder last spring and kept ditching our movie nights for parties just like this one—but now I guess I've gotten used to it. The surprise and the hurt have both worn off, leaving a sort of resigned affection behind.

Unfortunately, I don't think Iris ever reached the same level of equanimity. She's in the process of counting out cash and slamming it onto the table like the founding fathers have personally wronged her when my dad materializes at her side, his arms full of dirty plates from the party of two. He probably hasn't asked anyone else to come in, if he's bussing the tables himself; he'll probably wash the dishes himself, too, even though every time my dad spends too much time on his feet he gets terrible back pain and has to take Tylenol just to walk the next day.

There's no room for pride when running a business, he always used to say; except he'd say it in Chinese, and I only figured out what it meant after Jianyu heard it one evening and translated it for me.

"No charge, no charge," my dad says, waving her off. "Jianyu not coming? No dumplings?"

"Jianyu's not coming," Iris says, grimly. "And Mr. Zhou, the whole point of this is to help the restaurant, and it's hard to help the restaurant when you're giving away food for free—"

"Family doesn't pay," my dad says, and Iris says, "Mr. Zhou" again, a little heartbroken.

"Come back soon," my dad says. "And come to house! We miss you. You bring cat, too, Kenny's mom can do more photo shoot—*ha, ha.*"

The one time we cat-sat for the Mutisyas, my mom had taken one look at Princess Moonlight, cooed, "Oh, how *pretty!*" and then spent three hours taking photos of her for her blog. My mom now insists that Princess Moonlight is one of the most popular cats on Chinese social media, but unfortunately my second-grade Chinese reading comprehension limits my ability to witness her stardom for myself.

"I will, Mr. Zhou," Iris says. She pulls the straps of her backpack over her shoulders. "We'll come over next week to plan the fundraiser. Me and Jianyu both."

"Yes, yes, Jianyu," my dad says. "So busy with homework! Such a good student."

"Yeah," Iris says, smiling thinly: "Homework."

But my dad doesn't clock the bitterness in her voice—just says, "Take care," and heads off with the dirty dishes.

"Where is my mom?" I say. "He shouldn't be working shifts alone, even if it is a quiet night."

The screen goes dark before my dad reaches the kitchen, Alice still sitting alone at the table. And then it brightens again, and I get my answer.

20 | the medium

My mom is in an office.

It's small, but densely decorated: the walls lined with abstract art and the floor blanketed by a thick woven rug. All warm colors—reds, oranges, yellows. I can practically feel them radiating from the screen and leaching into the bone white of our walls.

There's one other person in the room with her: a woman with brown shoulder-length hair, wearing a patterned tunic that sweeps the floor.

She looks about my mother's age. She looks kind.

"What do you think?" Caroline says. "A shrink? A grief counselor?"

"Maybe?" I say.

Back during the good old days in the glorious land of the living, I never would have imagined my parents going to counseling. I could barely convince them to go to their annual physicals, even when their symptoms—my mom's persistent fatigue, my dad's back pain—were debilitating. Isolated instances of emotional distress, like disappointment over a bad test grade or anger at a particularly unpleasant customer at the restaurant, were generally triaged with porridge and good humor, and ongoing problems of that nature simply never came up. But perhaps this, like so many other things since my death, has changed.

The two women are sitting around a small, circular glass table in the center of the office: my mom with her purse still clutched to her chest; the therapist with open shoulders, her hands on the table, palms facing up. A stick of incense burns between them on the table, sending long fingers of smoke into the air.

There's a third chair in the room that's conspicuously empty. I'm surprised that my dad isn't there. I'm surprised that my mom would make an appointment without him.

But then the grief counselor—who is not a grief counselor after all—says:

"Eva, did you happen to bring a photograph of the person you're hoping to reach today?"

My mom pulls a photo out of her purse, slides it across the table. It's a picture I recognize from the living room windowsill: me, at age four, sitting on a swing with my legs kicked out in front of me. Midflight; midlaugh.

The shot is one in a series of photographs my grandmother took while she was here for six months, helping take care of me while my parents launched the restaurant. There are two others from that set on the same windowsill: one taken as I walked to the bus stop, my backpack almost larger than my torso; the other as I stood in the candy aisle of the nearest Chinese grocery store, looking mournfully at a box of lychee jellies.

"She's a medium," Caroline breathes. "See, Kenny? The phone call worked. Somehow, your mom knows it was you.

Oh—but this is *wonderful*," she adds, and I can sense the full wattage of her beam aimed in my general direction even if I can't look away from the screen long enough to see it. And even though I usually find Caroline's brighter moments more alienating than contagious, this time, I feel it, too. The glowing certainty that my mom heard me—not just as a glitch in the power grid or a series of prank calls, but as *me*. As her son.

"Kenny," my mom says, and sets her purse down on the empty chair next to her.

"Kenny," the medium repeats. She looks at the photo and then places it at the center of the open circle formed by her arms, her hands. "Yes," she says. "Yes, I can feel Kenny with us here now." Her eyes flutter shut; my mom leans forward in her chair.

"So young," the medium murmurs. "He passed last year?"

"December twelve," my mom says.

"Can't believe it's been so long already," Caroline says, and I'm about to interject—because how is she supposed to know how long it's been, when we don't have any clocks?— except then the screen freezes. It doesn't go staticky, like it normally does, or shut off. It just . . . stops. Like someone's hit pause on the video.

"What?" I say.

"This is new," Caroline remarks.

A note flutters onto my shoulder. PLEASE SEE MONITOR, it says.

"What monitor?" Caroline says.

Then a computer materializes next to the sectional with a loud *plonk*: the kind I've only ever seen in the pages of our history textbook, in the chapters about the information revolution and the advent of the computing age. It's massive, with a separate desktop monitor, keyboard, and CPU tower. I think it might be almost as big as the phone booth.

"A phone booth from the eighties, a computer from the nineties, and a CD player from the early aughts," I say, as the two of us walk over to the desktop. "Turns out God is a hipster."

Caroline snickers. A note flutters to the ground in front of me. It reads:

I'VE ALWAYS HAD ECLECTIC TASTE. SOME WOULD SAY IT GIVES THE ROOM CHARACTER.

The monitor is already on when Caroline and I get there, with a pop up in the center of the screen that reads:

Incoming divination request for Kenny Zhou (IDLES ID#459,839,094) from Angela Grimsley (ARCLAMPS ID #220482). Accept request?

Yes   No

"This cannot be real," Caroline says, from over my shoulder. "IDLES? ARCLAMPS?"

"That's what you're hung up on?" I say. "The abbreviations?"

But even as I say the words, there's another missive from above. Caroline unfolds it and reads:

IDLES: INTERDIMENSIONAL LOST ENERGIES & SOULS.

ARCLAMPS: THE ASSOCIATION OF REGISTERED CLAIRVOYANTS, MEDIUMS, PSYCHICS, AND SEERS.

"Huh," Caroline says. "Well, that's good to know."

"Is it?" I say. "Hold on, did the note say 'interdimensional'?"

"It also said 'lost,'" Caroline says. "Do you feel like a lost soul, Kenny?"

"I'm doing it," I say, and click YES. Immediately, the screen explodes into a shower of poorly rendered, multicolored confetti. A trumpet noise emanates from the computer speakers. Both the graphic design and the speakers are clearly of the same era as the computer.

"Oh, boy," Caroline says.

When the digital confetti clears, a second pop-up has replaced the first:

"Oh, no," I say.

ALWAYS READ THE FINE PRINT, the room says.

"The fine print wasn't legible!" I say. "Where's the button that says, 'Never mind'?"

"No way out but forward," Caroline says cheerfully, and presses Continue. Another pop-up replaces the previous one instantly:

"It wants me to answer, I guess," I say.

"The seeker—that must be your mom," Caroline says.

I type in *SON* and then hit Enter.

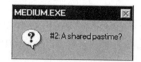

MEDIUM.EXE ☒

? #2: A shared pastime?

Over the next two minutes, a series of pop-ups appear in rapid succession, each with an empty short-answer field at the bottom. To make things difficult, an hourglass also appears that starts to count down the thirty seconds I have to write something before the next pop-up. To make things even more difficult, there's a fifteen-character limit on each answer. In the end, it feels more like a game of word association than anything else, with Caroline reading the prompts out loud and me furiously typing in the first thing that comes to mind while the clock runs down:

"#4: A sentimental object?"

I type in *DISHWASHER*.

"#5: A mutual loved one?"

My dad, obviously.

"#6: A message for that loved one?"

"How do I fit 'I miss you and I'm sorry and I'm doing everything I can on my end to buy you some time for the restaurant' into fifteen characters or less?" I say.

"We need Becca for this," Caroline says. "She has ten thousand followers on Twitter."

In the end, I type *GIVE IT TIME* and hope that gets the message across.

Unfortunately, some of the prompts aren't quite so straightforward. There's "#8: The eighth deadly sin?"

There's "#14: A fortuitous cardinal direction?" ("East?" I say, out loud. "Like, because we're Chinese, maybe?" Then the hourglass runs out before I have time to fill anything in at all.) There's "#21: Epoxy, a plague," which isn't even a question.

"It doesn't seem fair that I have to fill this out without knowing how Angela Grimsley is going to interpret them," I say. "I don't understand why I can't just write—you know—a letter or something."

DO YOU KNOW HOW MUCH ENERGY IT TAKES TO TRANSMIT A MESSAGE LIKE THAT ACROSS DIMENSIONS? the room writes. "A LETTER," HE SAYS. HOW QUAINT.

"You transmit literal furniture across dimensions!" I say. "Surely that takes a bit of energy!"

"Don't yell at the room, Kenny," Caroline says.

THE FURNITURE TRANSMITTED INTO THE ROOM IS AFFECT NEUTRAL, the room says. IT REQUIRES ONLY A ONE-TO-ONE TRANSLOCATION OF A PHYSICAL OBJECT ACROSS SPACE-TIME. LETTERS, ON THE OTHER HAND, ARE AFFECT NONNEUTRAL. LETTERS ARE COMPRISED OF THOUGHTS AND FEELINGS AND SUBJECTIVE EXPERIENCES, REQUIRING A TRANSLOCATION OF THE SOCIO-EMOTIONAL CONTEXTS IN WHICH THEY WERE FORMED BY THE SENDER, AND IN WHICH THEY WILL BE READ BY THE RECEIVER. LAVOISIER'S LAW OF CONSERVATION OF MASS—

I stop reading.

"I don't have time to get into the theory right now!" I say. The last three pop-ups have asked for "a beloved household pet," "a cocktail of choice," and "a board game that sparked insurrection," all of which I've had to leave blank.

"This must be why psychic readings are always so garbled," Caroline says. "I always figured it was because they were making everything up."

The last prompt is #30, and there's no box for me to write in at the bottom. It just says: "#30: Please take thirty seconds to reflect upon the circumstances of your departure from the mortal plane," and the hourglass tips over.

"I don't—" I say, but I can't finish the sentence. I don't know how? I don't want to? In general, I have tried to spend as little time as possible thinking about the circumstances of my departure, the circumstances *before* my departure, the people I've departed from, the looks on their faces at the funeral, my father's eyes, haunted by the realization that his only child was really—his only child had really—his only child—

And then, right on cue, there's the self-loathing, which is why I had wanted to avoid this particular train of thought in the first place.

Mercifully, the hourglass runs down, the short window of time for once a blessing. The pop-up disappears, and we're looking at the default Windows XP desktop background. There's another shower of confetti, neon worms raining down on an oversaturated rendering of a meadow, and another chipper little *doot-doot* from the speakers. It all feels considerably absurd.

"I don't know how Angela Grimsley is going to make sense out of any of that," I say, feeling defeated.

"I thought you did pretty well, all things considered," Caroline says. She tugs me out of the desk chair and back to the couch, where a note has landed.

SHE DOESN'T NEED TO MAKE SENSE OF IT. SHE JUST NEEDS TO MAKE IT SOUND PROFOUND.

"Don't be mean," Caroline says, and it's bizarrely satisfying to hear the familiar refrain directed at someone who isn't me.

SORRY, the room writes.

"Caroline," I say. "I think God just apologized to you."

"Don't say stuff like that," Caroline says, blushing.

If the bad thing about being stuck in this room with Caroline is that she forces me to spend a lot more time than I'd prefer thinking about the mortal plane, the good thing is that she's not actually terrible company.

I should tell her, I think. I should tell her that the circumstances of my departure from the mortal plane were very different from the circumstances of her departure from the mortal plane. And it's a good moment for it, with Caroline feeling all sunny over her special relationship with the man above. But then the television screen un-pauses, and—like no time has elapsed, like my mother has just said the date of my death—Angela Grimsley says, "So recent. So terrible, Eva, I'm so sorry for your loss. But Kenny is here with us today, and he's showing me—he's showing me a kitchen. It's got a blue-tiled backsplash, and he wants—he wants me to point out the dishwasher. Does that mean anything to you—a dishwasher?"

And my mom—who already *believes* in my existence—still looks shocked. "Yes," she says. "It means something to me."

Angela Grimsley stays silent, as if to say: *Go on . . . ?*

My mom hesitates before continuing. "We don't use dishwasher at home. Instead we put in the clean dishes after washing by hand—save water, save time. Better for dishes, too. One day Kenny come back after school, go straight to dishwasher, open it, turn it on, and say, *'This thing washes the dishes for you?!'* One of his American friends had told him."

My mom's impression of my outraged shout is pretty accurate: I couldn't believe I had spent so many years of my life washing the dishes after dinner as a chore when there was literally a machine that *washed them for you* three inches away. Even after I explained that the dish washer didn't *actually* use more water than doing all the dishes by hand, my mom still refused to use it, and would mutter, "So wasteful. So wasteful," every time I brought it up.

"That's a fond memory for him, too," Angela Grimsley says. "I can feel his energy here with us—he's smiling."

Caroline looks over at me. I stop smiling.

"I thought—" my mom starts. "Sometimes he seemed embarrassed. Not just of dishwasher. Other things, too."

"Perhaps he was embarrassed at the time, but isn't anymore," Angela Grimsley says. "Or perhaps the shame you remember is something you feared more than he felt." And then: "I'm hearing a J name—a Jason, perhaps a Jay. Do you know anyone with that name?"

"My husband," my mom says. "Kenny's father. It's his American name. Like my American name is Eva. His Chinese name is—"

She cuts off, realizing, perhaps, that Angela Grimsley has not asked.

"Go on," Angela Grimsley says.

"It's Zhou Jun," my mom says, looking a little embarrassed.

"Kenny is saying Zhou Jun is a good man, a good father. He just needs time."

"Time to turn the restaurant around," I say, as if I can will the rest of the message across, but my mother just furrows her brow, considering Angela Grimsley's words.

"And what about penguins?" Angela Grimsley says. "He's showing me penguins—what does that mean to you?"

PENGUINS had been my response to "#12: A serendipitous animal?" because of the long-ago memory that had flashed into my mind, unbidden, when I had first read the question. In the memory, my parents and I are at the Antarctica exhibit of the local zoo. There's an illustration of two emperor penguins huddled around a chick; being only seven years old, and thus too young to feel embarrassed by this sort of childishness, I shout, looking up at my mother: "It's like us!"

On-screen, my mother frowns. "I don't know," she says. "Kenny liked science. Many interesting science facts, maybe something about penguins . . ."

She doesn't remember the zoo. I suppose at this point it's been almost ten years. I probably should have gone with a rabbit, which is the Chinese zodiac animal of my birth year. But Angela Grimsley just says: "Perhaps the significance isn't meant to become clear until later," and continues with a prediction about my mother finding the answers to her questions by "looking East."

Angela Grimsley sits with my mother for another twenty minutes, taking my words and phrases from the Mad Libs exercise and turning them into messages, memories, predictions, using some combination of surprisingly astute psychological observation and, yes, cryptic bullshit. But despite the imperfect interdimensional translation—and the lack of "socioeconomical context," as the room put it—there are a good number of messages that *do* seem to get across. Moments when I can feel the connection between me and my mother stretching across space-time, as real as if I was sitting at the kitchen table with her, drinking tea and trying to find the words to tell her about my day.

Toward the end of the session, Angela Grimsley says: "Kenny thanks you for the red envelopes, and he wishes they weren't the last gift you gave him. He knows you've been feeling very lonely since he's been gone, and he wishes that he could be with you now."

She says it unassumingly, almost as if it's an afterthought—but my mom looks stricken.

"I didn't write that anywhere," I say, taken aback.

"Well, don't you?" Caroline says. "Maybe some things she really does just know."

"And finally—"

Angela Grimsley pauses. With her eyes still closed, she traces the edge of the photograph with her finger.

"And finally, he wants to tell you that it wasn't your fault. What happened—it wasn't your fault."

My mother clasps her hands together so tightly her knuckles go white. "Does he know?" she asks. "Can he see us? Is he here with us now?"

"He's been here with us," Angela Grimsley says. "I can sense his presence, his spirit, his joys, his sorrows. The whole of his person, an imprint of what he experienced when he still inhabited our plane. But in many ways, mediumship is a one-way street. We can sense them, but not how much of us they can sense in turn. If they're watching us—or even if they're listening. But I have to imagine that they are. That he is."

My mom nods. She reaches for her purse, sitting next to her in lieu of my father, and pulls out a pack of tissues.

Angela Grimsley opens her eyes.

"I'm sorry," she says. She really does sound sorry. "But unfortunately we've reached our time for today. I hope this brought you some measure of solace. Knowing Kenny is still with us, even if he's somewhere else."

My mom blots the table before responding, then blows her nose.

"Can I come back?" my mom says.

"We advise that clients take some time for themselves between sessions," Angela Grimsley says, gently. "It's important we maintain our relationships with loved ones on this plane, too."

"How much time?" my mom says. "I can bring my husband. He misses our son, too. And he needs to see this. To experience. To believe."

A beat. Angela looks thoughtfully at my mother. I don't know what I'm hoping for—do I want her to come back? Do

I want her to bring my dad? The objective of reaching out was always so she'd feel comforted enough to move forward, not to keep her returning to the past over and over again.

"Next month," Angela Grimsley finally says. "The twelfth. A mensiversary—that will be powerful."

"Thank you," my mom says. She picks up the photograph and slides it back into the purse—slowly, carefully, like it's something fragile.

"Should I bring different one next time?" she asks. "New photo? I have many. Kenny older, Kenny younger. Many photo."

"Oh, you don't need to," Angela Grimsley says. "It's just so we can get a sense of their spirit, the first time. And Kenny's is so strong. I can still feel him so clearly."

"Thank you," my mom says again. She picks up her purse and walks with Angela Grimsley to the door, where she sinks into a little half bow before leaving.

"Be safe," Angela Grimsley says, shutting the door.

Angela turns around, walks back to her chair in the center of the room and sinks into it. She crosses her legs and closes her eyes. After a moment, she murmurs: "Oh, Kenny. I'm so sorry."

"What's she doing? Why's she sorry?" Caroline says.

"I don't know," I say, even though I'm increasingly certain that I do. But it doesn't feel like the right moment to talk to Caroline about it anymore—not right now, at least, with everything that's going on.

"You poor boy," Angela Grimsley says.

On the table, the incense is still burning.

CAROLINE

21 | the green-eyed monster

After we watch Kenny's mom's visit to the medium, there's a long break in the television stream. It's a good thing, too, because I'm starting to feel like I'm losing my mind.

I miss restaurants. I miss the park. I miss being *outside*.

Kenny thinks I'm jealous of Iris because I think that Dom might be interested in her. But the truth is I'm jealous of Iris because she's *alive*. I'm jealous of Dom, too, in that respect—in fact, I suppose I'm jealous of everyone we ever see on the television, Iris and Dom and Cooper and Jianyu and Kenny's mom and Kenny's mom's psychic and all the other people who get to move through a world of dinner parties and wisteria trees and sports games while we're confined to 1,500 square feet of drywall and linoleum.

No matter how magical those 1,500 square feet are, it's still just a room. And it's still the same room every day for God knows how many days now. And I don't even want to think this, because thinking it feels like admitting defeat—but how many more days is it going to be? Everything the room has taught us to do so far has been about helping our friends and family move on. Helping them come to terms with our deaths. Helping them build new lives without us. And if we were just biding our time until we got the return-trip light-beam ticket back to planet Earth—well, we wouldn't need to do all that, would we?

What if Kenny and I are literally stuck in purgatory for the rest of our lives? And what if "the rest of our lives" is literally the rest of eternity? Our bodies don't function here like they do in the real world—one time, as an experiment, I drank twelve cups of coffee just to see what would happen, only to find that *nothing* happened; not so much as a headache. What if we're not aging—what if we never will?

Across the room, in the library, Kenny doesn't look like he's doing much better with his thoughts than I am with mine. He's staring blankly into the pages of his physics textbook, his expression frozen in place save for the occasional deepening of the crease between his eyebrows.

"Hey," I say, and walk over to where he's sitting. The mug appears in my hand as I'm halfway there; by the time I hand it to Kenny, it's steaming. "Here, drink this."

Kenny extends his arm, takes the mug, lifts it to his lips—all without looking up from his textbook. His movements robotic, like he's going through the motions without actually tasting anything. He's drained half of the drink before anything seems to register—but then he looks up at me, eyes wide.

"How did you know?" he says.

"I just asked for the same thing that you got me last time," I say. "I liked it. Tea, right?"

Kenny takes long sips this time, savoring it.

"It's my parents'," he says. "And I think this is the real thing. I think the room actually got it straight out of our kitchen cabinet."

He stares down into the mug, watching as the drink replenishes itself, watching as the water line rises. He lifts the mug to his mouth again, the scent of the tea wafting up toward me as he drinks, and then he puts the mug down on the table and says, "I feel like we're not doing enough."

"I know," I say. "But we're making progress, aren't we? We've figured out that time is passing differently. We've figured out that we're in another dimension. We've even figured out our superpowers."

Kenny doesn't respond. But my mom always says the most valuable element in the world is a silver lining, and so I forge ahead: "And they've *worked*. With Dom, with your mother. So if we can just get my parents through the hearing, and Iris and Jianyu through the fundraiser . . ."

"Yeah," Kenny murmurs. He's staring into his drink again, and I can tell he's not really listening. "Hey, I wonder if . . ."

A plate of dumplings appears before him. Then a bottle of vinegar. Then a bottle of chili oil with a portrait of a stern-looking Asian lady on the front.

"Every time," Kenny says, "every time, I'm surprised."

Kenny starts mixing the vinegar and the chili oil in a sauce dish, but not before biting into one of the dumplings. "Also the real thing," he says, his words thick with disbelief, and also thick with half-chewed food. "Definitely Dad's. How are you *doing* this? Doesn't anyone *notice*?"

Kenny catches the note in midair before it can flutter down and into the sauce. He reads out loud:

OF COURSE THEY NOTICE. BUT PEOPLE FIND EXPLANATIONS WHERE THEY CAN. A SPOUSE'S LATE-NIGHT CRAVING. A FORGOTTEN DINNER FROM EARLIER IN THE WEEK. A TRICK OF MEMORY. THEY ALWAYS HAVE.

Kenny puts the note down. "While I have you on the line," he says, and then there's a little blitz of paper scraps falling from the ceiling, all with the same text:

UNABLE TO FULFILL REQUEST. ERROR CODE #204.

UNABLE TO FULFILL REQUEST. ERROR CODE #204.

UNABLE TO FULFILL REQUEST. ERROR CODE #204.

"What'd you wish for?" I say, while Kenny looks crestfallen.

"A timer, a stopwatch, and a pendulum," Kenny says. "I was pretty certain we wouldn't get the timer and the stopwatch, but I thought, with the pendulum—because it's not technically a timekeeping device, see . . ."

Kenny brightens. "But in fact, pendulums are one of the oldest and most accurate ways of keeping time—because they oscillate at incredibly precise intervals based on their length." Then he deflates again. "But I guess they wouldn't work here because we're in an extra-temporal dimension. Would they oscillate at all? The physics is just gnarly."

"Gnarly, yeah," I say.

Kenny starts working his way steadily through the dumplings, plunking them into the sauce with every bite, the chopsticks moving easily between the fingers of his right hand. He's eaten half a dozen when a guilty expression flashes over his face and he says: "Do you want any? I should've asked."

"That's all right," I say. "I'm not hungry. Room biology, you know."

"You can eat for reasons other than hunger," Kenny says, his mouth twisting upward into a wry, sad smile.

And as he resumes eating I watch that smile transform into something softer, something that perhaps proves his point. The stress lines between his eyebrows smooth out and the tautness at the corners of his mouth relax until he starts to look comfortable—until he starts to look at home, almost. Like he's wholly present in the moment, in each dumpling he eats, in each reassuringly familiar bite, all questions about time, infinity, eternity temporarily rendered irrelevant.

I want to paint him, I realize. I want to paint the familiarity that has developed between Kenny and me over the course of our time here, wherever we are. I want to work on something other than the portraits of my brother and Dom—which began as my own testaments to love but now feel more like altars of grief. Every time I look at them, every time I catch Dom's eye on the easel—it feels like I'm losing them all over again.

"I'm gonna—" I start, motioning back to the easel, and Kenny just nods. He flips the textbook open again, starts riffling through the pages—but with more energy this time, jotting little notes down on the graph paper next to him in a messy scribble I can't read and probably wouldn't be able to understand even if I could.

It feels like I spend the next couple of hours working on the portrait—first roughing out the lines of Kenny's body, then the shape of his face, then the delicate arch of his fingers around the chopsticks. I'm just starting to sketch out his surroundings—the heavy oak desk, the bookshelf resting half empty above it, the plate of dumplings pushed up against the textbook—when the television year and cried again making it in junior year; it's where I opened the letter telling me I had gotten into the U on a full athletic scholarship just a couple of months ago, the rest of the table erupting into cheers when I read it out loud. I've spent more of my life over the past four years at WHS than at home, and within WHS, the cafeteria was always the place where I knew I'd be able to find my friends, somewhere to sit, and hot food that occasionally didn't even suck.

I glance over at Kenny, whose eyes are also scanning looking for Jianyu, probably, and Iris. Jianyu's not hard to find—he's the only Asian boy left in the grade. He's sitting with the Model UN kids, which is a group so large that the seniors occupy a whole corner of the cafeteria, three tables they've annexed for themselves. Jianyu is at the table with the most popular of the MUNers, gesticulating animatedly with a forkful of noodles held aloft in one hand that's dripping sauce onto the table. And Iris—

Iris is walking up to a table with Dom.

The video zooms in on the two of them, who make their way to an empty table on the south side of the cafeteria, on the opposite side of Dom's usual spot with the rest of the varsity hockey team.

"This OK?" Dom asks, and Iris nods.

"Thanks for having lunch with me," Dom says, as the two sit down. He unzips his lunchbox, looks down into it, and makes a face. "She always forgets we aren't allowed to use the microwaves," he says, and pulls out a Tupperware full of stew.

comes on again. Kenny and I both look up at the s
which is broadcasting a stream of lunch period at s

It's a wide shot—as if a camera has been placed i
the ceiling corners—that captures practically ever
ber of the senior class, making their way from the
doors to the lunch line or straight to a table, fo
paths so familiar and ingrained the movements
well be scripted, the tables preassigned. I can se
her backpack slung loosely off one shoulder, her l
wrapped in compression tape, where Tyler and B
Christian are already seated, and where Molly D
sitting in Adam Nichelsen's lap so there'll be m
at the table.

"Molly was JV at the last practice," I say. "She
been called up after I—"

I stop.

"Caroline," Kenny says, gently, "You need to
to saying it."

But it's hard—it's always been hard—and
cially hard now, watching everyone's lives un
the same rhythms, the same lunch tables, the s
groups, the same dumb, loud posturing from th
team, the same dark sneers from the snobby ar
for some reason sit next to each other despit
animosity that's probably existed since WHS'
in eighteen forty-whatever.

It feels like the cafeteria is where so much
has happened. It's where Maddie and Becca
from teammates into best friends; it's where I
missing the cutoff for the varsity team in

"No problem," Iris says. She doesn't respond to Dom's comment about the cafeteria amenities; in fact, she looks pretty skeptical of this entire situation.

"So, what's going on?" Iris asks.

"I wanted to talk about Kenny," Dom says, and Iris blanches.

Dom has never been the best at subtlety. It was something we were working on.

"And Caroline," Dom adds.

"You called me to ask to get lunch so we could talk about Kenny?" Iris says.

"Well, I called your other friend, too," Dom says. "But he didn't answer, and then he didn't respond to the text I sent explaining why I had called in the first place, so."

At that, Iris softens. "Don't take it personally," she says. "Jianyu isn't a great texter. Or a great communicator in general. Actually, right now, he's not a great anything."

She stabs at her own lunch, a chicken salad.

"I'm really sorry," Dom says. "I'm sure your friendship is under a lot of stress right now."

"He stood me up at dinner the other night," Iris says. "After he promised— he promised—"

Iris sighs, gives up. "Never mind. Let's not get into Jianyu right now; I'll lose my appetite."

"I'm really sorry," Dom repeats.

"It's fine," Iris says. "You know, he's probably going through his own shit right now."

Dom nods. "Everyone responds differently to grief," he says, with the kind of naked earnestness that would get him made fun of by his teammates.

"Your boyfriend talks like a self-help book," Kenny tells me. He's watching the screen anxiously, like he half expects Dom to whip off his shirt at any moment and ask Iris to the prom.

"I honestly don't know where it's coming from," I say. "I tried to get him to talk about his feelings all the time when we were dating, and sometimes it even worked, but this is just beyond. Maybe he's been seeing a therapist."

Dom says: "That's what my therapist tells me, anyway."

"You've been seeing a therapist?" Iris asks.

"Since last month," Dom says.

"It's been a month," Kenny says, looking shocked.

"It's been *more* than a month, since he definitely didn't start going right away," I say. A month. A month stuck here in purgatory, and how many more? Panic crawls up my spine. "But time is weird here, you know, so maybe—"

Kenny shushes me so we can hear Iris's response. "I should probably go to one, too," she says, sighing. "I know the school has them on call for us. I just haven't been able to bring myself to schedule an appointment. It's tough. Sometimes it feels like there's nothing anyone could say that would make me feel better. And sometimes it feels like it's a betrayal to even want to feel better in the first place."

Dom eats some of the stew, frowns, and pushes his Tupperware aside. He'll probably buy a few slices of pizza before lunch gets out and then scarf it down before practice. Then after practice he'll be starving again in time to go out for dinner with his teammates. I always used to tell him that the best part of being a hockey player was getting to eat like a hockey player.

"You don't think Kenny would want you to feel better?" Dom asks.

"Of course Kenny would want me to feel better," Iris says. "He'd want me to do all the dumb senior year stuff like ditch day and the prank and prom. And then he'd want me to go on some stupid road trip over the summer like everyone does before they start college. But that was all stuff we were supposed to do together, you know, with the three of us, and now Jianyu and I barely talk and Kenny is— Kenny is—"

Iris hasn't gotten used to saying it either.

"Sorry," she says, when she can't continue.

"Don't apologize," Dom says. "It's actually kind of nice. It's not nice that you're upset, obviously. But it's nice to hear someone else put into words everything that I've been feeling."

Iris looks taken aback. Her shock is slightly insulting, actually. But I figure now is not the time to call out Kenny's best friend for stereotyping athletes.

"So what have you been doing?" Iris asks. "You know— when things get—bad."

"Hockey helps," Dom says. "Gets me out of my own head. Reminds me that I can still do things that make me feel happy, even if while I feel happy I also feel kind of sad."

"I wish Science Olympiad was like that," Iris says. "But everything about it reminds me of Kenny. Jianyu invited me to apply for Model UN, actually, but I didn't because that whole crew is just—"

Her eyes flick over to the Model UN tables, where Jianyu's whole group has just burst into raucous laughter.

"—a glorified fraternity."

"You don't need to be friends with people to be on a team with them," Dom says. "I'm not friends with most of the guys on the hockey team, but I still like being on the team."

"You're not friends with most of the guys on the hockey team," Iris repeats, flatly.

"No!" Dom says. "I mean, I like them all right. We hang out, I go to their parties. But I've never been close with them—not really, not in the way Caroline was close with the softball team. Honestly, I think most of my teammates got along with Caroline better than they got along with me. Sometimes a little too much better."

Dom scowls. He's thinking about Harry Clarkland, who was always a little too excited to show off his wrist shot whenever I hung out at practice.

"So who are you close with, if not the hockey guys?" Iris says.

"These days? Mostly Cooper," Dom says. "He gets what we're going through. I mean, it's a lot worse for him, obviously, because she's his sister, and I guess things are kind of weird between his parents right now . . ."

Dom trails off as the warning bell rings, signaling three minutes until the end of the lunch period.

"Anyway," Dom says. "I'm going to go buy some pizza before sixth period starts. Thanks for getting lunch, Iris. I'm sorry if it was kind of a downer."

"Oh," Iris says, like the end of the period has snuck up on her. "No, not at all. It was nice, actually. I feel better. Thanks for listening. And for understanding. Like you said, it's kind of nice to hear someone else talk about the way you're feeling."

Dom looks happy. Genuinely happy. Not just determined, like he looked on the ice. Not just amazed, like he looked out on the driveway. Happy. I haven't seen him like this since—well. Since the other side.

"We should do this again sometime," Dom says. "Maybe I'll ask Cooper if he wants to join. God knows he needs someone to talk to."

"Yeah, and I can bring Jianyu," Iris says, and then adds, "If he can spare the time," rolling her eyes a little. Dom shoots her one last commiserating smile before heading off to the pizza line, and then the volume of the video starts to decrease, the raucous chatter of the cafeteria growing softer and softer until it's all just a buzz of background noise.

"Did your boyfriend and my best friend just become friends?" Kenny says.

"I think they did," I say. Iris is still sitting at the table, looking consideringly at Dom's retreating back, and now *I'm* feeling a little twinge of anxiety. But this is a good thing, I tell myself. It really is. It's good that Dom is filling his life with people like Iris and Cooper and his mother—people who will be there for him in the way I used to be there for him; people whom he'll let himself love in the same way he once let himself love me.

With Dom, it was never a question of finding people who wanted to care about him. Hell, Principal Meyers cared about him, not to mention every single hockey coach who took one look at him and decided it might be fun to play surrogate father for a couple of seasons. It was always just a matter of finding people he trusted. People who stuck around long enough to earn their way into the small, private universe he had lived in alone for so long.

There was a time when that list was a party of one. When it was just me. But a person can't live like that—I told him as much constantly—and if the only thing that comes out of my death is that Dom fills the vacuum left behind with the compassion and the tenderness and the affection I felt for him, but three, four, fivefold—then it's worth it.

Then I'm happy for him.

22 | some days it's all I imagine, too

We find my parents' SUV on Route 9, heading away from town and toward Cottonwood. It's well past sunset, the car's high beams cutting sharp lines of light through the darkness.

There aren't many other cars on the road. It's late.

They're about five minutes from home, stopped at the intersection right after Lake Street, when I feel my entire body go cold, my hands starting to shake before I even register why. Then the memories start, echoes of that night, that intersection reverberating through my mind: the windshield wipers, frenetic against the downpour; the cacophony of impact; the neon of the police lights.

There are new sensations, too: things I didn't know I remembered until now. The stinging, so sharp it almost felt like a burn, as the windshield broke, glass whipping across my face. The ache of my collarbone where my seat belt had caught and forced me back into my seat. The oblivion of unconsciousness, which didn't descend all at once but instead gradually, like the world was being pulled away from me little by little.

Kenny comes over and puts his hand on my back. I flinch, and he says: "Easy, I'm just—" and then presses down a little, his open palm underneath my shoulder blades.

"I know it's hard, but you should try to breathe through it," Kenny says. "I can count the breaths out, here—"

And then he does, taking deep, exaggerated breaths to match mine while he counts to ten.

"Thanks, Kenny," I say. "It's just—that intersection—"

"I know," Kenny says.

My parents park the SUV in the driveway, leave the garage door unopened. I wait for everyone to spill out of the car, wondering if Cooper has managed to accomplish his lifelong quest of poaching default shotgun rights from my dad now that I'm not there as a secondary source of competition. But instead it's just my mom, who exits the car unaccompanied, wearing her nicest wool coat and matching heels. The video tracks with her as she walks up the porch steps, then through the front door, the graininess of the nocturnal footage flaring, almost painfully bright, as she steps into the entryway.

My mom walks through the house, not bothering to kick off her shoes. The kitchen is even more of a mess than it was the last time we saw it: The dirty dishes have overtaken the sink and are now starting to migrate across the countertop. There are plastic takeout containers and cardboard pizza boxes peeking out from underneath the lid of the trash can, their edges darkened by grease.

In the living room, my dad is watching ESPN, where four pundits are embroiled in a vigorous debate over whether or not steroid usage should disqualify Major League Baseball players from the Hall of Fame. Cooper is sitting on the floor, doing homework on the coffee table.

"Amy," my dad says, when she comes into view.

He says the name too slowly, the syllables coming apart in the middle like they're separate words. *He's drunk,* I think, looking around at the cans of Bud Light littering the living room, at his red-rimmed eyes, at the jittery, repetitive motion of his hands—or perhaps it's just the grief, parasitic and debilitating, consuming more and more of him over time.

"Where were you tonight, Roy?" my mom says—demands, really, and Cooper's face registers instant alarm.

My dad doesn't respond.

"Roy," my mom says. "Tonight's meeting was for *your* benefit, not mine. Kriminsky and I have gone over my statement hundreds of times. The whole point of this evening was so he could give notes on yours."

It seems to take a while for my mom's words to reach my dad, as if they need to penetrate first through the heavy tension that's suddenly descended into the room, and then through the fog of apathy that shrouds my father from everyone else.

"I—" my dad starts. He pauses. "I haven't written it yet."

My mom stares at him. "Roy, the hearing is in two weeks!"

"Guys," Cooper says, warily.

My dad cranes his neck so he can look around her, back at the television, where the pundits are now forecasting the likelihood of a lockout before the basketball season begins, something about salary caps and the CBA and league-wide parity.

My mom walks over to the coffee table, picks up the remote, and mutes the television.

"Tell me what you're thinking, Roy," my mom says. "Tell me what's going through your head. Because I really have no idea."

"Guys," Cooper says again. "Maybe if you told me what was going on, I could help—"

But the sudden silence seems to set my dad off, as if the ambient noise from the television was the only thing keeping him calm.

"Maybe," my dad says, "you would have more of an idea what was going through my head if you were ever here. When's the last time you spent an entire day in this house? A weekend? You're too busy running around with Kriminsky, planning your big moment in court, happily oblivious to what Cooper and I are going through at home—"

"Speaking of Cooper," Cooper interjects. *"He's right here.* Dad—"

"My 'big moment in court'?" my mom says. "Are you referring to the statements we *both* agreed to give? The ones in support of our daughter?"

"Mom—" Cooper says. He stands up and places himself in between my parents, but it's no use. They continue to argue around him.

"And it's not like you've been there for me either," my mom says, bitterly. "Has it ever occurred to you that I can't spend more time at the house because I'm out taking care of the press and the paperwork and the finances that need to be taken care of after Caroline's death—*by myself*? This week I met with the school board because they want to start a scholarship in Caroline's name, I met with the church to thank them for all the support they've given us over the past couple of weeks, with a reporter from the paper because they want to write an in memoriam, and yes, with the lawyer, because the driver who *killed*

Caroline in a drunk driving accident in the first place has a sentencing hearing in two weeks, and our voices deserve to be heard as part of that process! You want to talk about Cooper? Who's been making sure Cooper gets to school, to practice, to therapy? Who's been—"

Cooper picks up a vase and throws it to the floor so that it shatters into a mess of glass and water and loose petals. More lilies, I register dimly.

My parents fall silent, shocked.

"Just—just stop," Cooper says.

"Go to your room," my mom says.

Cooper splutters. "I'm not—I'm not a *kid* anymore, Mom, you can't just send me to my room—"

"Adults don't throw tantrums," my mom says. "Go to your room."

Cooper grabs his keys off the counter and walks out of the house.

My parents both stare in the direction of the front door, reeling, as if wondering whether or not someone should go after him. Then they look back at each other, the anger burning down into wariness, into exhaustion. I've never seen them like this; it makes me want to turn the television off.

"I just can't do it, Amy," my dad says. "I can't write the statement. It's too much, it's unnecessary, it's vindictive—"

"Vindictive?" my mom says, her spine going straight. There's a whole world of emotion in that small movement, and in the fleeting expression of hurt that crosses her face. "We're not trying to punish anyone, Roy, we're not out for *revenge*. But we owe this to our daughter. Her last moments, Roy—last night I read the police file, the description of the crime scene, the medical examiner's report—you can't even imagine what she experienced, how she must have felt—"

"Some days it's all I imagine," my dad says, quietly. "And now you're asking me to relive it on *purpose*, now you're asking me to go up in front of a judge and *talk about it*—I just—I just want this to be over, Amy. I just want it all to be over. That's all I've ever wanted."

"It'll be over soon," my mom says, and even I know that's a promise she can't possibly keep. My mom sinks down into the spot where Cooper was just sitting so her legs are crossed on the floor, the stilettos of her heels peeking out from beneath the skirt of her dress. She reaches across the coffee table and takes my dad's hand in hers. "All I need from you is to stand with me this one last time. To stand with Caroline this one last time."

My dad doesn't respond, but neither does he pull his hand away.

"And besides—shouldn't we be united in this?" my mom says. "We made that promise to each other when we first had Caroline, don't you remember? That as parents we would always present a united front, even if as people we might not completely agree."

My dad looks at her, wavering.

"I know this is hard for you," my mom says. "And I wish I didn't have to ask. But who else is there? Who else is going to fight for our daughter? It's us, Roy. It's only us."

And even through the haziness of his expression, the glassiness of his eyes, a product of drinking or a portent of crying or both, his answer is written clear as day on his face. What is less clear is what this will cost them.

"You say you wish you didn't have to ask," he says. "But you'd ask me to do this even if you knew it would destroy me, wouldn't you?"

"Of course I would," my mom says. "That's what it means to be a mother."

Her words settle, heavy in their room; heavy, even, in ours.

"I'm going to—find Cooper," my dad says. He stands up from the sofa and his hand slips out of my mother's. "I don't think he'll have gone far. Didn't hear his car start."

My dad looks at my mom for a moment longer, and then walks out of the living room. Suddenly my mom looks tiny, all alone in the anarchy of the living room, all dressed up in a debris field of litter. And then, still sitting on the floor, still in her dress and black heels from the meeting, lily petals and broken glass still strewn across the floor, she starts to cry.

KEПΠY

23 | toad?

Caroline is quiet for a long time after the television turns off. With each passing moment, the knowledge that I should say something to break the silence mounts, but so, too, does the pressure to say the *right* thing. I try to think back to the evenings I used to spend lying on Iris's couch, too miserable to even explain why I was miserable, and the words she'd say to coax me out of those long, pregnant silences.

"What are you thinking about?" I ask.

"Um," Caroline says. She looks down at her hands, which are folded in her lap. "It's hard," Caroline says. "To see everyone like this. Especially my mom, you know—because we've always been really close."

"Yeah," I say, thinking about the number of thoughts Caroline starts with *My mom always said that . . .*

"And I get where my dad is coming from. Maybe emotional distance is the right way to move on. Maybe it's the *only* way to move on. But I'm still having flashbacks from that night; I can't even think about Route 9 without going to pieces. It's not so easy for me, and maybe it's not so easy for my mom either, who's now fighting this battle all by herself."

Caroline falls silent again. Minutes go by. Maybe hours, as I scour my brain for something reassuring to say, something that won't sound empty, hollow.

The problem is that I've been where Caroline is right now, and everything sounds empty and hollow.

"Do you want some more tea?" I ask, a little desperately. "Do you want to paint?"

"I don't really want anything," Caroline says.

And then it's silent again. I start to feel increasingly helpless, increasingly frustrated; then, on top of all that, I start to feel increasingly *guilty*. Is this what it had been like for Iris? Months on end of this helplessness, of this frustration, which I had been unable to appreciate because I couldn't see past my own misery?

We need some kind of distraction, I think, and I don't even realize that the sentiment could be construed as a request until the note lands on my shoulder.

YOUR WISH.

Caroline looks at me, confused, and I start to say, "I didn't mean—"

But then my explanation is drowned out by a blare of noise—several orders of magnitude louder than the *pop* of an incoming message, and nothing like the indistinct *bzzt* of an incoming video. No—this is loud, melodic, *insistently* cheerful.

It's the *Mario Kart* theme song.

"This is not what I asked for!" I say, looking at the television, where a whole host of cartoon avatars are jumping up and down, beckoning the two of us to start a game.

But Caroline is smiling. "Don't chicken out now," she says.

"It's not that I don't have the courage," I say. "It's that

I don't have the *skill*. I am terrible at *Mario Kart*. I never played video games as a kid, and now—"

"I'm always Toad," Caroline says, which makes my head spin, because—*Toad*? "And I think you should be Yoshi. You've got similar vibes."

And then I guess we're playing *Mario Kart*, because a controller appears in her hand, and one in mine.

"Hold on," I say. "You think you've got similar vibes to Toad?"

"Yeah," Caroline says. "Sort of hapless and cute."

"And I'm Yoshi, because he's . . ."

"He's fun, he's charming, he just wants to help his friends."

"I—" I start, and then realize I have no idea what I want to say. If anyone else ever said anything like that to me, I'd have to avoid talking to them for a few days just to let the awkwardness dissipate. But Caroline's just fiddling around with the controller, making her little Toad avatar jump up and down and land in various poses. I wonder what it's like, to be able to give and receive compliments so easily.

"You're a good person, Kenny," Caroline says. "I don't know why you're always trying to pretend otherwise. I mean, you're here, aren't you? I doubt there's very much *Mario Kart* being played in hell."

"Ah," I say. A familiar flash of guilt. "I think that may have been a bookkeeping error. I don't know that I deserve—well. What I mean to say is, if this is in fact purgatory, then—"

Caroline throws a pillow at me. "Quit it!" she says, and I stop short at the look she gives me. It's not unlike the one we've seen on her mother, actually: certain, steely, intimidating. But it's not so steely that it's without vulnerability, and it's not so intimidating that it's no longer human. It's not a look that makes me too scared to argue. It's a look that makes me realize it's OK not to.

I like Caroline's mother. I hope she wasn't alone in the living room for a very long time.

"Thank you," I say.

"You're welcome," Caroline says.

The two of us look at each other, apprehensive in the newfound seriousness of the conversation.

"Well, should we—" Caroline says, and I sputter, at the same time, "Do you still want to—"

Then the note appears.

PLEASE, it says. DON'T GET MAUDLIN ON ME NOW. I WAS SO LOOKING FORWARD TO THE GAME. AFTER KENNY'S SELF-EVALUATION, I LIKE MY CHANCES.

"You're going to play?" Caroline says. Sure enough, on the screen, a third character has been selected.

"You're going to play as Princess Peach?" I say.

PRINCESS PEACH IS FUN, the room says.

Caroline laughs, but there's a faint note of hysteria in it. I wish, for the umpteenth time since Caroline's arrival, I could borrow just a fraction of her determined optimism.

"All right," she says. "Which course should we do?"

"Just pick a random one," I say.

Caroline cheers up considerably after that. I guess it's hard to stay dispirited for very long when you're racing through a giant colosseum as an anthropomorphized mushroom on a go-kart.

"Wow," Caroline says after we're one minute into the game and she's already lapped me. "You weren't kidding. You really are bad."

I lose another quarter of a lap after that because I chuck my controller in her general direction, and even our "superpowers" (*I wish the controller was back in my hand instead of across the room on the floor*) cost me a precious ten seconds of time.

The room does a much better job of keeping up with Caroline. Princess Peach stays just a few paces behind Toad for the rest of the game, the course exploding periodically into various Nintendo whizbangs as they approach the finish line. But then Toad chucks a little blue shell that blows up right in front of poor Princess Peach, who goes toppling over the side of the track.

"You didn't mention you were a *Mario Kart* prodigy," I say.

"I am *not*," Caroline says. "I've never won a game against Cooper, not once. But somehow I've found the only two players in the world—in all the worlds!—who I'm better than."

She's right about to zip through the finish line when the game disappears—just blacks out on the screen.

"What just happened?" Caroline says. She looks from the television to my face to the television to my face again, as if I'm responsible for the untimely end of our game. Then, when the television fails to turn back on, she says: "What the hell!"

Caroline swears so infrequently that to hear her do it with so much vitriol over a video game is pretty funny.

MY APOLOGIES, the room says.

Then, static. Caroline's face lights up, and she swivels toward the television screen, anticipating certain victory in *Mario Kart*.

But it's not the game. It's my parents.

24 | the plea

The blinds are down at the restaurant, the tables wiped clean, the menus stacked by the register. The hum of fluorescent light bulbs fills their room, then ours.

Suddenly the *Mario Kart* game feels very far away, decidedly childish in its frivolity. Cartoon fungi and smiling dinosaurs. The adrenaline rush of a meaningless competition.

My parents are talking at a table near the back of the dining room, their voices low but urgent. My dad is cradling a teacup, the liquid flushed dark green with leaves and peppered with wrinkled, red-orange goji berries; my mother, a glass of baijiu, which is clear enough to see the tiny fissures that have started to spiderweb across the bottom of the glass.

"Come with me," my mom is saying. "Come with me on the twelfth. I know you don't believe, but once you meet her, you will."

"The twelfth," my dad repeats, with an edge to his voice that suggests we've been dropped into an argument that's been going on for a while. "The night of the fundraiser. I've been reminding you of it for weeks, Xiao Ye. And now a woman sells you a convenient fantasy about dishwashers and penguins and you forget all about it—"

"Subtitles," Caroline says, quietly, and the translations appear.

It's not a fantasy, my mom says. **She knew our traditions. Kenny's favorite book. Your name—she knew your name.**

Ye Yining, my dad says. **We run a business. Our names are on the internet. How could you be so—so—**

My dad looks like he doesn't understand how they've gotten to this point. Of the two, my mom has always been the more level-headed one, quick to bring my father down to earth when his ideas sometimes took on ambitions of their own. I wouldn't know what to make of her sudden spirituality either if it weren't for the fact that she's actually correct.

My mom sets her jaw, looking more determined than hurt by my father's dismissiveness. **Lao Zhou, I just have this feeling, I have this intuition, that there's something more. A mother always knows these things. And Angela said she could feel him, too—his presence, his spirit. Still with us.**

At first my dad doesn't respond, and I think that maybe he's going to indulge her. Then he says, his voice unexpectedly emotional and laced with a bitterness that makes him sound like someone else entirely: **I just don't understand why you insist on bringing Kenny into this.**

Kenny _is_ this, my mom says. **Don't you see?**

What I see, Ye Yining, is that we are running out of time and money, and instead of focusing on how we can keep our business open, you've been wasting money on a sham magician because you think some prank calls and a power outage were some kind of divine intervention!

I understand that you don't understand, my mom says. **But I think—I feel—I _know_ our son is still out there. Lao Zhou**, my mom adds, and her voice is consoling and imploring, full of grief and hope at once: **Don't you want to believe?**

Of course I want to believe, he says, hoarsely. He drops his head into his hands and takes stuttered, shallow breaths. When he looks up again, his eyes are watery. **And maybe you're right. Maybe Kenny is out there somewhere watching over us, and I hope that if he is, he feels some measure of peace, wherever that is. But the restaurant is *here*. The restaurant is here, the same place that it's been for the last ten years. And it needs us.**

Kenny needs us, my mom says. **He needs *you*. He's reaching out for you. Come with me, Lao Zhou, then you'll see.**

Xiao Ye, my dad says. He takes a deep breath, like he's winding up for a long explanation, like he's going to let her down gently. But then he just says: **No.**

My mom says: **Lao Zhou.**

My dad says again: **No.**

He stands up out of his chair. He makes to leave.

Lao Zhou, my mom says. Her voice is brittle, but her words are sharp. **The restaurant isn't Kenny.**

You don't understand, my dad says. **You don't understand, because you're so confused. You don't understand that it's all we have left of him.**

The scene ends. This time, we do get our *Mario Kart* game back—paused exactly where we left off, with Caroline's Toad barreling toward the finish line, the room's Princess Peach tumbling off the track, my Yoshi several laps behind. So, too, returns the music—trumpets and maracas that are now insultingly, infuriatingly cheerful.

Caroline sits down next to me. She drops her head so that it's resting on my shoulder.

Caroline has been wearing the same clothes since she arrived in the room, but she smells like fresh laundry. It's not a strong scent. I've never noticed it before. But now, with her hair splayed across my shoulder, with her arm pressed against mine, it's just enough to remind me that I'm still here.

25 | the reveal

Caroline stays beside me for a while—so long that at a certain point it becomes unclear whether she's comforting me or I'm comforting her. It's a little bit of both, I suppose, given the last couple of times we've tuned into Terrestrial TV.

We've really been racking up the bad news lately: Caroline's parents fighting, and Caroline herself more unhappy than she'd ever been in real life; my parents fighting, and myself about as unhappy as I'd always been in real life. *I should be working harder to maintain a brave face,* I think, *as the only one between the two of us who's experienced this sort of prolonged misery before.* But what's the point? That's something else I know that Caroline doesn't: At a certain point the sadness settles around you, thick and impenetrable as late-summer fog, and there's no amount of coffee or tea or dumplings or *Mario Kart* that can get through it.

The next time the television turns on, I brace myself. Caroline does, too—I can feel it without even looking at her—and then she lifts her head off my shoulder.

Iris is standing outside Jianyu's front door in the middle of the night, her car parked crookedly in the driveway. She's wearing a windbreaker and jeans and an expression of blind fury.

"I know this street," Caroline says. "Maddie moved to this neighborhood with her dad and her sister after the divorce."

"Sounds about right," I say.

Jianyu's house is a two-story, three-car-garage McMansion that went up a couple of years ago in a newly constructed subdivision called Winterton Grove. His family bought the house when they were first laying the foundation and moved in the moment the paint dried; then, over the course of the next year, his dad bought two new cars to fill that garage, his mom swapped out all her fake Louis Vuitton handbags for real Louis Vuitton handbags, and Jianyu started lifting weights.

Jianyu answers the door wearing fleece pajama pants and nothing else.

"Oh," Caroline says.

"Oh, no," I say.

"It's two in the morning," Jianyu says.

"I've been texting you," Iris says.

"I'm sorry," Jianyu says. "You must have missed the part where it's two in the morning. I've been asleep."

"I've been texting you since yesterday night," Iris says. "Have you been asleep since yesterday night?"

"No," Jianyu says, and sighs. "I've been— Look, why don't you come in?"

"I don't want to come in," Iris says, even though she's shivering.

Jianyu rolls his eyes. "Iris, come into the house. I'm not going to let you stand outside wearing a T-shirt and a windbreaker in the middle of February."

"I don't need you to *let* me do anything," Iris snaps.

"Iris, I will still respect you as an independent self-reliant free-thinking feminist if you come into the house to get out of the cold, can we *please not do this right now*—"

"February?" Caroline interrupts, wrinkling her nose. "No, that can't be right."

"Look at all the snow," I say. "And look at the sky—look at the stars."

Even depressed, even dead, I am amazed by the stars.

"You can always see the stars," Caroline says.

"Not like this," I say. "In the winter they're sharper, because the air's not as humid."

"But that's before—" Caroline starts.

"Let's talk about this later," I say, because Jianyu has finally succeeded in coaxing Iris over the threshold and into the house. We move into the foyer with her, and then through the hallway and into the kitchen, where Jianyu pours her a glass of water from a teakettle on the stove.

"Do you want anything to eat? We have oranges, bananas. I think some grapes in the fridge."

"Jianyu," Iris says. "I didn't come here to be plied with fruit."

"There's pork left over from dinner, and some beef stew my mom made a few days ago . . ."

"Jianyu!" Iris says. "You can't just make this go away by pretending nothing is wrong!"

Jianyu pulls out one of the swiveling bar seats that line the kitchen island and sits down. The entire counter is marble, and spotless, with the basket of proffered fruit sitting neatly on one side.

I liked Jianyu's new house, because it meant we had somewhere to do Winterton Chinese Thanksgiving that could actually fit all three Winterton Chinese families, and because it meant that *during* Winterton Chinese Thanksgiving, the kids—who were all teenagers by that point—could sneak a few bottles of beer down to the finished basement and watch a movie while the adults played cards upstairs. But Iris generally responded to my yearly invites to Chinese Thanksgiving the same way I generally responded to her yearly invites to Christmas Mass, and I knew that going to Jianyu's house had never stopped being weird for her. The three of us had lived within a five block radius for as long as we had known each other, and now Jianyu was over on the other side of town in a house that had five bedrooms and heated toilet seats.

"Look," Jianyu says, quietly. "I get you're mad because I haven't been responding to your texts, and I'm sorry. I probably deserve it. But could you wait until tomorrow to yell at me? It's late; my parents are asleep. It'll be more satisfying to chew me out in the cafeteria, anyway, where you'll have an audience."

"Sorry," Iris says. She takes a breath.

"Have a banana," Jianyu says, and passes her a banana.

"I don't want—"

"Just eat something, Iris, you'll feel better."

"I'm not— this isn't—I'm not *hangry*, Jianyu. Raising my blood sugar isn't going to make me any less upset."

"OK," Jianyu says. "What would make you less upset?"

"It would make me less upset," Iris says, through gritted teeth, like she's talking to a toddler, "if you were *sorry*. If you were *there*."

"I just said that I was sorry!" Jianyu says. "And I've apologized hundreds of times for forgetting about dinner last week, but if you want me to do it again, I will, Iris. Here you go: I, Jianyu Zhang, am truly, deeply sorry I missed a previously scheduled dinner appointment with Iris Mutisya, and will henceforth strive to—"

"It's not just about the texts!" Iris says. "It's not just about dinner! How can you possibly be this dense?"

"Well," Jianyu says, "I'm sorry again, I guess, for being this dense." He spreads his hands out on the table: placating, deferential. "But help me understand, Iris, because I really want to. What's going on? What is this all about?"

"What is this all about?" Iris says, not at all placated. "What is this all *about*? This is about the fact that you—don't—care," she says, and punctuates each word by thumping the banana on the table.

Jianyu removes the banana from her hands and puts it back in the basket.

"How can you think I don't care?" Jianyu says. "I talked on the phone with you and Kenny's dad for literally two hours the other night to help plan everything out. The invite list. The menu. The location of the donation box. The fundraiser is going to be fine, Iris, it's going to be great."

"How can you say that?" Iris says. "We still haven't sent the finalized schedule of events to Kenny's parents, we only have twenty RSVPs even though we need to fill the entire dining room—"

"People will come," Jianyu says.

"And if people don't come, Jianyu? What's the plan then?"

"We can check in on the RSVPs in a couple of days when we're closer to the event. If the numbers still aren't looking great, we'll figure something out."

"'We'll figure something out,'" Iris parrots. "Except what you really mean is that *I'll* figure something out, because you'll be too busy hanging out with your cool new MUN friends, or getting drunk at a party, or—or strutting around shirtless to impress your own reflection in the mirror!"

"Iris," Jianyu says. "It's the middle of the night. These are *pajamas*."

"You weren't there for Kenny when he needed you, and you're not here for me now that I need you, and it's only a matter of time until some poor Model UN kid who thinks you're a true friend needs you only to realize that you're not there, that you've moved on to the next, shiny thing, because that's just who you are now, that's what you do."

Jianyu sits back—or as far back as he can sit without falling off the backless stool, anyway.

"Are you done?" he says.

"No!" Iris says. "No, I'm not done!"

And all of a sudden I know exactly where this conversation is going; I can see the path that it's going to take light up in front of me like floor lights on an airplane, like radiation streaming out from a dying star.

I look at Caroline, who's watching everything on-screen unfold with wide, sympathetic eyes. Who's spent the last hour with her head on my shoulder, smelling like shampoo and detergent. Who called me a good person and wouldn't let me argue.

"I don't think we should watch anymore," I say. "How do we stop it? Where's the remote?"

"Kenny," Caroline says, gently. She puts her hand on my arm. I don't know when we've gotten so touchy-feely; I don't know how we've become so close. "Kenny, there's no remote. There's never been a remote."

"I would like a remote," I say. I even look up at the ceiling. A note lands in my lap, but I already know what it says: If the room were going to give us the remote, it would have appeared by now.

UNABLE TO FULFILL REQUEST. ERROR CODE #162.

"I know it's hard to watch your friends argue," Caroline says.

But that's not it at all.

"You know," Iris says, "after Kenny—after Kenny died, I cried nonstop for two weeks, thinking to myself that there must have been something more I could have done, that there must have been something more I could have said. It haunted me, Jianyu. It still does. And it just occurred to me—you've never thought about any of that, have you?"

"Iris," Jianyu says quietly.

"No, really," Iris says. "Have you ever thought about how things might be different if you had just *talked to Kenny* about how he was feeling? If you had just *hung out with Kenny* during some of his shifts at the restaurant? If you had maybe *invited Kenny* to one of those stupid parties you spent all summer going to? I mean, this is your best friend from childhood we're talking about, not some random kid you met in history class! Do you ever think about how that must have made him feel—to be blown off, week after week, weekend after weekend?"

"Iris," Jianyu repeats. "My parents—"

But Iris has finally gotten to the point she's wanted to make all along—the reason she drove to Jianyu's house in the middle of the night, the reason she stood banging on his front door in the freezing cold, too furious to wait until school tomorrow morning. *It's something she's wanted to say for a while, I think, even if she's only fully realizing it now.*

"I bet you haven't," Iris says. "Because if you had—if you had stopped to think about any of that—just for an hour, a passing minute, a second of your precious, popular time— you wouldn't be able to get to sleep either. You'd be up all night, just like I am, and it'd be a thousand times worse; it'd be excruciating; the guilt would destroy you. Because you'd realize that maybe, if you weren't such a useless excuse for a human being, your so-called best friend wouldn't have killed himself, and I'd still have mine."

26 | the fallout

There is some part of my brain that processes the rest of the conversation, which is short and curt and heavy with the weight of Iris's accusations. "I should go," she says, and Jianyu replies, "Yes, I think that would be for the best," and then Iris is walking back out of the kitchen, back down the hallway, back out the front door and into the cold, away from Jianyu's new house in Winterton Grove and everything it's made of him.

Mostly, though, I'm focused on Caroline, who has scrambled up and off the couch and is now standing between me and the television, her expression of wide-eyed sympathy rapidly morphing into one of wide-eyed horror.

"Is that—" she starts.

"What Iris said," she tries again. "Was that—"

It's possible that I manage to nod: a quick jerk of the head, a twitch that confirms the answer to the question I know she's asking. But I can't say for sure, because I feel dissociated, far away from my body, and it's possible that's all the confirmation she needs, too.

"I thought it was a medical condition," she says. "I thought it was a freak accident. The newspaper said—"

"My parents would have wanted to keep it private," I say. And why wouldn't they? They had done everything for me, given me every possible reason to want to live.

"The newspaper said your heart just gave out one night, sometime over winter break," Caroline says.

"My heart *did* give out," I say. "I went into cardiac arrest."

"But it wasn't an accident," Caroline says.

I hesitate.

"No. It wasn't an accident."

Caroline backs a few more steps away, then starts to walk toward the library, then turns around and faces me again, like she's just learned that I have some sort of communicable disease and she can't figure out how far away she needs to be to stay out of the transmission radius.

"I don't understand," Caroline says. "Why?"

I sigh. The truth is that there *wasn't* a why, or at least there wasn't a why that I could make sense of. If there was, I could have fought it, I could have changed things, I could have fixed it. But instead of a *why*, there was an *is*: an immutable fact of my existence that had come on slowly and then solidified, like running magma hardening, midflow, into rock.

"There isn't a reason," I tell Caroline.

"How can there not be a reason?" Caroline says. Quiet, disbelieving. "How could you kill yourself without a reason?"

I flinch.

"I'm sorry," Caroline says. "I'm sorry that you felt—the way you must have—if you did that. But I guess I just don't understand."

"There wasn't a *discrete* reason," I say, growing defensive despite myself. "More an accumulation of miseries.

Persistent existential dread. Debilitating self-loathing. You know."

"I don't understand," Caroline says, "what any of that means."

"It means I was depressed, Caroline," I say. Of course Caroline Davison has no ability to conceptualize the idea of self-loathing. She's probably never felt it before in her life.

"But," Caroline says. "But you weren't—it's not like you were—this isn't like the articles you read on the internet about kids who were bullied or abused by their parents or, or—"

"Oh," I say, sarcastically, "so if I had been bullied, then you'd understand. Maybe if I'd been shoved into a few more lockers, had my lunch stolen a few more times—"

"That's not what I'm saying!" Caroline says, hotly. "But people liked you, the school newspaper wrote about you, I just don't get why you would—"

"People knew I was the captain of the Science Olympiad team!" I say. "That's not a personality trait! That's not being liked, or being known—not for anything real."

"It's high school!" Caroline says. "Who's liked or known for anything real? This is your problem, Kenny: You take everything so seriously, and you're always so in your head all the time—"

"Oh, *that's my problem*," I say. "I take things too *seriously*. I'm always *in my head*. Well, maybe if I floated through the hallways on a cloud of adoration like you did, I wouldn't have to be so serious all the time. Maybe the reason why I can't get out of my head is because I've spent my entire life feeling hopeless and disoriented, with nothing to be proud of and nothing to look forward to—"

"Nothing to look forward to?!" Caroline says. "What about graduation? What about college?!"

"I didn't want to go to college!" I say. "I didn't want anything! I'm sorry, Caroline, if you can't understand, but that's the truth of it, that's all there is! I didn't want to—I didn't want. And I couldn't control it, and I didn't know why it was happening, and I was making everyone around me miserable, and I just—I saw a way out and I took it, OK? That's your reason. That's your why."

Caroline looks at me like she's looking at me for the first time, like she looked at me when she first appeared in the room, convinced I was a fever dream, a hallucination. Then she says, almost breathless, almost in wonder:

"I would give anything. Anything. To be alive right now. To have my life back. And you just—you just threw yours away. Just like that."

She laughs a little—all shock, no humor. "Just threw it away," she repeats.

"It's not like it was an easy thing for me to do, Caroline," I say, quietly. I think back to the fall: the days growing shorter and shorter, the nights spent in increasing desperation. Flow charts, Venn diagrams, entire notebooks of pros and cons. But you couldn't reason your way out of reasonless despair.

"You had a choice," Caroline says. "And I—"

I can see the memory of the car accident flashing over her face as she cuts off, her whole body stiffening.

"It's not a choice when you don't have any other options."

"There are always other options, Kenny!" Caroline says, her voice rising again—but in obvious anger this time, rather than in shock. "You should have gone to therapy. You should have tried medication, you should have—"

"Therapy!" I say, and laugh. "Do you know how expensive therapy is? How could I have asked my parents to pay for something like that? The restaurant was barely breaking even until a year ago, and by the time it was breaking even I was so busy that—"

"I would have paid!" Caroline says. "If you had reached out to the school or something, if you had asked—"

"*Are you kidding me?*" I say. "You had never said a single word to me until we wound up in this room together. And why would you have? I'm just some guy you read about in the school newspaper."

"It doesn't matter," Caroline says. "If I had known, I would have helped. I would have—"

"And I'm sure that would have been great for me," I say. "Who wouldn't want to become another one of your little projects—"

"What are you talking about," Caroline says, each syllable now bitter, each word an accusation.

"You know what I'm talking about!" I say. "The way you talk about Dom—it's like he's some kind of *project*, like he's a house you're renovating."

"Shut up," Caroline says.

"*Oh, Dom is terrible at talking about his feelings,*" I say, pitching my voice up an octave in imitation. "*But we were working on that. Oh, Dom's table manners were just awful* before we met—thank God he has me now, to train him up, like he's a dog—or a circus elephant."

"Shut up," Caroline says.

"You know what *your* problem is, Caroline? You can't imagine the fact that not everyone in the world lives your exact blessed life, with teachers who know who you are before you've even taken their classes and buildings downtown named after your family. You don't *want* to imagine that fact, because then you might start to feel bad about it, and God forbid anyone makes Caroline Davison, Winterton darling, feel bad."

"*Shut up!*" Caroline shouts.

I shut up.

"No," Caroline says. "I can't imagine wanting to kill myself. But it's not because I was popular at school. It's not because some distant relative of mine was an architect. It's because of my parents. It's because of Cooper. It's because of my team. It's because there were people in my life who cared about me. People I loved. And you know what, Kenny? You had that, too, even if you obviously didn't appreciate it."

"I appreciated it," I say. "Don't preach at me about my own feelings. You obviously don't have a goddamn idea."

"No, you didn't appreciate it," Caroline says. "Because look at them now. Your parents are a wreck. Iris is a wreck. You knew this would destroy them, but you did it anyway. Because you think being sad is an excuse for being selfish."

I get up off the couch. I storm through the curtains and into the bedroom Caroline created for me, days, weeks, maybe months ago—a bedroom that is, of course, about three times larger and nicer than my actual bedroom in real life, because what else has she ever known? *I want to be alone*, I think.

The room gives me the next best thing—a door. I slam it.

CAROLINE

27 | how can there possibly be more than two hundred error codes?

Kenny shuts the door hard, and the sound echoes around the room's high, vaulted ceiling, which feels like it's closing in on me despite being at least twenty feet above the floor. It's like I'm in the car again, boxed in on all sides, the police lights painting the insides of my eyelids in primary colors, the sirens growing louder and then slipping away. It's like I never escaped the car at all, like I've been trapped in it this whole time. I'm hyperventilating again, breathless with claustrophobia, but this time Kenny's not here to count me through my breaths.

And I don't know what stings more—the fact that Kenny hid the truth from me through weeks and weeks of being my only company, my video game partner and confidant, my superhero teammate and shoulder to cry on, my actual *friend*; or the fact that he did it in the first place. That he made a choice to take his own life, just months before I had mine stolen from me.

I went into cardiac arrest, Kenny had said, his voice flat, like it was nothing, like dying was nothing, like I didn't go out in a hurricane of terror and pain and flashing lights—

I AM SORRY, CAROLINE, the room says. The note lands in my lap, startling me out of my thoughts, saving me, probably, from another total meltdown. WOULD YOU LIKE TO SEE YOUR FRIENDS?

Yes, I think. The answer to that question will always be yes.

The television screen lights up, and it's not just my friends—it's Kenny's friends, too: Dom and Cooper and Iris and Jianyu all at Wisteria Park, which is buzzing with the energy of incipient spring. Flower buds and small leaves stud the tree branches; dewdrops glisten on the blades of fresh grass; the air is filled with birdsong—the high, staccato chirps of robins and the sweet trilling of red-winged blackbirds. And then there's the smell, which surfaces in my memory so abruptly and with such vividness that I may as well have just lit a candle: snowdrops and irises, perennials unearthed from beneath the winter snow, their fragrance floating over the sharp, clean scent of the still-cold air.

Everyone is sitting together on one of Cooper's picnic blankets. They're eating sandwiches.

". . . and Jianyu makes four," Dom is saying. "Hey, I think we have enough people to start an official WHS club now. What do you think, Cooper? Do you think we could convince the student council to give us funding?"

"We could if Caroline were here," Cooper says, glumly. "Admin loved her."

Jianyu looks a little uncomfortable, actually—like it might be his first time hanging out with the group. I'm surprised he's there at all, given what happened the last time we saw him with Iris. But Kenny did say that their friendship had always been tumultuous; perhaps they've made up—again.

Iris, on the other hand, looks totally at ease: She's sitting next to Dom, leaning back on her elbows with one shoulder pressed against his.

And Cooper—well, Cooper gets along with everyone, fits in everywhere. He always has.

"We probably could if Kenny were here, too," Jianyu says. "We'd be the most diverse student group in the school. They'd have to give us funding for that alone."

Jianyu and Iris exchange fond, nostalgic glances. Some inside joke, a reference with history. Either they've made up, or they're much better actors than Kenny gave them credit for.

"I wish I'd known him better," Cooper says, ruefully. "All the times I ate at Eastern Wind, and I never thought to shoot him a text, ask him how things were going at the restaurant . . ."

"He would've been mortified," Iris says, sounding bemused at the very prospect. Then her smile drops into a worried frown, and she turns to Jianyu. "You haven't heard from them at the restaurant, have you?" she says. "I went to see Mr. Zhou on Wednesday night, and the door was locked and the lights were off, even though it was only six P.M."

"You don't think they've had to shut down, do you?" Dom says. "Didn't you say you bought them at least a few months with all the fundraising money?"

"Six months," Iris says. "I ran the numbers with Mr. Zhou a few weeks ago. All thanks to the deep pockets of the

MUN kids—or the deep pockets of the MUN kids' parents, anyway." She shoots Jianyu an appreciative look, which lasts for about three seconds before the crease between her eyebrows reappears. "Still—maybe you should have your parents give them a call, Jianyu—make sure they're doing all right."

None of this is making sense. Since when does Dom know about Kenny's parents' restaurant? And the fund-raiser has already happened? Then I remember Iris at Jianyu's door, her breath appearing in front of her in little puffs of vapor, Jianyu's exasperated attempts to usher her into the house. *I'm not going to let you stand outside in the middle of February*, he had said. And now: the picnic blanket on dry grass, the flower blossoms on the trees in front of me.

"I'm—am I seeing a scene from the future?" I ask, out loud.

UNABLE TO FULFILL REQUEST. ERROR CODE #204.

"Thanks," I say. "That's very helpful."

"How are your parents, Cooper?" Iris asks.

Cooper has been wearing the same morose expression since the video started. Upon hearing Iris's question, he falls backward onto the picnic blanket and throws an arm over his face.

"Ah," Iris says. "That bad, huh?"

"I thought it'd be better to stay with Dad because he spent less time obsessing over Caroline's death," Cooper continues, and—wait, *what?* Has dad moved out? "But now I've realized that just because he isn't obsessing over Caroline's *case* doesn't mean he isn't obsessing over

Caroline's *death*. Dad spends most of his time looking at photo albums and her old paintings, working his way through six-packs of Bud Light. Most days he doesn't even talk to me."

"After my dad died, my mom didn't talk about it for a good six years," Dom says.

"Great," Cooper says. "Just five years and ten more months to go, then."

"You know you can always crash on my couch," Dom says.

"Or in one of my guest bedrooms," Jianyu offers.

"*One* of his guest bedrooms," Iris says, rolling her eyes. Dom laughs, which seems to set Jianyu more at ease. And I don't know the last time Dom made someone feel more comfortable.

"Thanks," Cooper says. "I might take you up on that."

The conversation stalls, and Cooper sits up, starts plucking individual blades of grass out of the ground and piling them up in front of his crossed legs. "The worst thing is that neither of them will tell me what's going on," he says. "They won't tell me why the hearings have all been closed to the public. They won't even tell me the identity of the driver, even though it's all going to come out in a week, anyway."

"I'm sure they're just trying to protect you, Cooper," Iris says, gently. "They probably don't want you thinking about it too much, with everything else going on—"

"What else am I supposed to be thinking about?" Cooper says. "What else is going on that matters as much as this? Sometimes I get back to Dad's apartment after practice and then I do all my homework and then I order a pizza and then I make sure he hasn't passed out on the couch and then it's nine P.M. and I'm just like—what now? The other day I scheduled some college tours. *College tours.* My sister is dead, and I'm planning a road trip to New York."

"I don't think there's a 'supposed to' in this situation," Iris says. "That's why we're all here, isn't it? Because there isn't anything we *can* do, much less anything we're *supposed* to do. So instead we just sit at the park and pretend that life goes on as normal."

"*Normal,*" Cooper says, like the word is in another language, and then sighs. "Real bang-up job we're doing."

But that's the thing—they *are* doing a bang-up job. The evidence is all over the screen, has been all over the screen for a while now. They're moving on, they're living their lives, they're healing.

And maybe that's why the sirens have been so much louder in my head recently; maybe that's why I've spent so much time struggling to breathe that I might ask the room for an inhaler. Each step they take toward healing is a step they take away from me, and each step they take away from me is a step I sink further into the arrested present of March 12.

Because I'm not going back to the real world. I'm not going back in time; I'm not going to erase everything that's happened between then and now so I can run it back, start over, do it better this time. How could I? Even if it were possible, even if Kenny's dog-eared textbook found us a way, I couldn't do it. Not when Dom has finally started to forge a real relationship with his mother. Not when Cooper is about to go to college. Not when I'm watching the four of them become fast friends right before my eyes, sprawled out on a picnic blanket in Wisteria Park, my ex-boyfriend and my brother and two kids they never would have met if not for my death.

"New York is great," Iris is saying. "I'd probably be going to NYU in the fall if Howard hadn't offered me that scholarship."

"It'll be nice to get out of state," Dom says, and Cooper murmurs his assent.

So Cooper will go to NYU or St. John's or Fordham—somewhere in the city, like he's always wanted. He'll play baseball, of course, and he'll go to parties and make new friends and come back home for the holidays. One winter he'll tell my parents that he's bringing his girlfriend, and my mom will insist my dad take the taxidermy deer off the wall—*"For goodness' sake, Roy, we don't want to scare the poor girl away before we've had the chance to sell her on your cooking."*

Cooper will pick out a major, and then change his mind, and then change his mind again, and at that point my parents, who will have made up, will have one of their joint conniptions. But it'll turn out fine: He'll get his diploma, all's well that ends well. I won't be there to cheer him on in person—not for his graduation, not for any of it—but he'll still be my baby brother, because there are some things you can change your mind about, and there are some things you can't.

One day he'll come back to Winterton and the town won't even feel like anything is missing anymore. One day it'll feel like that for all of them.

KENNY

28 | the fundraiser

The great thing about being trapped in an extratemporal dimension where you don't have to eat or drink or shower is that it makes it much easier to lock yourself in your bedroom and never emerge. Beholden to no bodily demands, I'm free to lie in bed indefinitely, replaying my argument with Caroline over and over again, fuming with newfound energy at her accusations and coming up with sharper and sharper retorts that I wish I'd thought of in the moment.

You think being sad is an excuse for being selfish, she had said, and I think:

Yeah? Well at least I don't think being happy is an excuse for being cruel.

At least I don't think being pretty is an excuse for being dumb.

At least I don't think being liked is an excuse for being—

I don't get the chance to finish that last one, because a scrap of paper floats down from the ceiling and lands on top of my face. I unfold it, equal parts resentful and grateful for the interruption.

I AM SORRY, KENNY, the note says. WOULD YOU LIKE TO SEE YOUR FRIENDS?

"Now?" I say. Because I do—of course I do—but I don't want to have to go outside to do it. I don't want to have to sit in the living room with Caroline, feeling her eyes on my face, knowing she's thinking about all the things I've done wrong, all the people I've hurt. I don't want to open the door and watch her scramble up and off the couch, recoiling away from me on instinct.

"NOW" IS SUBJECTIVE, the room replies. BUT YOUR NOW— YES.

"I've had enough interdimensional technicalities for a lifetime," I say. "Or two, I suppose. But fine. Any chance I could get a screen in here?"

THERE IS ONLY ONE TRUE MIRROR, the room says. BUT I CAN CREATE A TEMPORARY CLONE.

"A temporary clone," I repeat. "You know, there really should be some kind of manual."

There's a *thump* and a little puff of dust, and then a leather-bound tome lands at my feet, like something out of a medieval library.

"*Now*?" I say. "You couldn't have given this to us earlier?!"

I THINK YOU AND MS. DAVISON HAVE EARNED THE CLARITY, it says. AND I CAN ONLY HOPE YOU'LL BE ABLE TO PUT IT TO GOOD USE. BUT YOU MUSN'T FORGET THE ORIGINAL QUESTION. THE MOMENT IS PASSING, AND I BELIEVE YOU SAID YOU WISHED TO SEE YOUR FRIENDS.

And then a little hologram appears in front of me—the television screen in miniature, colors wavering a little before snapping into place.

"God," I say. "I do wish Iris could see this."

The shot in the hologram is of the front of the restaurant's dining area, which has been separated from the rest of the room by a thick blue curtain and repurposed as a ticketing station. There's a plastic foldout table draped in a black silk tablecloth. On top of it, a card stock sign reads:

KENNY ZHOU MEMORIAL BENEFIT DINNER
DOORS OPEN AT 5:30 P.M.
PLEASE CHECK IN HERE

Iris is sitting behind the foldout table, laying out stacks of paper, anxiety written all over her face. She's wearing a dark-blue dress with a blazer over it. Her go-to tournament outfit.

The thought triggers a rush of memories: our first competition in the fall of freshman year, when we'd sat next to each other on the school bus from Winterton to Pinedale and run through flash cards together, so focused on the questions that we'd forgotten to ask for each other's names. The state championship the next year, when I'd sat with her in the bathroom while she almost threw up from nerves. Nationals the year after that, when she'd sat with me in the bathroom while I *actually* threw up from nerves.

"I don't see how this is any different from the last one," she had said.

"I'm the captain of the team now," I had said. "Which means if we embarrass ourselves, everyone will know it's my fault."

"If we embarrass ourselves, everyone will be too busy being embarrassed to even think about you," Iris had said.

And the thought had been comforting, in a grim sort of way.

Our last tournament together had been in mid-November, right before Thanksgiving break. Iris had just gotten her driver's license, and the two of us had taken her car there, giddy with the freedom. We'd spent the entire time fighting over the music before finally settling on a podcast about piracy in the South China Sea. We'd stopped at two different fast-food chains for lunch, only cruising past a third because Iris had said, "*No*, we cannot throw up at tournaments *four years in a row*; I refuse to allow it."

"But I want KFC," I had said, sadly, watching the exit sail by.

"We'll get it on the way back," Iris had said.

But on the way back, we had been too busy celebrating: We had won that tournament, and we were headed back to Filippo's house for pizza and whatever beer he managed to sneak out of his parents' garage. As Iris and I drove back, it hit me with increasing, horrible finality that there was something seriously wrong with me, because as she whooped with joy and recounted each of her rounds in glorious detail, practically glowing with delight, I mostly just felt—removed. Like I was inside a bubble, insulated from the joy of the moment and from everything else.

I hear the familiar *ding* of the restaurant door (*Welcome to Eastern Wind—we're so glad that you'll be dining with us tonight*, I think, the line so rehearsed it's almost instinctive), and watch as Iris stiffens. Then Ian and his girlfriend, Shannon, come into frame—two familiar faces—and Iris relaxes again.

"Oh, hey guys," Iris says. "You're the first ones here."

Iris looks down at a sheet of paper on the table in front of her—the RSVP list, I realize—and marks off two rows with a Sharpie.

"OK, so—here are your wristbands, which will allow you to enter and exit the dining area for the evening. And here is a menu of tonight's courses, which includes some background on the history and origin of each dish. And here is a description of today's program, which is really just a little tribute that Kenny's dad and I wrote for Kenny, and a couple sentences about Kenny's parents and the history of the restaurant, and some family photos because we thought it was getting a little text heavy and oh, God, I'm going to have to give this speech, like, fifty more times."

Iris's voice speeds up as she talks; by the end, she's practically panting.

"Whoa!" Ian says. "You gotta relax, Iris. Everything's going to be fine."

Shannon takes the wristbands, the menu, and the program from Iris. "Everything looks amazing," she says. "The decorations, the menu. Really. Kenny would be proud, Iris. And grateful. And probably also a little embarrassed."

It is a little embarrassing: everyone dressed up on my account, looking through baby photos and reading a *tribute* as if my death was some sort of great tragedy. It's horribly pretentious. It's way over-the-top. It's—

It's for the restaurant, I remind myself. It's for my *parents*. I'd dress up in a tuxedo and learn to tap dance if it meant helping my parents.

"We're going to head inside," Ian says, and Iris has just waved them through the curtain when the front door chimes again and Casey and Filippo come through, along with two girls I don't know. Neither of them had girlfriends last I checked, so these must be . . . other friends I'd never met? Random classmates who heard about the event and wanted to come?

"Damn, Iris," Casey says. "Place looks great. Do you need, uh—"

He holds out a printed sheet of paper.

"Oh, right," Iris says. "No, that's fine—we have a list. So I have you down, and Filippo, and Emma, and Bee . . ."

She scans the guest list, adding little check marks as she goes. There look to be about fifty rows in total—so that's most of the Science Olympiad team, and then half a dozen or so other kids, people like Emma and Bee who must have been lured here by whatever sob story Jianyu and Iris put out.

That's not bad, I think. Probably not as many as the number of people who sent the Davisons condolence gifts—maybe not even as many as the number of people who sent the Davisons condolence pastry baskets—but it's still pretty good. If each of them is donating a hundred bucks or so, that's a few thousand dollars. That'll buy my dad a month or so, which will hopefully be enough time for some of the customers to start coming back.

I'm not that memorable, after all. It's only a matter of time until people start forgetting. It's only a matter of time until people have forgotten altogether. And then the restaurant will be fine, freed of its unappetizing association with my death.

Over the course of the next half hour, most of the guest list arrives. Iris settles into an easy rhythm of greetings and introductions; sometimes, it even looks like she's having fun. Most of the attendees are Olympiad kids, but a lot of them bring girlfriends or boyfriends I've never met, and occasionally there's a straggler who comes in alone and aggressively mispronounces my name.

Then Corey Loman shows up, and things start to get a little weird.

To say that Corey Loman and I weren't friends when I was alive would be accurate but imprecise. It isn't just that we weren't friends—it's that we didn't exist in the same universe of Winterton High School. It'd be like trying to define the relationship between polar bears and jungle cats.

"Hi," he says, upon entry.

"Hi," Iris says. She regards him with a barely concealed look of suspicion, one of those rare instances when I wish she were better at hiding her feelings.

"I'm here for the fundraiser for Kenny," Corey says.

"Right," Iris says. She makes a show of checking the guest list for the next minute, even though Corey can clearly see that the guest list is only one page long.

"Sorry, Corey—I'm not actually seeing your name here . . ." Iris says. "Did you—I mean, uh, is it possible that—"

"Yeah, uh," Corey says. "Jianyu said I'd be able to make the donation at the door . . . ?"

"Jianyu . . . ?" Iris says.

"Yeah, Jianyu Zhang . . . ?" Corey says. "Asian dude, kinda tall?"

Having the identity of one of her best friends explained to her by a lacrosse bro seems to bring Iris back to lucidity. "I know who Jianyu is," she says. "I just didn't know—anyway. We do have room to accommodate additional guests, so I'm happy to sell you a ticket at the—er, door."

Her eyes float around the makeshift reception lounge, which does not, in fact, have a door.

"Our suggested donation amount is eighty dollars per person," Iris continues, "though of course we recognize that everyone's ability to contribute varies, and we encourage those who may not be able to meet the suggested amount to donate what they can—"

"Sweet," Corey says. Iris loses the rest of the sentence and instead mouths the word *sweet* a few times, looking increasingly bewildered.

Corey digs around in his pocket and pulls out his wallet. Then he digs around in his wallet and pulls out a check, which has been folded into quarters and is lodged somewhere in between credit cards and paper bills. "Here you go," he says, handing the check to Iris.

Iris looks at it. She does a double take, but just barely. "Great!" she says. She gives Corey an orange wristband, a copy of the menu, and the program for the evening, and says, all in one breath:

"This is your wristband it will allow you to enter and exit the dining area here is the menu there's also some additional information about the origin of each dish and finally here is a program that Kenny's father and I put together in his memory."

Iris lets out a huge exhale.

"Sweet," Corey says again, and heads through the curtain.

"What—" she says, picking up her phone, but before she can call or text Jianyu, another group arrives at the desk. This time it's three boys on the Model UN team, one of whom I'm eighty-five percent certain is named Larry. The other two might also be named Larry, for all I know.

"Hi," Iris says.

"Hi," says Larry. "We're here for the benefit dinner."

"Right," Iris says. "I assume you want to buy tickets at the door . . . ?"

"Yeah," says Larry number two. "Jianyu mentioned—"

"And he's absolutely right," Iris says, smoothly. "So our suggested donation amount is eighty dollars per person, though of course we recognize that everyone's ability to contribute varies, and we encourage . . ."

A steady stream of people I've never met before in my life keep coming through the door: more lacrosse bros, half the Model UN team, a group of a dozen theater kids who have somehow managed to make formal wear look avant-garde. Most of them pay in cash, but a few besides Corey give Iris checks, too. What kid our age carries around checks?

When the digital clock on the check-in table reads 5:25—five minutes before the event is supposed to start—Jianyu arrives. Iris stands up behind the desk the second he walks in, surely ready to tell him off, but then a second person walks in on his heels.

Iris sits back down.

Jianyu is accompanied by Patrick Doherty, who rounds out the Model UN senior class.

"Oh, hey, Iris," Patrick says, like the two of them are old friends.

"Hi, Patrick," Iris says. She's too tired from checking in swarms of other guests to bother having an attitude with Patrick, but not too tired to give Jianyu the cold shoulder. "I'm guessing you'd like to purchase a ticket to the benefit dinner?"

"Got it in one," Patrick says, flirty, and winks.

Jianyu and I make the exact same face at the same time.

"Great," Iris says. "So our suggested donation amount is eighty dollars per person, though of course we recognize that—"

"Gotcha," Patrick says. It takes him a minute to extract his wallet from his back pocket, on account of the fact that he's holding his coat in one hand and a tote bag in the other, but as soon as he's managed it, he slips out a hundred-dollar bill and hands it to Iris.

"You don't need to give me change for that," he says, as Iris reaches toward the register.

"OK," Iris says.

"This is such a great cause," Patrick says.

"I know," Iris says, now sounding faintly irritated.

"Right," Patrick says. "Of course."

He smiles at her, all straight white perfect teeth; not a hint of offense taken. Poor Iris. First Dom, and now

Patrick Doherty. Soon there won't be anyone at school for her to project her general misanthropy on to.

"Oh," Patrick says. "And I wanted to pass something along from my parents, too. We, uh—we used to eat here a lot, actually, and obviously they feel terrible about everything that happened."

He pulls a box of chocolates out of his tote bag—the fancy kind, Swiss French on the label. Attached to the chocolates is a white envelope that has my parents' American names written on it in loopy cursive.

"For Kenny's parents," he says.

"Wow," Iris says. "Wow, thank you. Uh."

"Sure," Patrick says.

Jianyu is watching the whole interaction play out like it's second Christmas. "You go ahead in, Patrick," he says, as Iris hands him his wristband. "I'm going to stay out here with Iris for a bit, make sure we catch anyone who's coming in late."

"Sounds good. See you later, man," Patrick says.

The two of them fist-bump, and then Patrick heads into the dining area, leaving Iris and Jianyu in the front with a box of expensive chocolates sitting between them.

"Everyone's checked in," Iris says. She waves the RSVP list, where a column of red check marks runs down the left side. "I don't think we're expecting anyone else, unless there's more of your crew—"

"I don't think so," Jianyu says. "I told them dinner started at five so they'd be on time when they ran late."

"Clever," Iris says, flatly.

"Thanks," Jianyu says.

Part of the reason why it's so difficult to stay angry at Jianyu is that he never seems to notice that you're angry at him, and by the time you've realized how much work it'll take to make him understand, it doesn't even seem worth it anymore.

"Hey," Jianyu says. "Hey, we should read what Patrick's parents wrote. I'm curious."

"What?" Iris says. She wrinkles her nose. "But that's private."

"They didn't even bother sealing the envelope," Jianyu says. "C'mon, I wanna know."

Iris looks at the envelope, which is, in fact, tantalizingly unsealed. "Well, all right," she concedes, and Jianyu grins.

She pulls out the contents—a check, which she hands to Jianyu, and a letter, which she unfolds. Jianyu whistles when he sees the amount on the check, but before he can tell her how much it's for, she starts to read.

Dear Jason and Eva,

We started coming to Eastern Wind when Patrick and his brother, Calum, were both young. Those days it was hard to go anywhere as a family without risking a tantrum or a mess, and Eva was one of the few people who treated us like a young family just doing our best and not a band of criminal interlopers jeopardizing everyone's peace and quiet on purpose. We were regulars after that, even after Patrick and Calum largely outgrew family dinners, and even after we lost Calum six years ago, when he returned four weeks early from a one-year tour of duty overseas. Encased in cherry-wood, draped in an American flag. Gone from us at nineteen years old.

We can't tell you that the pain of losing a child is something that ever fully heals. The fact of it is that it simply remains with you forever, the grief ebbing and flowing with the passage of time, the wound staunched and reopened in turns by the procession of birthdays and Christmases and New Years that somehow continues despite the world having one less person in it to celebrate them.

The pain is something that Tim and I still carry with us. That we continue to wake up with every day. But we can tell you with the certainty of having lived it that it is survivable, and we hope that in the moments when you are in doubt of that fact—in the moments when it feels like the loss has stripped you down to your bones, has turned you into a creature of regret and sorrow and anger—that you'll give us a call. That you'll stop by our house. That you'll let us share a meal with you, as you've shared with us so many times over the years.

Our very best,
Tim and Ellen

Iris puts the letter down.

"We shouldn't have read that," she says. Her voice is so hoarse it's almost a whisper.

"I didn't know," Jianyu says. "Patrick never . . ."

Then he looks at the check.

"Well, this should dry your tears," he says, and hands it to Iris.

Iris takes one look at it, and then puts it down on the table, as if expecting it to burst into flames. "That's—"

"I know," Jianyu says. "Though I guess it's not the most surprising thing. I gave Patrick a ride here, and they live in Cottonwood Circle, that cul-de-sac with all the huge Victorians."

Iris slides the letter and the check back in the envelope, puts the envelope back on top of the chocolates, and shoves everything back into the tote bag. "I suppose you're expecting that I'll forgive you now," she says.

"I wouldn't say 'expect,'" Jianyu says. "But—hoping, yeah."

"It doesn't—" Iris starts, and then sighs, like she can't believe she has to explain this. "It doesn't make it OK that you've been blowing me off just because you got the people you've been blowing me off *for* to come to the fundraiser."

"It's not an excuse," Jianyu says, quickly. "I've been a shit friend. And I'm sorry."

Iris is clearing off the ticketing station, stuffing the remaining printouts and wristbands into a box under the register. There aren't very many left. She leaves two sets of materials out: one for herself, one for Jianyu.

"As for the MUNers . . ." Jianyu says. "Look, I hang out with them because I like them. They're cool guys—nice guys—you met them tonight, they're great."

"They're fine," Iris says. "They all have very nice teeth."

"They have very nice *personalities*," Jianyu says, and then, when Iris looks mutinous: "Look, all I'm trying to say is that it's not just about the—the—"

Jianyu waves a hand in the air, in a motion I suppose is meant to encompass the peacoats and the crew cuts and the teeth.

"But you can't deny that it *helps*, Iris, to be friends with people like that, because then you can share the things you care about with them, and then they care about those things, too. And that's what politics is, Iris, so you're going to have to get used to that if you want—"

"That's not my politics," Iris says, darkly. "And you know why? Because it's not *real*. Because these people don't *actually* care. If they actually cared, they'd have RSVP'd weeks ago, when we first posted about the event in the Facebook group."

"They didn't *see* our post about the event in the Face-book group," Jianyu says. "There are like six hundred posts every hour in that group, and the vast majority of them are people asking for the answers to math problems! When I told Patrick about the event, he said he hadn't seen anything about it!"

"That's exactly the problem!" Iris says. "They're not looking! These are the same people who never spared Kenny a second glance when he was alive, and I didn't see a single one of them at the wake. But now—now you've made it *trendy* to care about Kenny, and now they show up with their checkbooks and their chocolates and think that just because they've donated a few hundred—"

"Or thousand—"

"—dollars means that they were suddenly best friends with Kenny all along, that they're good people now."

I think about my parents sitting at home eating left-over fried rice, the counters bare save for piles of unsorted mail, while the Davisons worked their way through weeks of gift baskets.

"Well," Jianyu says, "Aren't they?"

"No!" Iris says, vehemently. Jianyu raises an eyebrow. "Well, not *no*—they're not *bad* people, but they're also not—just because—it's complicated," she finishes weakly. "Look, we should go in."

The clock on the table reads 5:35. They're late to their own event.

"Yes, we should," Jianyu says. He lifts his elbow up as if Iris is supposed to give him her arm. Instead, she gives him a dirty look, and he lowers it again. "Oh, well. After you, I guess."

The video follows them as they slide through the curtain. On the other side, my dad is standing at the front of the dining room, a microphone in his hand. He's wearing the same suit he wore to my funeral, but it's too big on him now—he's lost weight.

"Jianyu!" he calls. It comes out way too loud, and my dad adjusts the volume on the microphone. "Iris!" he says. This time it's too quiet. My dad makes a disapproving noise in the back of his throat and puts the microphone on the floor.

"I'll just talk like this," he says, and then, for a second time, as if there aren't fifteen full tables of other people in between them: "Jianyu! Iris!"

"Hi, Mr. Zhou," Jianyu says.

"Now we start," my dad declares, and Iris looks faintly amused as she says: "Yes, go ahead. You really didn't have to wait for us."

"Thank you so much to everyone for coming to this benefit dinner in honor of Kenny," my dad says, and scans the room. Now that he's taken his attention off Jianyu and Iris, he looks suddenly nervous—like he, too, was unprepared for the number of people who have come to the event. It doesn't help that everyone is so dressed up and that half of them are staring up at him with somewhat bewildered expressions, like they can't figure out if that whole thing was a bit.

"My English is not so good," my dad says. "So I am sorry for that. But if you have trouble understanding me, just shout, and we'll have Jianyu translate."

I know and Iris knows and Jianyu knows that my dad is one hundred percent not joking—but no one else in the room knows, and it gets them laughing, loosened up. Jianyu dips his head a little bit, faking bashfulness, working the audience, and there's another collective peal of laughter right on the tails of the first.

"Mrs. Kenny's mom and I started the restaurant many years ago, maybe before some of you were even born," my dad is saying. Pleased, if confused, by the warm reception. "We are originally from Hunan province of China, very beautiful, very much history. It is a land of rivers, surrounded by green mountains. In the summertime, the air is filled with the sounds of playing bugs and the frogs that eat them. It is very humid place, lots of rain . . ."

"I've never heard this story," Jianyu whispers.

And neither have I, for that matter. My parents had never talked about their childhoods very much, if at all; their oral histories tended to begin with the part where they sacrificed everything to move to America. Sometimes my white acquaintances would go on about their extended families, describing great-aunts and second cousins, drawing lines and dotted lines between last names until they got all the way back to Ellis Island. It had always seemed so foreign to me—to have a sense of self so grounded in the past, to have an understanding of family as a tightly drawn net rather than one flung across oceans.

"People are eating this up, though, look," Jianyu says, and he's right: The crowd is rapt, totally absorbed in my father's words. Bee is tearing up (already?). Patrick is jotting little notes down on his program.

Everyone loves a good origin story, I suppose, especially if it's one that doesn't look like your own.

"When we moved to America," my dad is saying, "we missed a lot of things. We missed our brothers and sisters. We missed going to grocery store and speaking in Chinese. English was much harder when we first moved here, and me and Kenny's mom spent several years only talking to each other. Most of all, we missed the food of the Hunan province, the best food in all China, except for maybe the fried pork bun in Shanghai, which is also very good."

"I just wish Kenny's mom were here," Jianyu says. "It's too bad she had that—"

The hologram distorts for a moment, then resets, like it's been rewound by ten seconds.

"It's too bad she had—"

Another glitch.

"It's too bad she—"

CAROLINE

29 | but she's still wearing her wedding ring

My mom meets my brother at High Rollers. It's not exactly the obvious choice.

High Rollers hasn't always been High Rollers. Ten years ago, it was Rock 'n' RollerVille, an eighties-themed roller rink frequented exclusively by 1) elementary school students whose parents didn't want to shell out for a birthday party at Chuck E. Cheese and 2) stoned teenagers. But then someone got the bright idea that people might like to eat in between sprained ankles, so they retrofitted a diner into half of the building, and now it's High Rollers: Come for the grease, stay for the people watching.

Dom and I had planned a date here last fall, just to see what all the fuss was about. But he'd taken one look at the interior—which was neon and patterned and space-themed all at once—and demanded we go to the burger place down the street instead.

"It's *pastiche*," I had told him, irritated. I had heard they made a killer Margherita pizza. "That's the aesthetic; that's the *point*."

The place is crowded with people when Mom and Cooper arrive, and both of them look taken aback as the door swings shut behind them and they take in their surroundings. Perhaps Cooper, like Dom, had been confused about the definition, or perhaps the extent, of "pastiche."

My mom orders—*One large pepperoni pizza,* she says, her card already halfway into the hand of the kid working the register, *just water for me and an iced tea for my son*—and then they sit down at a booth up against the wall. A plastic card on a shiny metal stand declares their order number 35.

I miss them. I miss them I miss them I miss them. It's the only thing there is to say.

"How are things with your father?" my mom asks.

"They're good," Cooper says, though what he said at the park the other day suggests this is far from the truth.

"You know you can come back home anytime you'd like," my mom says. Her voice cracks around the syllables of the word *home.*

"Of course, Mom," Cooper says.

It makes my chest ache to see my mom like this. When I was growing up, she was always surrounded by family members or friends or other parents, drinking in the attention so gracefully you almost didn't realize she was the center of it. And now she's sitting in a booth at High Rollers of all places, desperate and vulnerable, trying her best not to cry in front of my brother.

A server comes by, setting a pizza and their drinks on the table and whisking their order number away.

"Cooper," my mom says. She takes a deep breath. She steels herself. "I know you've been frustrated with how little information your father and I have shared with you regarding Caroline's accident."

Cooper pauses, a slice of pizza halfway to his mouth. A piece of pepperoni falls to the plate.

"We've been trying to protect you, of course—to keep you insulated from some of the more grisly, more sordid elements of the legal proceedings. But your father and I have reflected—"

There's the slightest pause here, which makes me wonder about how the reflection between "your father and I" was distributed.

"Your father and I have reflected, and we think you're right. If you want to know more about the driver, about the trial, about why it's so important to us to speak at the sentencing hearing—it should be your decision to make."

"I want to know," Cooper says, instantly.

"Of course," my mom says. She hesitates, and then continues: "All right. Why don't I start from the beginning."

I feel a twist of nausea low in my stomach, a reaction evidently not shared by Cooper, who has now finished his first slice of pizza and is well into his second.

"The accident occurred at 5:54 P.M. on Friday, March 12," my mother says. "The police arrived at the scene seven minutes later at 6:01; the paramedics arrived one minute after the police at 6:02."

The memory comes together in my head as she describes it, more vivid than it's ever been before. This time, I'm not just remembering the physical reality of that night, the sensory details of the rain and the sirens, the metal and the glass. I'm remembering the experience of it, the crash as it unfolded inside my head.

I had been listening to Dom's playlist. I had been thinking about dinner. Dad had promised us lasagna that morning, and I didn't want the dish to come with a lecture on the side.

It was all the Honda Odyssey's fault, the fact that I was going to be late. Well—the Honda Odyssey, and also the rain, which was coming down in sheets, now making it hard to see even though the windshield wipers were on the highest setting.

At least it's not snow, I had thought, approaching the intersection.

I had seen movement out of the corner of my left eye and wrenched the wheel to the right. There had been panic so sharp and fierce that even a split second of it felt like a lifetime. The pain had been—the pain—

And then it was all just gone.

"After Caroline was taken to the hospital, one of the police officers at the scene conducted a DUI assessment of the other driver," my mom says. "The officer noted that the driver was unable to successfully perform two out of three of the field sobriety tests, which led him to administer a Breathalyzer exam. However, the Breathalyzer recorded a blood alcohol level of 0.04, which is well under the legal limit. This led the officer to conclude that the physical impairment noted during the field sobriety tests was likely due to trauma from the accident rather than alcohol or other substances. It also meant that the vehicular manslaughter case was prosecuted as a misdemeanor rather than a felony."

"But—" Cooper says, "But he had been drinking. When he—"

When he hit me, I think. *When he hit me; when he killed me.*

I'm definitely going to be late to dinner now, I had thought, and my temples had been searing; my face had felt wet, wet, wet.

"Yes," my mom says. "And in my opinion that should absolutely factor into the sentencing, even if it wasn't enough to warrant a felony conviction. Which is part of the reason why it's so important to your father and me to speak at the hearing. We're going to advocate for the maximum possible sentence."

Cooper nods, looking numb. I can't blame him. Sometimes it feels like I've only barely come to terms with my death, and I've got the flashbacks as a constant reminder that it actually happened.

My mom's breath catches, like there's a thought stuck in the back of her throat.

"There is one other thing," she says.

She hesitates again, drinks out of her glass of water. Her pizza remains entirely untouched, though she's been blotting at it absent-mindedly this entire time with a napkin that is now fully saturated with grease.

"Another reason why your father and I have kept you in the dark is because we worry some of the details might make the case feel quite personal, Cooper," my mom says.

"And the last thing we want is to complicate your relationships with your classmates."

"Personal?" Cooper repeats. But my mom forges ahead without pausing, like she needs to complete the thought before she changes her mind.

"You see," my mom says, "On the night of March 12, the driver—"

KENNY

30 | the medium, part ii

—And then I'm looking at my mom, parking her car in a strip mall in the rain.

I don't think she's in Winterton anymore. Even the run-down parts of Winterton are nicer than this.

My mom stands up out of the car and onto the asphalt, which has been poured unevenly, which is littered with cigarette butts and broken glass. Dilapidated storefronts loom in front of her: a check-cashing place, a seedy-looking bar, an electronics store with windows so reflective it's impossible to see inside. She makes her way to an unmarked door near the middle of the row, carefully stepping over a pile of trash on the sidewalk.

There's a sign taped to one of the windows that reads:

Trying to find someone on the other side?
Angela Grimsley, Certified Psychic Medium, Energy Healer,
Grief Recovery Specialist

My mom pushes on the door, but it doesn't open. She tries pulling; still no dice. The door is locked.

Maybe Angela Grimsley has gone out of business, fallen victim to the high turnover and crime rates that often plague strip malls. Maybe she's traded in mediumship for a less depressing pseudoscience. Or maybe she just forgot. Either way, the fact remains: There's no one there for my mother.

"No," my mom says. And then, the words becoming a chant, "No, no, no!"

I understand my mom's despair because I've felt it myself. Standing in the phone booth, a receiver pressed to my ear, my words dissipating unheard into thin air. Even in life—moments when I've wanted so desperately to be heard, to be known, to be *felt*.

"Kenny," my mom cries, like I'm four years old again, like the name will summon me to her from across the playground or too far into the ocean at the beach. She sits down on the steps, paying no mind to the rain soaking through her clothes, the trash littered around her, and pulls a water bottle out of her purse. She takes a long drink, and then grimaces.

I don't think the bottle is filled with water.

Oh, shit, I think.

I had seen my mother drinking at the restaurant that night with my dad—the cracked glass cup cradled between her hands, the open bottle of baijiu next to the register. But here? Now?

She looks back at the office and its locked door, the unfulfilled promise on the other side. "I need to go to the restaurant to help your dad now, Kenny," my mom says. She takes one last drink and throws the rest of the water bottle away. "But I will come to you later, I promise; I will find another way to reach you. Angela is not here but I will find another way—"

And then she's climbing into the car, her wet shoes

squelching underneath her weight; she's pulling out of the parking lot, away from the uneven asphalt and the blinking fluorescent signs of the strip mall; she's winding through the side streets and on to Route 9, the video locked in place in the passenger's seat of the car.

Thank God, I think, sagging with relief.

My mom keeps up a steady stream of babbling over the next fifteen minutes, alternating between my dad's name and Angela Grimsley's name and mine, saying, "Kenny, I will find another way, I will find another way," over and over. At some point she starts crying again, and then she's driving through the rain and through her tears, and all I can think about is how I'm so close to her, how I should be able to reach out and touch her, brush her hair off her shoulder and out of her eyes, say, *Mom, I'm right here. You've already found me. I'm right here.*

It's a quarter to six when she first crosses back into Winterton, which feels wrong somehow, in an undefinable way that I can't place. But then my mom runs through the stop sign at an intersection, and I forget about the time altogether.

Take it easy, Mom, I think, but it's too late: There's another car rolling through the intersecting street, its back tires kicking up two streams of muddy water, accelerating while my mother accelerates, then swerving while my mother swerves. "Kenny, 宝贝, 妈妈来了, 马上就来了," my mom is saying, and then her whole face freezes with sudden realization and she slams on the brakes—too late, I register, way too late—and then there's the *crunch* of metal hitting metal and the other car is spinning out, spinning out, spinning out, the whole driver's side caved in, smoke pouring out of the windows, my mom screaming and screaming, my whole body frozen with shock, and then, seconds or minutes or hours later, the other car finally spins to a halt, its own momentum canceling itself out, the driver's body invisible through the smoke, but—

CAROLINE

31 | error code #204

"—on the night of March 12, the driver was on her way to a benefit dinner," my mom says. "A memorial for her son, who had passed away three months ago to the day. One of Caroline's former classmates."

Cooper puts his slice of pizza down.

"His name was Kenny Zhou," my mom says.

KENNY

32 | error code #204

—but I know, with crushing certainty, who it is.

"Caroline," I whisper, as the hologram goes fuzzy, and then black. I rush out of the room, but Caroline is already halfway to my door, her eyes wide with understanding and with horror.

PART III

KENNY

33 | block time

"Kenny," Caroline says. Her voice is even softer than mine—barely audible, even in the ringing silence of the room. "What's going on?"

"I don't—" I start. "I can't—"

Everything feels slow, sluggish, like the last three months of consecutive all-nighters are finally starting to register with my brain.

"What's going on, Kenny?" Caroline repeats, and she doesn't even sound angry with me anymore. She sounds desperate—childlike, almost—like she's pleading with me to give her an explanation that makes all of this make sense. That makes all this OK.

"There's an—an interpretation of Einstein's theory of relativity," I say. "Well, it's not so much an interpretation of the theory so much as it's an interpretation of an *implication* of the theory, which is that time is just another fixed dimension within four-dimensional space-time, and our experience of moving 'through' time isn't an objective reality but instead a subjective illusion that arises from the limits of human perception. That the past, the present, and the future all exist at once, independently, without the causal links that—"

"OK," Caroline says. "But *what is going on*?"

"I don't know!" I say. Panic mounting. "I need to look at my notes, I need go to through that chapter again, maybe ask for supplementary materials on Minkowski space-time—"

My notebook appears in my hand. A stack of spiral-bound essays lands at my feet. I start riffling through the notebook—flipping through pages and pages of scribbling about string theory, simulation theory, wormholes. Then the brief detour I took into the major religions and their notions of the afterlife; then time dilation and relative simultaneity, until finally—

"OK, here we go: Minkowski space-time. If we accept Hermann Minkowski's geometric model of special relativity, then everything that happens in the past, the present, and the future exists simultaneously, just at separate coordinates in a four-dimensional block of space-time. We *perceive* different events as 'different times,' just as we perceive different stops on a bus route as 'different places,' but all those times and all those places are equally real and equally fixed, even if we're not there to perceive them. The bus stop six stops ago doesn't cease to exist just because we're not there anymore; the bus stop six stops from now doesn't only come into existence when we get there. Similarly, the past doesn't disappear just because our senses have left it behind, and our future is already out there even if our senses haven't caught up to it yet. Everything happens *at the same time*, which is to say, in no time at all."

I'm not sure Caroline is keeping up with what I'm saying; I'm not even sure she's listening. But it feels good to think out loud. It feels good to *solve* something, because that means this is a problem that can be solved.

"We've been watching events from two different time-lines," I say. "Well, there's no such thing as a 'timeline' in this theory, because time doesn't progress linearly—but we've been watching events that people on Earth are experiencing as two different causality streams."

I walk up to the whiteboard and draw two parallel lines, the one on the bottom starting where the one on the top ends.

"The first is the set of events that occurred 'after' my death, including Jianyu and Iris planning the restaurant fundraiser and my parents arguing about the validity of supernatural phenomena."

I label the first line KENNY EVENTS.

"The second is the set of events that occurred 'after' your death, including Dom transforming into Mr. Congeniality and your parents arguing about how to handle the legal proceedings."

I label the second line CAROLINE EVENTS.

"The two sets of events conjoin at this point in time—"

I connect the two the lines with a dotted vertical line—

"—which is the— the—"

Screaming metal; thick columns of smoke. My mother repeating my name, over and over and over again.

"The accident," I finish, and then force myself to forge ahead. "But the sequential nature of it all is only an illusion. And that must be why—when I tried to ask for a clock—whenever we tried to ask for *anything* time-related—oh, but that reminds me—"

And then the television manual lands at my feet, too, as tall as the entire stack of supplementary reading.

"I need to go through this book," I say. "The room gave it to me when I asked for a manual for the TV, and at first I thought—*Great, another piece of useless junk from our landlord who is maybe God*. But then I realized—"

"Kenny," Caroline interrupts. "We need to talk about what's happening. We need to *slow down*."

"We don't have time to slow down, Caroline!" I say. I haul the book into my lap and flip the leather cover open, which sends us both into coughing fits as plumes of dust roll off its pages and up into the air.

"How is it possible we don't have time to slow down when you just told me that time *literally doesn't exist*?"

"Time does exist," I say. "It's just fixed. And it's only fixed to an objective observer. But the people down on Earth—my mom, your mom—they're not objective observers. And we can figure out a way to help them, but first I need to understand all the rules."

"Them?" Caroline says, and the blank shock on her face has started to condense into something else. Something flammable. "Help *them*?"

I blink at her.

"Kenny, your mother killed me! You can't just stand there and pretend that didn't happen!"

"I'm up to my elbows in quantum physics here!" I say. "Does it look like I'm pretending nothing happened?"

Then the television turns on.

"Is there no way to pause?" Caroline snaps, exasperated, only—

UNABLE TO FULFILL REQUEST. ERROR CODE #162.

I page through the book with my right hand and wave away additional dust clouds with my left. "Error Code 158, 159 . . . Oh, here it is. '162: Once initiated by the interstitial regulator, the flow of information through an Einstein-Rosen mirror cannot be interrupted, reversed, or altered.'"

"Huh," I say, after a brief moment of contemplation. "That's interesting."

"How can you—" Caroline starts, her voice rising. But then the static clears and the retort dies on her lips.

We're looking at my parents. They're standing in the parking lot in front of the town jail, next to a green Chevy.

A rental car, I realize. We only ever had the Toyota.

It's midday, the sky clear and cloudless, the sunlight glancing off the thin layer of snow on the ground and making the whole scene too bright, overexposed. My mom has collapsed into my dad's arms, buried her face in the crook of his neck as she shakes with tears, her hair so tangled that in places it's started to mat. I wonder if they let her shower before they threw her in jail, or if she's had to spend the nights enveloped in the smell of smoke and burnt rubber, trapped in a second, sensory prison within her cell. My dad is crying, too, the tears leaving wet tracks down his cheeks, his chin, as they drip down his face and land on my mother's head. Their embrace is a sight unlike anything I've ever seen, even in the privacy of our home.

"I'm sorry," my mom says, in Mandarin. "I'm so sorry, Lao Zhou, I'm so sorry."

Subtitles appear; Caroline must have asked for them.

"Xiao Ye," my dad says. He's crying so hard his words are unintelligible; so hard that I, too, have to read them off the screen.

It would have killed me, my dad says. **You know that, don't you? Surely you must know. I wouldn't have survived it. I couldn't have lost you, too.**

34 | the reveal, part ii

And then the scene changes. Eliding over days, weeks, months of perceived time, for all we know.

We're in the Rhododendron Lawn of Wisteria Park, watching as Iris pulls foil-wrapped sandwiches from Arcetta's out of a paper takeout bag. "And the roast beef is yours, Cooper," she's saying. "Hey, can I steal your pickle again?"

But Cooper is gazing off into space, oblivious to Iris's outstretched hand and the sandwich she's trying to give to him.

"Oi," Dom says, and swings his foot over so he can kick Cooper in the shin.

Cooper startles. "Sorry," he says. He takes the sandwich out of Iris's hand, not quite managing to look at her as he does so.

"Your parents again?" Iris says, and makes a sympathetic face.

"How does she know about that?" I start. "When did they—"

"You missed the last video," Caroline says. "I think they've all become friends. And Jianyu was there, too, but I don't see him this time . . ."

"Uh," Cooper says. "Sort of. It's—they're . . ."

"What's going on, dude?" Dom says.

"Sorry," Cooper says again. He licks his lips. "Everyone's just prepping for the hearing . . ."

"Oh, right," Iris says. She's unwrapping the foil that encloses her own sandwich, though I already know it's a BLT. "You said that was next week, right?"

"Thursday," Cooper mumbles.

"Cooper can't keep a secret for his life," Caroline says, and sure enough, it's only a second or two of silence before Cooper blurts out "It-was-Kenny's-mom" all in one breath, like the sentence is physically forcing its way out of him.

"I really shouldn't have told you that," Cooper says.

"What?" Iris says. "What was Kenny's mom?"

For a second, I have the craziest thought, like—*Maybe I can stop him from telling them.* But how could I? Caroline and I have only ever been able to use the three tools the room has given us—the telephone, the computer, the CD player. We can't change what they know. We can't change what they want.

"My mom said," Cooper says, quietly, "that the driver of the car that hit Caroline's was on her way to a memorial dinner. A fundraiser. In honor of her son."

Iris and Dom stare at Cooper. Then:

"They haven't been answering their phones . . ." Iris says. "Even last week, when Jianyu's parents called, they didn't—oh, God."

"You're shitting me," Dom says. "You can't be serious. Are you serious?"

Cooper finally looks up at the two of them, his expression a wordless confirmation.

"But how could—" Dom starts. Then he rounds on Iris. "Did you know?" he demands.

"Did I—" Iris splutters. "Of course I didn't know! If I had known, I would've said something, I would've told you!"

"Would you have?" Dom asks. "Because it seems like you and Kenny's mom were pretty close!"

"We *are* close," Iris says. She turns to look at Cooper; says, beseechingly: "Cooper, are you absolutely *sure* it was her? I just can't imagine—I mean, Kenny's mom would never—"

"Kill someone?" Dom supplies. And then, when Iris and Cooper look shocked at the venom in his voice: "What? She did, didn't she?"

A beat of silence. Iris's eyes have welled up with tears.

"It's a vehicular manslaughter charge," Cooper says, with some difficulty. "Not a felony, because the Breathalyzer results . . . But we really shouldn't be talking about the case here," he says. He looks around at the other picnickers, many of whom are starting to turn in their direction. "Look, can we go to one of your places? I'd offer one of mine, but obviously, with my dad around . . ."

"I'm sorry," Dom says. He stands up, his face tight with anger. "I can't—I need to go."

"Where are you going?" Cooper says, as Dom walks off in the general direction of the parking lot. "You don't even—"

But Dom is already out of earshot.

"He doesn't even have a car," Cooper says, helplessly. "I'm sorry, Iris—I know it's a lot to process. But I need to go make sure Dom doesn't—well, I need to go."

"It was really Kenny's mom?" Iris says. Her voice trembles a bit as she says my name, pitched high with emotion. It's not quite shock, not quite sadness, certainly not anger—

It's fear, I realize. Iris is afraid.

Cooper hesitates, and then nods. "It was really her."

"I should go, too," Iris says, and then she, too, is stumbling toward the parking lot. We follow her into her car, where she lets her head fall onto the steering wheel, where she starts to take long, shaky breaths.

After a few minutes, she pulls her phone out of her pocket. She makes a call on speakerphone, which is forwarded to a voice mail greeting that I helped record, years and years ago, each cheerful and accented word etched into my memory by hundreds of subsequent listens.

Hello! You have reached Jason Zhou and Eva Ye. Sorry we cannot come to the phone right now! Please leave a message, and we'll return as soon as possible.

Iris hangs up. She sets her jaw. She wipes the tears off her face with the back of her sleeve.

Then she slides the key into the ignition, and she drives to my parents' house.

35 | welcome to hummingbird junction

It takes minutes of continuous knocking until my dad answers. But the longer her knocking goes unanswered, the more determined she looks, until finally—

"Iris?" my dad says, pulling the door open. "Is everything OK?"

"I'm OK," Iris says. "Are you and Eva . . ."

She trails off—unsure how to ask the question, unsure of the right question to ask.

"We are doing fine," my dad says. "But now is not a great time, unless it's an emergency. Maybe you come back next week, we make noodles, you bring cat—"

He has the door halfway closed already. "Wait, Mr. Zhou," Iris says, desperation in her voice, and he pauses.

"I know about the accident," Iris says.

My dad blanches. "How did . . . ?"

"It's not important how I know," Iris says. "But I know. Can I come in?"

My dad hesitates, and then ushers her through the doorway and into the house. Iris slips off her shoes, hangs her jacket in a coat closet by the door, grabs a pair of slippers from that same closet, and walks down the hallway, the whole routine so practiced that it's obvious how much time she's spent in my house.

Then, so abruptly that my dad almost walks into her, she stops short.

"Oh, Eva . . ." Iris says. Our video tracks past Iris and into the living room, where my mom is lying on the couch, cocooned in blankets.

I let my head fall back so it's resting against the couch, so I'm looking up at the ceiling instead of at the screen. Way, way, way back, when the room was still just four white walls with nothing between them—empty of furniture and electronics, absent the heaviness of knowledge and bad history—I had looked up at the skylights and thought maybe I could escape. I had thought that maybe this was all a dream, and that if it wasn't a dream, surely it was some kind of scientific marvel, some kind of miracle.

In a way, I had never been more hopeful than after I killed myself.

"Xiao Ye, Iris came over to see us," my dad says. "Let's go sit at the table with her for a few minutes—we can't be rude, can we?"

"Subtitles," Caroline says, and they appear.

"Ni hao, Xiao Ye ayi," Iris says.

"Iris?" my mom says. She pulls herself into an upright position; one of her blankets falls to the floor. My dad sits down on the newly vacant couch cushion and drapes the blanket back over her lap, every movement radiating tenderness.

"Just came over to say hello," Iris says. She crosses the living room and sits cross-legged on the floor, across the coffee table from my parents. "Tea? Should I make some tea?"

My mom looks at my dad. She says, in Mandarin: "She knows."

My dad nods.

"How could you ask her to come here?" my mom says, and though Iris doesn't speak the language, the despair in my mother's voice is universal. "What must she think of me, knowing what I did—"

"Xiao Ye, Xiao Ye," my dad says. "I didn't ask her to come. She chose to be here. With us. With you."

"It's OK, Eva," Iris says. "I'm here to help."

"Help," my mom repeats, and through her tears I can make out the contours of a thin, shaky smile. "Always such a sweet girl. But it's no good for you, spending time with me. Your parents must be so ashamed, must want you anywhere else—"

"My parents would want me right here!" Iris says, fired up. "Sure, maybe you made a—a mistake," Iris continues, stumbling slightly, "but no one lives a perfect life. It's how you respond to your mistakes that matters. It's how you come back."

"She won't come back," my mom says, and then, through a fresh wave of tears: "She's gone. Like Kenny. Gone forever."

And it takes me a minute, but I realize she's talking about Caroline.

"She is gone," Iris says. "And that—that is a terrible thing." She swallows. I wonder if she's thinking about Dom, about Cooper, all these newfound friendships that have made Caroline's death just as real and as tragic to her as mine was. Maybe even more so. "But you can't let that keep you from living the rest of your life."

"Gone forever," my mother says. "My fault."

"When was the last time you got out of the house, Eva?" Alice says. "We should go for a walk. Get some sunshine, fresh air. Maybe stop by the restaurant for some food. What do you say?"

At that, my mom really does laugh. When Iris just looks confused, she turns to my dad and says, "She doesn't know . . ."

"Not another thing I don't know," Iris says, wearily.

"Iris," my dad says. "We're not reopening the restaurant."

"What?" Iris says.

"We're shutting down," my dad says. "We're selling."

"But—but *why*?" Iris says.

"We don't have the money," my dad says, heavily. And then he says it again—"We just don't have the money"—and then I realize that this is it. That I can hear the capital letters in his voice. That this time, after years and years of saving and scrimping and scraping by, we really Don't Have the Money.

"But the fundraiser," Iris is saying. "Tens of thousands of dollars, surely that's enough to keep it open for a little longer—"

"Iris . . ." my dad says. "The dinner was incredible. Kenny's mom and I cannot express how thankful we are for what you and Jianyu did that night. It gave us so much, so many things more important than money. It gave us hope. It gave us new friends. It gave us Kenny back, if only for one night. He would have been—"

My dad pauses, choked up.

"He would have been so happy to see it. But the money—the money—"

Then he can't continue at all.

"Let me, Lao Zhou," my mom says. She clasps one of my dad's hands in hers. She says, in Chinese: "I should be the one to tell her. It's my fault."

"It's not—" my dad starts, but my mom waves him off.

"We had to use the money to pay the bail," my mom says, to Iris. "So now . . ."

"So now that's it," Iris finishes. "The restaurant's not coming back."

"None of them are coming back," my mom says, and my dad hunches over, the weight of all that loss settling over him. Iris crawls over to the foot of the couch on her knees and rests her head in my mom's lap, her tears dampening the blankets.

"Turn it off," I say, feeling dizzy, feeling nauseous, only now realizing that I, too, am crying, because this is—this is too much.

A note appears—"Error code #162—yes, yes, I remember," I say, not even bothering to unfold it—but the television turns off just a few seconds after anyway: I guess this was all we were meant to see.

Caroline stands up from the couch, where it feels like we've been frozen in place for days. She moves, off-balance and uneven, toward the bedrooms.

"Caroline, wait," I say.

She turns toward me. Her expression is a mask of shock, like she doesn't know what she's feeling enough to actually feel it.

"Caroline," I say. "I can't let your parents do it. I can't let them testify."

CAROLINE

36 | if only there were anywhere to go

"But—" I say, my head spinning. "But—she killed me."

"I know that you're upset," Kenny says. "But you have to understand: Your mom will ruin them, Caroline."

And I can't believe—after everything that's happened—after everything we now know—the fact that it was *his mother* who killed me—the fact that it was Kenny who *killed himself*—and then there's all this about *two different timelines*, which makes me feel like I'm literally going insane—

"Ruin them?" I say. "I'm *dead*, Kenny. I think that's worse than being ruined!"

"Caroline," Kenny says. "My parents aren't like yours. They barely survived paying my mother's bail. I don't know what they're going to do if my mom serves jail time. Certainly no one will buy the restaurant with all the bad press, which is maybe your mom's whole point in the first place—"

"That's not the point," I say. "She just wants to do what's best for me. That's all she's ever wanted."

"What's best for you? Caroline, you're dead!" Kenny says, and I hate that he says that; it feels cruel; it feels *true*. "But my parents—they're still out there, on Earth! And they don't deserve to have their lives destroyed just because—"

"What *they* deserve?" I say. "What about what *I* deserve, Kenny? I deserve to be *alive*! I deserve to go to college next year, I deserve to get married, I deserve to have kids, I deserve to get old—"

"Of course you deserve to be alive!" Kenny says.

"—And what about what my family deserves? My parents gave their whole lives to watch me grow up, and now that's all been taken away from them! What do they deserve?"

Kenny's face is tear-streaked, vulnerable, pleading, and I don't want to see that; I don't want to see any of this. Because maybe if he hadn't killed himself, then his mom wouldn't have been rushing to the fundraiser, and if his mom hadn't been rushing to the fundraiser, then I'd still be alive right now, sitting in the cafeteria with my friends and going to softball practices and making faces with Cooper every time my parents kissed.

"Of course you deserve to be alive," Kenny repeats. "But we can't change that now, Caroline; it's already happened. But my parents can still move on from this. My parents can still be *happy*. If your mom would just—"

"Don't pin your parents' unhappiness on my mom," I say. "You know what would probably make your parents happy? If their son hadn't freaking *killed himself*—"

"Stop," Kenny says, and his voice is so harsh, so ragged, that I do. "You think I don't know that? You think I don't think about that every single waking minute of every single day—which is every minute, by the way, because we *never, ever sleep*, because there's *no way to get away from it*—to forget, to move on—"

"Oh, this is so like you," I say. "To make everything about *your* feelings, like everything that happens in the whole wide world happens for no other reason than to make you miserable. Well guess what, Kenny? Maybe you're not that important. Maybe my parents are doing this for *me*, their *dead daughter*, not to feed whatever bizarre victim complex you've got going on—"

"Caroline," Kenny says. "I do not give a *fuck* what happens to me. You could tell me I was doomed to spend the rest of *eternity* in this room, miserable and guilt-ridden, and you know what? I wouldn't even care. But I care about *my parents*. And I know, *I know*, that they would be happier if I hadn't killed myself. And every minute of every day I wish there were another way things could have played out."

"I hate when you do that!" I shout. "You act like you didn't have a choice, just like you're acting like your mom didn't have a choice—*she chose to drink, she chose to get in that car!*"

"She wasn't drunk!" Kenny says. "I would know, Caroline, *I was there, I saw the video*—"

"Well, I was there, too," I say. "In case *you've* forgotten. I died that night."

Kenny falls silent.

I think back to what my mom said to my dad, sitting in the kitchen of a home where they no longer live together. *Her last moments, Roy—you can't even imagine.* But how could either of them imagine? How could either of them know what it's like to feel your body come apart while you're still inside of it? To feel that pain, that panic, and to be *grateful* for it, to cling to it, because you know if you let yourself give in to the relief of unconsciousness, you're never coming back?

"Sometimes, I think I'm still in that car," I say. "Sometimes I think I'll never get out."

"I know," Kenny says. "Caroline, I know. And I'm sorry. You must know that."

"Like I said," I say. "This time it's not about you."

And then I walk away.

37 | there's a class at WHS called "introduction to philosophical inquiry" for people who are into this sort of thing. I did not take it.

The claustrophobia intensifies when I first step into the bedroom. I haven't been here during several weeks of real-world time, and I've forgotten how small the space is, how the dark-green curtains absorb so much light it's perpetually movie-theater dim.

I need water, I think, casting about for things that might pull me out of the spiral: *I need air, I need to go for a run, I need to paint.*

Four *pops*, and there's a glass of water in my hand, a bag of oxygen on the floor, a treadmill in the corner of the bedroom, and my entire art station in front of me, transplanted perfectly, half-painted canvas still resting on the easel, oil paints still arrayed on the palette.

It's the oxygen that makes me feel better—the sight of it on the floor, the absurdity of it. "Thanks," I say, amused. And then, feeling kind of stupid but knowing there's never going to be a better time to ask—

"Hey," I say. "This is a weird question, but—are you real?"

The note appears almost instantaneously.

QUESTIONS OF ONTOLOGY ARE DIFFICULT TO ANSWER, it says. WHEN HUMANS SAY "REAL," THEY GENERALLY REFER TO OBJECTS AND PHENOMENA THAT EXIST MIND-INDEPENDENTLY. A PERSON IS REAL. A GHOST IS NOT. THE COLOR BLUE IS REAL. THE SMELL OF BLUE IS NOT. THE SOLAR ECLIPSE OF 2134 BCE WAS

REAL. THE DRAGON THAT WAS SAID TO HAVE CAUSED THE ECLIPSE BY DEVOURING THE SUN WAS NOT.

BUT THE TAXONOMY QUICKLY GROWS MESSY. IF OUR POLTERGEIST, STARVED FOR ATTENTION AND TIRED OF BEING DISMISSED AS A CHILDISH FANTASY, BEGINS TO FLING HOUSEHOLD OBJECTS AROUND, DOES HE THEN BECOME REAL? THE COLOR BLUE IS MYSTERIOUSLY ABSENT FROM THE WRITTEN RECORD UNTIL THE TIME OF THE ANCIENT EGYPTIANS—WAS THE COLOR NOT REAL UNTIL WE NAMED IT?

AS FOR THE DRAGON—HE MAY NOT HAVE BEEN REAL IN THE CONVENTIONAL SENSE, BUT THE CHINESE ASTRONOMERS WHO WERE BEHEADED FOR FAILING TO PREDICT HIS APPEARANCE SURELY CURSED HIM REGARDLESS.

"Right," I say. "Right, never mind. Maybe it doesn't even matter."

QUESTIONS OF EXISTENTIALISM ARE ALSO DIFFICULT TO ANSWER, the room says. WHEN HUMANS SAY "MATTER," THEY GENERALLY REFER TO ONE OF THREE CATEGORIES OF SIGNIFICANCE. THE FIRST IS OBJECTIVE. THE SECOND IS NORMATIVE. AND THE THIRD IS ETHICAL. IF YOU'D LIKE, I CAN PRESCRIBE A BASIC READING LIST THAT COVERS THE FUNDAMENTALS OF EXISTENTIAL INQUIRY, RANGING FROM THE ANCIENT GREEKS TO THE CONTINENTAL PHILOSOPHERS TO CONTEMPORARY ANALYTIC THINKERS (THOUGH THE LATTER GROUP DOES TEND TO BE RATHER DISDAINFUL OF THE FIELD AS A WHOLE).

"That's all right," I say, and resolutely do not comment further, lest another offhand comment like "Maybe it doesn't even matter" triggers a bout of rigorous philosophical interrogation.

By this point, I've been in the room for long enough that my eyes have adjusted to the darkness, and I can make my way over to the newly relocated art studio and the paintings around it. The last portrait I'd been working on—the one currently propped up on the easel—was of Kenny: his fingers curled around a pair of chopsticks, his mouth half-open in anticipation, radiating an odd sort of peace. But I don't want to look at that—*can't* look at it anymore without being reminded of everything that's gone wrong between then and now—and so it disappears with another *pop*, off to God-knows-where.

The other paintings are all from the *Winterton, Evening Hours* series. There's Becca, mid-dive in the outfield; Cooper, a blur of motion at sunset; Dom, a radio at his feet, wonder in his eyes; and my parents, together and in love— lives and moments rendered in two dimensions, because I'll never, ever get the real thing back.

And that's what Kenny doesn't understand. I don't want his parents to be unhappy any more than I want anyone else in the world to be unhappy. But it doesn't feel right that the world could just keep on turning, blind or else indifferent, after someone's life and all its constituent love just disappears forever. Shouldn't that kind of loss carry some weight? Shouldn't it carry some sort of consequence?

The portraits in the series are in various half-finished stages, but the furthest one from completion is the one of my parents. It's a re-creation of a memory from last summer, when my father had turned on the television one Sunday, taken one look at the score of the baseball game, and declared that the rest of the afternoon was better spent on an impromptu barbecue. Around dinnertime, as Cooper was manning the grill, my father realized we'd forgotten to prepare any vegetables and sent my parents into the house to get some. They'd reappeared at the sliding door a few minutes later, carrying onions and peppers and asparagus, only to realize that their hands were so full neither of them could open the door. My dad had tried first, and a few red bell peppers tumbled to the ground; then my mom tried, and though she succeeded in nudging the door open, she also lost half of her asparagus in the process. The next time I looked up, there were vegetables rolling across the deck in all directions, and my parents were both alight with laughter, having shared some joke that Cooper and I, standing across the backyard, could only imagine.

"Tell me that we have not become the adults in this situation," Cooper had said to me, as my parents raced around the deck trying to reharvest their vegetables before they rolled off the edge and into the backyard, and I had said, "I think that we have. S'mores for dinner?"

I'm so lost in the memory I don't even notice when the room tries to send me a message—one note, at first, and then a whole parade of tiny scraps of paper, raining down from the ceiling and accumulating at the foot of the easel. It's not until I hear a tide of static from the living room—the sound so jarring it's impossible to ignore—that I realize what's happening.

"Crap," I say, and the motion sends a few pieces of paper cascading out of my hair. I don't even have time to think about how awkward it's going to be to see Kenny again; how maybe it's for the better that we'll have something on-screen to focus on instead of each other.

The static clears just before I sit down on the couch, and when I look up at the screen, Dom is already there, sitting across a table from my mother.

38 | dom is all about their macarons, but he refuses to admit it no matter how many times I tell him that there's no such thing as a "girly" dessert

My mom meets Dom at Arcetta's. My favorite bakery in the entire world.

They're there for me.

"Dominik," my mother says. "Thank you for meeting with me. I appreciate it."

"Thank you for the croissant, Mrs. Davison," Dom replies, each word stilted with self-consciousness. Poor Dom—he doesn't even like croissants. Even after all this time, being around my mom still makes him nervous.

"Please," she says, "Amy."

"Of course, Mrs.—Amy," Dom corrects.

"Right," my mom says, looking amused. "Well, your time is valuable—oh, don't make that face, Dom, your time *is* valuable—so I'll get straight to the point."

Dom gets halfway through a weak-kneed "sorry" before my mom waves him off and continues.

"Dominik, I'm about to give you some information that should be held in strict confidence. The police department has kept most of it away from the press thus far, but it's only a matter of time until it's public, and I want you to hear it from us. Do you understand?"

"I understand," Dom says.

"The woman who struck Caroline with her car was convicted of misdemeanor vehicular manslaughter two months ago," my mom says. "Her sentencing hearing is on Thursday."

"Oh," Dom says.

A beat of silence.

Dom starts a little, and then adds: "*Really?*"

My mom raises an eyebrow—just the one on the left. "Cooper told you," she says.

"No," Dom says, and then, when my mom's other eyebrow jumps up to meet the first: "By which I mean, yes. Sorry, Mrs. Davison."

My mom sighs. "Well, that's all right, I suppose—as long as he hasn't gone blabbing to the entire school about it. How are you taking the news?" my mom says.

Dom blinks. "What do you mean?" he says.

"I mean—how are you feeling?" my mom says, and then, when Dom still doesn't respond: "I'm sure it's been difficult for you, Dominik. It's certainly been difficult for Cooper. I can't thank you enough for being there for him. It's made me and Roy feel so much better just to know that he's not going through this alone."

My mom smiles at him, softening. She used to smile at me like that all the time—whenever I offered to say grace at the dinner table without being asked; whenever I helped Cooper study for exams in classes I'd already taken. Sometimes she'd smile at me like that for no reason, as if it were some kind of blessing just to be in the same room with me, just to be my mother.

I miss her very much.

"Cooper's been there for me a lot, too," Dom says. "I'm glad that I've been able to talk to him."

My mom nods.

"As for how I'm feeling . . ."

Dom pauses, considers.

"Well, honestly, I'm feeling pretty pissed off."

Another pause.

"If that's something you don't mind me saying," he adds.

"That's fine, Dominik," my mom says. She smiles wryly. "I, too, have spent much of the spring feeling 'pretty pissed off.'"

"Right," Dom says. He sits up a little straighter, emboldened by my mom's validation, and continues: "At first, I was devastated, obviously, because Caroline is the best thing that's ever happened to me, and to lose her is just—it's like losing a limb. I don't know how I'll ever feel whole again."

My mom looks surprised—touched, even—by Dom's sudden expressiveness.

"But then Cooper told me it was actually Kenny Zhou's mom who killed her," Dom continues. "And that she'd been drinking. And from what I've heard from Kenny's friends, it seems like she's been going off the rails for a while, you know? So she never should have been in that car in the first place. And because she made that stupid decision, I lost—we lost—"

"A miracle of a human being," my mom says.

"Yes," Dom says. "It's not fair. It's not right."

"It isn't," my mom says, quietly.

The two share a moment of reflection. My mom, newly moved. Dom, stewing in old angers.

"Caroline's father and I will each be making a statement at the hearing," my mom says. "It's our belief that the defendant should have been charged with a felony on the basis of the field sobriety test, even if the Breathalyzer results were under the legal limit. And while we can't advocate for a harsher conviction, we can ensure that the judge understands just what a tragedy it was to lose our daughter, and ask for the person who took her away from us to receive the maximum one-year sentence."

"That's the maximum sentence?" Dom says. "One year? That's it?"

"Yes," my mom says. "I'm frustrated by that fact as well. After all, Caroline received a life sentence. In a way, we all did. There's no equivalent of parole for us; we don't get Caroline back as a reward for good behavior. She's gone, and I'll never—"

She cuts off, her eyes starting to brim.

"You'll have to excuse me," she says. "It's still not easy to talk about."

"That's all right," Dom says. Slowly, and ever so clumsily, he slides a napkin across the table to her.

"Thank you, Dominik," my mom says. She blows her nose with the napkin, even though she always carries tissues in her purse.

Then she says: "I wanted to ask if you'd consider making a statement at the hearing as well."

"What?" Dom says. So surprised that it tempers his fury.

"It doesn't have to be long. The plan would be for you to go before Caroline's father and me, just so the judge hears a few different perspectives. Just a few paragraphs—or even sentences—about how Caroline impacted you. And about how losing her impacted you."

"I'm not a very good public speaker," Dom says. "Or a very good writer. I'm not a very good anything. It's not that I don't want to do it, it's just—have you thought about choosing someone else?"

"It's not my choice that matters, Dominik," my mom says. "It's Caroline's. And Caroline made the choice one year ago, when she started dating you."

Dom gets a little weepy at that.

"I'll give you some time to think about it," my mom says. "I understand it's quite the request, and you may want to consult your mom before—"

"What?" Dom says, and the weepiness evaporates. "No, I'm in."

"What?" my mom says.

"I'm in," Dom says. "I'll do it."

"I appreciate your—enthusiasm," my mom says. "But I really do understand if you need to take some time to think it through. This will be very public, Dominik, and there are risks that come with that."

"What, like people writing mean comments about me online? Yeah, genuinely could not care less."

"It's not just mean comments online," my mom says, taken aback. "There might be social ramifications. This will likely make Kenny's friends feel sad, perhaps even hurt; not to mention the effect it will have on his parents.

Now, those are trade-offs that I'm comfortable with, because I believe they're being made for the right reasons, for my daughter. But Roy tells me not everyone will feel that way. I want you to be able to make an informed decision."

"I don't care about Kenny's friends," Dom says, the edge creeping back into his voice. "And as for his parents—they *killed my girlfriend*. If it were up to me, they'd have it a lot worse than a one-year sentence and a news article."

"I see," my mom says, and now even she's registering the anger, the darkness, the recklessness—all the things I spent the better part of a year trying to convince my parents Dom was so much more than.

"And Cooper?" Dom says. "Will he be there, too? Is he working on a statement?"

My mom sighs. "I asked, of course. But it seems Cooper has gotten into his head that he's some kind of pacifist."

Dom rolls his eyes. "Cooper can be such a—"

An ever-so-slight pause, just barely noticeable—

"—such a pain sometimes."

Now my mom looks uncomfortable—like she's not sure she should have made the request in the first place. Like maybe she's miscalculated.

"I do admire his principles," she says, "But of course I wish he would stand with the rest of our family."

"It's all right, Mrs. Davison," Dom says. "I'll talk to him. Leave Cooper to me."

39 | the last fight

And in many ways, it's like déjà vu all over again, a phrase that Iris used to remind me was redundant every time I said it. "Déjà vu *means* all over again," she'd say: "It's like saying ATM machine or six A.M. in the morning."

Iris is in front of Jianyu's house again—first cloaked in the mansion's long shadows, then thrown into sharp relief as the automatic porch lights come on. But the snow is fully melted now, revealing the long-dead grass that a team of landscapers will soon be working to get rid of, and when Jianyu opens the door it's with none of the warm concern I remember from their last late-night doorstep encounter. He looks weary, guarded.

"I've been calling you," Iris says. "Did you get my voice mails?"

"I did," Jianyu says.

"What a mess," Iris says. "I just don't know what to do."

"We should hold off on making any judgments until we have all the facts," Jianyu says.

"I just can't believe it," Iris says. "I remember thinking it was weird—how she was never around when we were doing all that planning with Kenny's dad, and then the fact that she wasn't at the fundraiser at all. But this is just—I mean—*Caroline Davison*—"

"We should hold off on making any judgments until we have all the facts," Jianyu repeats.

"I almost didn't believe Cooper, when he first told us," Iris continues. "But then I went to see them, and she could barely look at me. Both of them were *wrecked*, Jianyu, they were terrified—and I would be, too, if I were them! Facing down the Davisons and their fleet of lawyers—God, they probably can't even read the court documents properly—"

"Iris, just—just give me a second, OK?" Jianyu interrupts, and disappears behind the door before Iris can respond. When he comes back, he's put on a pair of sneakers, and he steps outside so that he's standing with Iris on the porch. He shuts the door behind him.

"And then they had to use the money from the fundraiser to pay bail," Iris continues, "so now they can't keep the restaurant open, and even if they *could* keep the restaurant, I don't know how Mr. Zhou would run it alone. They're trying to sell it. But no one in Winterton is going to buy it once people find out what happened—you know what this town is like. Everyone's always so on about how much *Caroline* did for Winterton, how much the *Davisons* do for Winterton, but what about what Kenny's parents do for Winterton? They run a restaurant, for God's sake! They literally spend seven days a week serving the community. But no one cares, because it's not a shiny new gym for the high school, or a big performance at the spring fair.

"And even if they do find a buyer—then what? This is what they've been doing their entire lives. It's not like they have any other work experience, and it's almost impossible to get hired with a criminal record. The good news is that I looked it up, and the maximum sentence

Kenny's mom is facing is one year. There's precedent that she might not serve jail time at all. So maybe, if we could just—if we could just—"

Iris looks meaningfully at Jianyu, as if there's something she's waiting for him to say.

Jianyu sighs. "If we could just what?" he says.

"I haven't totally figured it out," Iris admits. "But there must be something more we can do. Maybe we could get in touch with the public defender, help put together a case for Kenny's mom to be let off with community service. I mean, she wasn't *actually drunk*. And there are—there were—mitigating circumstances . . ."

"Iris," Jianyu says. He puts his hands on her shoulders; looks her in the eyes. "You need to let this go."

Iris stops short. I can hear, faintly through the television speakers, the electric hum of Jianyu's automatic porch lights, cutting through the silence of the night.

"What?" Iris says.

"You can't save Kenny's parents, Iris. His mom made a bad decision—made a bad decision that *killed someone*—made a bad decision that killed not just anyone, but *Caroline Davison*. There are legal ramifications for that kind of thing. You want to be a lawyer, Iris—you know that."

"I'm not trying to *save* them," Iris says. "I'm just trying to help. And I thought you'd want to help, too, given everything they've done for you—"

"Iris!" Jianyu says. "Listen to what you're saying right now! How quick you are to forget that whole fundraiser we put together—"

"That whole fundraiser *I* put together," Iris says. "All you did was show up. At the very last minute, mind you—"

"With half the attendees!" Jianyu says. "Who donated—oh, I don't know, ten thousand dollars or so?"

Iris's face goes cold. "You think that's what it means to pull your weight?" she says. "To show up after all the planning's been done with a bunch of your rich friends who only came so they'd look good in front of their dates?"

"Oh, here we go again," Jianyu says. "You think you're so much better than everyone else, just because—because what, because they have money? Because having money makes you a bad person?"

"Because throwing your money around doesn't make you a good person," Iris says.

"God, do you have any idea how sanctimonious you sound?" Jianyu says. "Except it's even worse than sanctimony—it's hypocrisy. Because when push comes to shove, you're more than willing to take money from the people you're too busy talking shit about to get to know—"

"Stop it!" Iris cries. "The fundraiser doesn't matter anymore, Jianyu—none of that matters anymore! If you saw the state Kenny's parents were in, you'd understand. Maybe you could talk to your parents. Maybe they could give them a loan or something—just until all this blows over, until—"

"Iris," Jianyu says. "I've known Kenny's family for a decade longer than you have. Believe me: I care. But Kenny's mother *killed someone*. She's been convicted of *manslaughter*. You think my parents would feel comfortable giving them money after all this?"

Iris takes a stunned step back. "I see," she says. Her voice, suddenly, is dead calm. "So, just to be clear. Just to make sure that I understand: You don't want to help the parents of your oldest friend, your so-called best friend—who just lost their son, and their jobs, and who now have to navigate a legal system that's stacked against them for multiple reasons—"

Iris takes a breath.

"—because your parents think it'd be bad for your reputation. Is that it?"

"It's not about our reputation," Jianyu says. "It's about picking our battles. Iris, there are thousands of causes in the world, there are millions of people who need help, and we can't just—"

"Right," Iris says. "Lots of battles. I get that. But—you're really not going to pick this one? The battle being fought by a family you've known literally your entire life? Who say, every time I go over, no matter how long it's been since they've seen you, 'Jianyu! Such a sweet boy! Always so busy with homework, such a good student!' That's not a battle worth picking?"

"It's not just about picking battles that are worth it," Jianyu says. "It's about picking battles that you can win. It's about picking the practical battles, not just the ones that are personal or sentimental. The hearing is on Thursday. There's nothing we can do for them in two days. And besides, we already *fought this battle*. We raised *twenty thousand dollars* for them. And now all that money, all that time, all that stress, all that work, is just—*gone*, because his mom made a bad decision."

"Just answer this for me," Iris says. "Do you believe in what you're saying right now? Do you honestly think what your parents are telling you is right? Is fair? Is just?"

Iris looks at him—really *looks* at him, as if she can will him into returning her gaze, and as if by returning her gaze he'll suddenly see the person that she sees in him—that she knows he can be—reflected in her eyes.

"Iris," Jianyu says—almost gently, now, his voice full of the love that the three of us once felt for each other, the memories we created and the future we imagined that we'd share. All those movie nights, all that laughter. All that history, laid bare in the tenderness of his words; rendered, by those very same words, meaningless.

"Iris, I'm sorry," Jianyu says. "But I think you should go."

Iris stares at him.

"I—you—" she starts, mouth closing and opening in disbelief. Then she nods—a quick jerk of the head, not so much registering comprehension as compliance.

"I'm sorry," Jianyu says.

Iris takes one step off the porch, then two. She's standing on the concrete path that cuts from the front door, through the yard, to the driveway.

"You were like a son to them, you know," she says, turning back.

But the door is already shut, and the impact of Iris's last, cutting remark to Jianyu dissipates into thin air.

40 | a very bad IDEA

Iris gets on Route 9 after leaving Jianyu's, headed eastbound toward her house. The television stays on, stays with her, and it's like March 12 all over again, it's like that awful day playing out on loop, and each time I'm sitting in the passenger's seat, watching someone I love fall to pieces, unable to reach out, unable to help.

But I could reach out, I think. While Caroline was busy stewing in her room, I had started reading through the manual. I had put together a model of our interdimensional engagement attempts—or "IDEAs," for short. The key was the television screen, which the manual had called an Einstein-Rosen mirror—or "ERM," for short—and the old CD player, the even older computer, and the downright Jurassic phone booth the "conduits." Caroline and I each got one engagement attempt per conduit—which was why the CD player had disappeared after we had both used it. Technically, I had already used mine for each conduit—the Chinese song I had played Jianyu and Iris; the phone call I had made to the restaurant; and the interaction with the medium—but there was a loophole, which I had exploited that very first intervention without even knowing it. Shorting out the restaurant had been an accident—a function of improper use—but it had done *something.* And the fact that it wasn't *technically* an intervention meant the same limits didn't apply.

Iris sails past the street her house is on, and I think that maybe she's going to my house; maybe she's going to see my parents again. But then she drives past my house, too, only rolling to a stop a few minutes later when she arrives at a familiar duplex.

"She's at Dom's," Caroline breathes.

Iris rings the doorbell, and I don't care how many times Dom and Iris get lunch or go for picnics at the park—the beam on Mrs. Novak's face as she pulls the door open is bizarre. "Iris!" she exclaims, like she could not be more thrilled to see her, like Iris is a person that she definitely knows, that she has definitely met at least one other time.

"Very good timing," Mrs. Novak continues. "I made borscht, and I made too much. Though Domek likes to say any borscht is too much borscht."

Her beam dims a little.

"Oh, that's all right," Iris says. "I had dinner already. But thank you, Jola."

"Nonsense," Mrs. Novak says. "There is always room for borscht. Come in, come taste."

She peers more closely at Iris's face, and then frowns. "Is everything OK?"

"Everything's fine," Iris says, still not crossing the entryway. "I'm just here to see—"

But the person Iris is just here to see has just appeared at the door, and he doesn't look like the feeling is particularly mutual. "Who is—oh," he says, and his voice flattens. "It's you."

Mrs. Novak looks from Dom to Iris, confused.

"Go inside, Mom, I'll handle this," Dom says, and slides past his mom out on to the porch.

"Of course I am going to go inside," Mrs. Novak says. "And so are you. It's forty-five degrees outside, and where is your jacket, Domek, honestly, it is like you think you are invincible just because you are young—"

"It's better if we talk outside," Iris says, and Dom shoots her an annoyed look even though she's agreeing with him. "Sorry, Jola," Iris adds, when Dom's mother looks betrayed.

"Well, all right," Mrs. Novak says. "If you're sure."

"We're sure, Mom," Dom says, and shuts the door.

"What are you doing here?" Dom says. His voice is so blunt I can feel the impact all the way from here, some unquantifiable number of dimensions and light-years away.

Iris blinks. "You're still angry," she says.

"Did your best friend's mom still kill my girlfriend?" Dom says.

"It wasn't—" Iris starts.

"Yeah," Dom says. "She did. So, yeah. I'm still angry."

"Dom," Iris says. "It wasn't her fault."

"The officer said she could barely walk in a straight line!"

"She wasn't drunk!" Iris says. "I went and saw them the other day, Dom, and she said she'd only had a few sips of Chinese wine before she remembered the fundraiser and stopped—"

"And what would you know about getting drunk, Iris?" Dom says. "Must be hard doing all that drinking at parties you're not invited to."

I didn't know Dom could sound like this. I mean, I knew Dom could sound like this, because of what everyone always said about Dom, but I didn't *really* know. Not for myself, not until now.

"What is wrong with you?" Iris says, and even though she should be angry, even though she has every right to be angry, she mostly just sounds sad.

"I'm sorry," Dom says. "But did you miss the part where your best friend's mom *killed my girlfriend*? And you're asking what's wrong with *me*?"

"It wasn't murder!" Iris says. "It was an *honest mistake*. Dom, you know I'm sorry about Caroline; you know I think it's terrible and tragic that she's not with us anymore, but—"

"I don't *care* if it was an honest mistake, Iris!" Dom says. "Caroline's mom says she's already getting off easy, what with a misdemeanor conviction instead of a felony, and that's why she has to say something at the hearing on Thursday—"

Iris opens her mouth to retort—and then shuts it again, looking thoughtful.

"Caroline's mom said that?" Iris says. "You talked to her?"

"Caroline was my *girlfriend*," Dom says. "And Cooper and I are friends, even if he is being a pussy right now. Yeah, she talked to me."

"But then," Iris says, "but then you can ask her to help us. You can explain the situation to her, that it wasn't Kenny's mom's fault. I mean, put yourself in her shoes," Iris is saying, the words only barely intelligible as she tries and fails to hold back a cascade of tears. "First she loses her son, which she's absolutely convinced is her fault, by the way, even though if anything it's *my* fault—Kenny never even told his parents he was depressed, whereas I'd known for months and still couldn't figure out a way to keep him alive, some best friend I am. Then there's another tragic accident and someone else in the community dies, which everyone else *also* blames on her, even though this time there's even *less* that she could have done—"

"Hold on," Dom says, and Iris must mistake his lowered volume for a sign that she's getting through to him, because she does. "Kenny killed himself?"

"Jianyu and I aren't supposed to tell anyone," Iris says, congested and miserable. "Kenny wouldn't have wanted anyone to know. And his parents—well, I don't know, I think they consider it to be—oh, but none of that matters. We're not supposed to tell anyone, and I haven't, until now. But don't you see? Can you imagine what his parents have gone through? What *she's* gone through? First their son, then their restaurant, now their—"

"Let me make this clear," Dom says, interrupting her. He takes a few steps forward so that he's literally standing above her; so that Iris is in his shadow, and she looks up, confusion and then fear flitting across her face.

"Just because your buddy killed himself before his mom's little joyride doesn't mean she's innocent," Dom says. "It just makes him equally guilty."

Iris gapes at Dom, this last, callous comment finally rendering her speechless.

"How can you be this *cruel*?" Iris says, and she's asking the question of Jianyu as much as she's asking the question of Dom. She's asking the question of Corey Loman and Larry, Larry, Larry LLP, none of whom have talked to or even looked at her since throwing a few hundred dollars in her general direction before the memorial dinner. She's asking the question of all the people who don't care about all the other people like me, like my parents, like her.

Hell, she might even be asking the question of me. I was, after all, the one who abandoned all of them in the first place.

"Iris is never going to survive politics," Jianyu had said to me once, when I was playing Switzerland in another one of their impenetrable arguments. "She has no ability to compartmentalize."

"You might be the only person I've ever met who would criticize someone for being too nice," I had said.

"Compartmentalization isn't being mean," Jianyu had said. "It's being disciplined. It's being smart. And I'm not criticizing her, Kenny. I'm just saying she's not going to survive politics. If anything, that's a compliment."

Switzerland, I had thought, firmly, and then refrained from saying what I had wanted to say, which was that by those standards Jianyu would be president by the time he was fifty.

"Just go home, Iris," Dom says. He turns and walks back into the house, slamming the door behind him, leaving Iris disconsolate atop the porch steps; leaving her final, desperate question unanswered in the air.

"Your boyfriend," I say, turning to Caroline, "Is a real piece of work. You know that?"

"Shhh," Caroline says.

"He's got anger issues, Caroline!" I say. "And now that you're not around to do arts and crafts with him, he's taking them out on *my* family and *my* friends—"

"*Stop!*" Caroline says.

"How can you possibly deny—"

"I'm not denying anything!" Caroline says. "I know he's got anger issues! And I know Dom is being—that he's being—"

Her whole face drops, like it hurts her to admit it.

"He's being awful. But it's still going, so if you could just—wait a couple of minutes before lecturing me—"

Instead of staying with Iris, the video has followed Dom into the house, where he's stopped at the entrance to the kitchen and is looking at Mrs. Novak and the enormous pot of borscht sitting in front of her on the kitchen table in a silent standoff.

Mrs. Novak says something in Polish, looking entirely nonplussed.

"Subtitles," Caroline and I say, in unison.

Do you want to tell me what's going on? the screen reads.

"Nothing's going on," Dom says, in English.

Domek, Mrs. Novak says. **I may be stupid, but I am not blind.**

"That joke," Dom says, "has never been funny. Not once."

See? Mrs. Novak says. **And neither am I deaf. Tell me what's going on, kochanie, or I will make borscht and nothing but borscht every night for the next month.**

"What's going on is that it's all their fault!" Dom shouts, his face contorted with sudden rage. "The whole family, they're all just—they're all crazy, is what they are, and I'm glad Mrs. Davison gives as good as she gets, because people like that deserve what's coming to them."

Mrs. Novak looks at him. **Did you call me crazy, Domek?** she says. **All those years, all those nights when you had dinner alone, before you met Karolina, because I had cocooned myself in my own grief. Were you so ungenerous to your own mother?**

Dom continues as if she hasn't spoken. "Her son—the one who died earlier this year. He killed himself. Caroline and I felt so bad for him when he died, and now all I can think is that he took her out along with him—"

Mrs. Novak walks over to Dom, puts her hands on his shoulders, and steers him into a chair.

How terrible, she says. **To be so young and to feel so hopeless, so alone. And his parents . . .**

Mrs. Novak trails off, her fingers drumming a delicate, absent-minded pattern on Dom's shoulders. **I should give them a call**, the screen reads. **I should send them an email.**

"How can you defend him?" Dom demands. "How can you defend something so selfish—you, of all people, should be angry, should be furious! People shouldn't *abandon* their families!"

Mrs. Novak keeps her hands on his shoulders, as if she can breathe her calm into his body, as if she can grant him her serenity through touch. What sort of love must it take, I wonder, to be so gentle with someone when there's violence written in every line of their body? To see a live wire and reach out your hands to grasp it?

Oh, Domek, Mrs. Novak says. **I've made peace with that, don't you see? Finally, I've made peace.**

"He shouldn't have done it," Dom says, swiping his palms along the tops of his cheeks. I hadn't even realized he was crying. "He shouldn't have done it, he shouldn't have left us. He shouldn't have left *you*. How could you ever forgive someone for something like that?"

Mrs. Novak blinks, as if surprised by the question. **It was you, Domek**, she says. **It was you who helped me, all those months ago, when we sat at this table and you said it was finally time to talk about what happened with your father.**

Caroline stands up.

"He never told me," she says, abruptly, and walks into her bedroom.

41 | faith, part ii

The ERM pixelates and then reconstitutes as soon as Caroline shuts the door, as if the room understands I'd much rather spend this time with Iris than with Dom.

Iris has gone to church.

I had read once that the architecture of churches was all about psychology: the high ceilings, the raised altar, the intricate artwork all meant to inspire feelings of wonder, to evoke the divine. I can imagine shafts of light slanting through the windows during morning services, absorbing the colors of the stained glass, painting the whole room in shades of red and gold. I can imagine what it would feel like to arch your neck to look up at the pulpit, the preacher on his mounted platform telling stories of damnation and absolution, the very act suggesting a sort of seeking. And I can imagine what it would feel like to bow your head in prayer after the sermon—the release of it, the emotional tension carried out with the physical.

Iris is standing up at the front of the church, near the altar, where a votive stand is empty save for three lit candles flickering at uneven heights. She strikes a match, then lights a candle of her own, the fire moving gracefully from matchstick to candlewick; and then she places the candle in the votive stand and takes a step back.

Last fall, as all my pros and all my cons seemed to be leading to the same inescapable conclusion, I had told Iris that I envied her for her religion.

"Because you really believe everything's going to get better," I had explained. "You really believe everything's going to be OK."

"You don't need to believe in God to know that things will get better," Iris had said. "You just need to believe in something. You just need to have faith."

And the idea had seemed so effortless coming from her lips, the words sweet with a missionary's conviction.

The problem was that the things that gave other people faith—the phenomena they attributed to intelligent design or divine intervention—I mostly attributed to science. People felt awe when they stood in churches because churches were designed to inspire awe. People felt belonging when they sang hymns because they sang them in groups, in unison, in harmony. People designated so many things as inexplicable when in reality they had *designed those things themselves*, designed them *to be* inexplicable, a pattern you could trace all the way back to the founding myths—created and transcribed by humans—that birthed religion in the first place.

"That's the problem," I had said. "I don't have faith."

"Well, I'll lend you some of mine, until you can find your own," Iris had said. "Hey, you should come with me to Christmas Mass."

That had made me laugh. "Oh, is it that time of the year again?"

"I'm serious!" Iris had said. "I think it'll be good for you, and besides, it's—it's something I really want to share with you."

Iris had gotten a little bashful at that, which was strange, because this was about the fifth year in a row she'd tried to get me to go to church with her.

"I'll think about it," I had said—which wasn't a lie, exactly: I really *would* think about it. I just already knew where those thoughts would round out.

On-screen, Iris has taken a seat in one of the pews, which are far enough away from the lambent candlelight of the altar that all I can make out is her silhouette. She's leaning forward, with her arms draped over the bench in front of her, with her hands clasped, and then she takes a breath and says:

"Dear Heavenly Father—"

And then she stops. She releases and rethreads her fingers. She lifts her head. I imagine her opening her eyes, suddenly at a loss for words, reaching for the reservoir of faith she's held within herself for so long only to find it depleted.

Iris bows her head and tries again.

"Dear Heavenly Father," she says. "I've never found it difficult to pray before. But there's a lot that's gotten harder this year.

"Firstly, I would pray, as I have prayed so many times before, for Kenny. I know you are a merciful God, a God of grace, and I pray you extend to Kenny the same mercy and grace you extend to all your children. He was—"

Iris chokes up.

"He was my best friend, and I hope to see him again."

In her conversation with Dom, while describing my mother's guilt over my death, Iris had instead taken the blame upon herself. *I'd known for months,* she had said, *and I still couldn't figure out a way to keep him alive.* But the truth was that she hadn't known—not everything, at least, because as many hours as I'd spent lying on her couch describing my depression to her in boring and self-indulgent detail, I had never, not once, told her I was suicidal.

If Iris had known I was thinking about killing myself, she'd have spent hours, days, weeks trying to change my mind; and then, when she failed, she'd have spent hours, days, weeks wondering what she had done wrong. I hadn't wanted that on her conscience, so I kept the thought within the pages of my green one-subject spiral-bound notebook, the same one that housed the pros and the cons, the flowcharts, the occasional incoherent journal entry. What I hadn't anticipated was that Iris would instead spend the time praying for the salvation of my eternal soul, which I suppose was because I hadn't believed I had an eternal soul to save in the first place.

Now, of course, I don't know what I believe. Because it's worked, hasn't it? By the grace of God or by the grace of Iris, I'm here, putting together crackpot theories and cutesy acronyms about interdimensional communication instead of being torn apart by harpies or whatever other special hell was promised to those arrogant enough to die on their own terms instead of on God's.

There's also the other thing, which is that no matter how many acronyms I manage to work into my theory of the room, I doubt it'll ever account for the notes.

"I also pray," Iris is saying, "that you may grant me strength and guidance. I want to help Kenny's parents. I want to fight for the justice and peace they deserve, but the more I struggle the more I wonder if this is a fight better left in your hands. If this is a time for acceptance rather than action. I sit before you today in humility and in hope, asking that you might light the right path before me, so that I will know it for what it is and so that I may take it.

"I say this prayer in the Lord's name—amen."

Iris keeps her hands folded, keeps her head bowed, stays motionless in the pew, and I know what I'm going to do before I do it. It's selfish, I suppose—to keep her on this quest to help my parents when it's already taken so much out of her, and when there's a good chance she'll be completing it alone. But they're *my parents*. There's so much I still want for them, and even the knowledge that those things might be impossible can't stop me from *wanting*. I want them to heal from my death, to wake up in the morning smiling again—and if that means hating me for what I did, then I hope they hate me for what I did; and if that means forgetting me altogether, then I hope they go through the house tomorrow and throw out every photograph I'm in. I want them to spend the rest of their lives doing what they love—running the restaurant together—and if it turns out that running the restaurant isn't what they love, then I want them to do something else. They could go back to China. They could be with their families again, now that they no longer have my education to worry about. I want them to shake off every shackle I've ever put on them, in life or in death.

And even beside the fact that it's my parents, it's *Iris*—Iris, who always finds a way, who always finds her faith. And even beside the fact that it's Iris, I'm already doing it. I'm already reaching out, letting my consciousness slip into the space on the other side of the ERM, feeling the power surge through me without the mediating force of a conduit.

Except—

"Is it OK?" I ask, out loud. "Is it OK if I do this? She's going to think it's you, you know—if it's really you, whoever you are."

The note falls into my lap.

IN A CERTAIN SENSE, it says, YOU ALREADY HAVE.

And then all the church lights come on at once, beams lancing down from the ceiling in long, straight lines; the altar haloed by the warm glow of the apse; the stained glass windows suddenly backlit. Iris's eyes fly open. She blinks rapidly, first from the sudden brightness and then from sudden tears.

Iris doesn't know that it's me, of course. She thinks that it's God, or perhaps one of the lesser angels, tasked with overseeing mundane human dramas. But the connection is there, from my world to hers—I can feel it, she can feel it, and what does it matter if she thinks it's through God and I think it's through science? It's the moment that

I wanted to share with my parents; the epiphany that I wanted to give to my mother; but in the end it's Iris, and maybe it's always been Iris. "I'll lend you some of mine until you can find your own," she had said, but my faith was always in her.

42 | the hail mary

Iris gets in the car and makes one last phone call.

"Hey, Cooper," she says. "I know it's late, but it's kind of an emergency. Can we meet up?"

CAROLINE

43 | she's right. if this is going to come down to dom, they are screwed.

In my room, I think about Dom's father. I think about how he died, about how Dom never *told me* how he died. I had never been under the impression that Dom and I shared everything with each other—he had his secrets, parts of his past he wasn't ready to talk about, and that was OK. But hiding something that important, about some*one* so important . . .

Had Dom's father felt like Kenny? Had he, too, felt like he had no other choice?

The claim had made me so angry just a few moments ago. But now I'm just blank, drained of either the will or the capacity to be mad. Maybe Kenny really was just doing what he felt like he had to do, just like my mom is doing what she feels like she has to do. Maybe that's the whole cruel joke of the room—that Kenny has to pay the price for all the decisions I have no choice but to make, and I have to pay the price for all the decisions Kenny has no choice but to make, and on and on and on, all the way back to his suicide, which was the choicelessness that had started this whole thing in the first place.

Kenny and I have spent so much time with our parents and Dom, Cooper, Jianyu, and Iris that sometimes it feels like the eight of them must be living in their own little bubble universe—one just as far removed from the rest of Earth as ours; one that's become entirely consumed by our deaths, just as ours has become entirely consumed by their lives. But there are so many other people we haven't seen at all—other friends and teammates, classmates and teachers. I think of the barista who used to work at Arcetta's every Sunday afternoon, the bus driver who takes the team to our away games. All these people whose lives have probably just moved on, moved forward, with nothing to do with Kenny or me or our inexplicable room in the sky.

I can hear Kenny's footsteps padding over to my door, as if summoned by the thought. And then his voice—hesitant: "Caroline . . . ?"

"I'll be right out," I say. And I meet him on the other side, where the television is already on—

—And where Iris is lying on Cooper's bed.

"Wow," I say. "The door's closed and everything. Mom would have an aneurysm."

It's not actually scandalous—Cooper is sitting six feet away in his desk chair, swiveling himself back and forth in little semicircles—but still: Mom would have an aneurysm.

It's weird, seeing all of Cooper's furniture transplanted into a bedroom I don't recognize. *That lamp should be on the other side of the room*, I think, *and the bed should be centered against the wall, not pushed into the corner like that.* And half of his clothes are on the floor, another thing that Mom never would have allowed, and he's left all his posters and photographs back at the house, so the walls are sad and empty, and it's—

It's wrong, is the thing. It's just all wrong.

"And that's when I called you," Iris is saying. She pulls herself up so she's sitting in a cross-legged position and pastes a fresh veneer of determination over the misery.

I like Iris—I think she's smart and fierce and loyal—but she needs to learn when to quit, if only for her own sake. I mean, is Kenny really worth all this? Is anyone?

"Jianyu won't support a cause until he knows how it's polling with the electorate," Iris says, "And Dom—"

"Dom's got his own stuff to sort out," Cooper says.

"Sure," Iris says. "That's one way of putting it. The point is, I wouldn't be here if I hadn't tried everything else, Cooper. I know she was your sister—"

"Is," Cooper says.

"I know she's your sister," Iris amends. "And you, of all people, have a reason to want revenge. But I just thought—if I could explain the situation Kenny's parents are in, maybe you would understand, and maybe then you could talk to your parents, and maybe then your parents would—"

Cooper laughs darkly.

"It's not going to work," he says. "I've already tried. But my mom has made up her mind, and when my mom makes up her mind . . ."

He sighs.

"You've tried?" Iris says, surprised.

"Of course I've tried," Cooper says. "But my mom believes the person who killed Caroline should face consequences. And that *we* deserve for the person who killed Caroline to face consequences. She says anyone else who lost their daughter would feel the exact same way."

"What do you believe?" Iris asks.

Cooper looks thoughtful. "I believe . . . I believe a longer sentence isn't going to bring Caroline back; it's not going to fix anything. It's just going to make more people more miserable for more time. People like—well, people like you," he says, and shrugs a little.

My mom was right. He really has gotten into his head that he's some kind of pacifist.

"Thanks, Cooper," Iris says.

Her expression softens for a moment—and then grows steely again.

"What if *I* talked to your mom?" she says.

"Uh," Cooper says. "I mean—you *could*. But she's kind of—"

"Terrifying, I know," Iris says, and then looks guilty. "No offense."

"None taken," Cooper says. "We actually like that about her."

"When the conversation is between you and your mom, it's always going to be about Caroline," Iris says. "What Caroline wanted, what Caroline deserves. But what we need is to find a way to make it less about Caroline, and more about Kenny. More about Kenny's *parents*."

"But it *is* about Caroline," I say. "I'm the one who *died*."

"I mean, that's what you said, right?" Iris continues. "You're against the sentence because you know me, and through me you know Kenny, and his parents, and the restaurant, and that entire universe your mom doesn't realize is valuable because she's never stepped inside of it."

"That's pretty good," Cooper says. "Except . . ."

"Except?" Iris says.

"It'd need to be both. Both my parents. My dad's heart isn't in this—his heart's not in anything these days, but he's still doing it, because he wants to believe that once he does, this will all finally be over—all the grief, all the anger."

"And you don't believe that?" Iris says, looking only very slightly afraid of the answer.

"I don't think it's ever going to be over," Cooper says. "I think I'm going to feel those things every day for the rest of my life."

"I'm sorry," Iris says, and then: "I know it's not the same, but I think I'm going to feel those things every day for the rest of my life, too," and then Cooper stops spinning his chair long enough to meet her gaze, both of them so sad and so commiserating and so, so irritatingly *noble*, and I don't like this. I don't like this at all. Cooper has *no idea* what he's doing; he has *no idea* what I want; he's so far up on his high horse than he's willing to *trample* my mother and my memory—and for what? For the sake of a family he doesn't even know? For the sake of the woman who killed me?

I get up off the couch and march over to the telephone booth. I consider trying to use the desktop computer, but Cooper doesn't have his laptop out—who knows how that would work. A phone call is imprecise, and the words will be garbled if it's anything like the one Kenny made, but this is my *brother*. He should know it's me.

Kenny races to the booth and gets there before me, tries to block off the entrance so I can't get inside.

"Caroline," Kenny says. "What are you doing?"

"I'm going to have a conversation with my dear brother," I say. "If you will kindly just—move."

I shove past him and into the phone booth.

"He's not going to be able to understand you," Kenny says. "You remember that, right?"

"We'll cross that bridge when we come to it," I say.

I punch in Cooper's cell phone number. And sure enough, he pulls his phone out of his pocket, checks the caller ID.

"Unknown caller," he says to Iris, while his phone vibrates in his hand. "Think it's spam?"

"Pick *up*, Cooper," I say.

"Then again," Cooper says, "what spam caller calls so late at night?"

Cooper picks up.

"Hello?" Cooper says.

"Cooper," I say. "It's me, your sister. Look, I know you can't understand what I'm saying *for real*, but I'm hoping that if you just—that if you just listen to this, you'll understand what I'm saying *in spirit*. That you'll—"

And then the line goes dead, because Kenny has edged his way into the phone booth and disconnected the line.

For a moment, we just stare at each other. Kenny looks as shocked as I am at what he's done.

"I'm sorry," Kenny finally says. "I just—I had to. It's my parents."

On-screen, Cooper moves his phone from his ear; looks at the screen, confused.

"Spam?" Iris says.

"No, weirder," Cooper says. "Some kind of prank call, maybe?"

I turn to look at Kenny, furious. "I have never," I say, "*ever*—interfered with your powers. Every single moment you've wanted to have with your parents, with your friends, I've let you have, because I know these moments are the only ones we'll ever have with them again. You *know what this means to me*—"

"It's my parents," Kenny cries. "Wouldn't you do the same, for yours?"

And in that moment, I know I've lost this fight.

Because I would. Because we both know that I would.

I think of my mom, losing sleep over this hearing; sacrificing her *marriage* for this hearing. Fighting this battle all on her own, with her son scheming behind her back, with her husband somewhere else entirely even when he's by her side. "This isn't about you," I had snapped at Kenny—because how could he think that my mother's determination had anything to do with him, or his mother, or his restaurant, or anyone or anything else other than the fact that *I was her daughter*?

There are some things that you can't justify. There are some things that you shouldn't have to.

"It probably won't even work," Kenny says, looking from me to Cooper, from Cooper to me. "Their plan probably won't even work, but I can't let you keep them from trying, Caroline—"

I walk away from the phone booth. I sit back down on the couch.

"I'm sorry," Kenny says, trailing behind me, and his voice is a little helpless, a little desperate. I wonder if this is how it is between my parents all the time now. Every interaction weighted with history, but with the wrong kind of history—animosity where there once was admiration, resentment where there once was love.

We had made each other tea. We had played *Mario Kart*. We had found moments of unexpected kinship in joy and in despair. And now—

"I'm sorry, too," I say.

A note flutters down from the ceiling.

TICKET #39,842,430, it says. CONDUIT 2 OF 3: CLOSED.

I don't need to look to know that behind me, the phone booth is disappearing.

"Hold on a second," Iris is saying. "What about Dom? Isn't Dom making a statement, too?"

"Is he?" Cooper says, looking genuinely surprised. "He hadn't told me."

"I wish you'd been there tonight," Iris says. "Except

I don't, because it was terrible. He was just yelling and swearing and—and *looming*."

"Yeah," Cooper says. "Dom is a loomer."

"If this is going to come down to Dom," Iris says, "we are screwed."

"It's all right, Iris," Cooper says. "I'll talk to him. Leave Dom to me."

44 | was that whole thing just an excuse to hug?

The scene changes. Cooper, standing at Dom's doorstep, wearing workout shorts and a compression shirt and holding a basketball.

Dom wrenches the door open. "What are you—" he starts, but then Cooper bounces the basketball across the doorsill, hard, and says, "Shoot around with me."

Dom looks down at the basketball, which he's caught reflexively. A slow smirk spreads across his face. "Well, all right," he says. "Give me a second to put on my shoes. Unless you need an advantage?"

"Yeah, right," Cooper says. "I've spent the last couple of weeks working out while you've been sulking." And then Dom throws the basketball back at Cooper with the kind of chest pass that gets people injured in gym class, and slams the door in his face.

Cooper heads back to the driveway, dribbles around the perimeter a few times. The house's garage door starts to rise, pulleyed up inch by slow inch, and then Dom ducks under it, his expression of grim determination looking even darker somehow in the warm, dappled light of the golden hour.

Cooper and Dom run through a few drills, neither of them speaking, until they're both breathing hard.

"I'm over this," Cooper says.

Dom snorts. "Tired already?"

"Bored," Cooper says, from the top of the driveway, and checks the ball to Dom.

Dom returns the check, signaling the start of the game, and then Cooper is off, driving hard up the asphalt, accelerating so suddenly that Dom's feet are still set when Cooper blows by him. Cooper gets to the basket, goes up for a dunk, and then—

Dom blocks the shot from behind. The ball ricochets off the backboard, lands well out of bounds, and then rolls back down to the driveway, where Dom is waiting for it.

"All right," Cooper says, nodding curtly. "Your ball."

"But this—this is not good conflict resolution," I say, appalled.

This time, Dom checks the ball. Unlike Cooper, he takes it up the driveway slowly, dribbling from hand to hand until he's eight feet away, at which point he feints hard to the right, spins to the left, and goes for the jump shot. It clangs off the rim, bouncing back toward the two of them, and Cooper grabs the rebound. He sprints toward their designated half-court at the edge of the driveway, only to get body-slammed out of bounds by Dom on the way there.

It's an obvious foul, but Cooper just laughs. "Here," he says. "I'll give you the extra possession since you're so desperate for it," and then he rolls the ball toward Dom, who's visibly seething.

It feels like it's been months since I've seen Dom like this—since his argument with his mother, probably, and the time before that would have been when I was still alive. *It means that he's been happier*, I think. Devastated, of course—grieving, disconsolate, heartbroken—but also somehow happier. He used to look like this all the time—like he was constantly being pulled under the rising tide of his own anger, his frustration, his resentment—and it's only the muted surprise of seeing it again and the uneasy anticipation that follows, which used to be so familiar, that makes me realize how much has changed since my death.

After the inbounds, Dom pushes Cooper forward until they're both under the basket and goes for the layup.

"That's one," Cooper says, as it drops through the net.

The two go back and forth for another six, seven, eight possessions, each growing more aggressive than the last. On the ninth possession, Cooper elbows Dom in the ribs while they're fighting for a rebound under the basket. On the tenth possession, Dom shoves Cooper into the base of the hoop stanchion. Cooper loses the ball but trips Dom when he goes after it, and Dom hits the ground hard.

"*This* is not good conflict resolution," Kenny says, appalled, and then his mouth drops open and his eyes go wide as Dom abandons the game entirely and takes a swing at Cooper.

"Oh, shit," I say, as Cooper ducks the swing.

"What the hell was that?" Cooper says. "Was that supposed to be a punch?"

"Cooper, *no*," I moan. Cooper plays *baseball*, for God's sake; everyone knows that baseball players can't fight.

Dom throws another punch, and Cooper dodges that one, too, stepping backward from the driveway into the front yard, at which point Dom catches him in the side with a right hook.

Cooper goes down, but he goes down laughing.

"God, your mom was right," Dom snarls, "you really have turned into a little bitch," and Cooper says, "And Iris was right, too—you really have turned into a fucking *psychopath*—" and then Dom goes for a kick and Cooper grabs his ankle and twists, pulling Dom on to the ground, too.

"Just because," Dom pants as they roll around, each trying to pin the other down, "just because you won't man up and do the right thing for Caroline—"

"Oh, that's rich," Cooper says. "Telling me to man up. Is this how your dad taught you real men behave?"

"Shut the fuck up," Dom says, and lands a punch straight to Cooper's mouth.

Now Cooper is laughing even harder, and all I can think is, *Oh my God, what is he doing, what are either of them doing?* Cooper, instigating this ridiculous game, egging Dom on, bringing up his *dead father*, which everyone knows is way off-limits. And Dom, turning into the worst version of himself, turning into a version of himself that he swore he'd never be again, that he swore he never *wanted* to be again.

"You think this is what Caroline would have wanted?" Cooper says. He gets one arm free and goes for Dom's eyes. Dom recoils reflexively, and Cooper hits him in the ribs while he's off-balance and scrambles off the ground.

"Of course it's what she would have wanted!" Dom shouts. Dom tries to stand, but he only gets halfway up before he has to bend over, one hand pressed to his side where Cooper hit him, wincing with every breath.

"Of course it's what I want," I whisper. But it's hard to put any force into it, looking at the two of them now, standing there with split lips and bruised ribs, staring at each other like they hate each other's guts.

"God," Cooper says. "God, I can't even—" but he can, I guess, because after he throws his hands up and looks around, he says, "Look at yourself, Dom! You're angry, you're ditching school, you're throwing *punches*, for God's sake—it's like sophomore year all over again. You think my sister would have wanted this for you? For any of us?"

"Caroline would have wanted us to do the right thing," Dom says. "Even if it was hard. And that—that was what I loved about her. Caroline was always willing to have the hard conversation, to make hard decisions, to—"

"Caroline would have wanted us to be happy!" Cooper shouts, and Dom moves forward with an expression like he's going to hit him again—like he's going to kill him. But the punch he throws this time is actually barely a punch, and Cooper catches it easily between his hands, and then Dom collapses in on himself, heaving with exhaustion or with tears, stumbling into Cooper, and Cooper throws his weight right back, puts his arms around him like he's using Dom to steady himself.

"My sister," Cooper says, and his voice catches a little on the word, "my sister would have wanted a nice funeral, with lots of sad speeches, and no photos of her from before she had braces. All of which she got."

He smiles a little, through a watery chuckle, and shakes his head.

"Caroline would have wanted us to cry at the wake, and to leave fresh flowers at her grave—but nothing purple, because she hated that color, and not too many, because she always felt bad when we drove by a cemetery and there was one gravestone hogging all the flowers. And then—and then she would have wanted us to move on. She would have wanted us to heal. She would have wanted us to be—happy."

Cooper looks at Dom, his face open and honest and awful. "We're never going to be happy this way, Dom," he says. "None of us are."

I think of Becca and Maddie, Susan the barista and Tony the bus driver, all the people outside of the room and its obscure mechanisms, to whose lives Kenny's and my deaths must have felt a sort of puncture wound: deep, but contained. Gruesome, but finite. A far cry from the grief lacerated across the lives of my parents, my brother, Dom. Are they happier? Have they healed?

"We're never going to be happy, anyway," Dom says, and Cooper snorts, says: "You're full of shit."

Give it a rest, Cooper, I think. But Dom just disentangles his limbs and sits down on the grass, looking exhausted.

"You're full of shit," Cooper repeats, and sits down next to him. "You know how I know that?"

Dom doesn't answer. Instead, he lies down so he's splayed out across the yard, so his shirt rides up a little, and I can see the beginnings of a bruise starting to form where Cooper had hit him.

"I know that because you *were* happy," Cooper says. "Sitting at the park. Making fun of lawyers. Offering to let me crash on your couch and not even getting annoyed when Jianyu one-upped you. You were happy; I know you were. I was there; I saw it."

And I had seen it, too, hadn't I? I had seen Dom at the park with them that day, eating a sandwich, laughing about Jianyu's spare bedrooms. I had seen Dom at lunch with Iris, asking her about Kenny, about her career plans, bright-eyed and thoughtful. I had seen Dom looking out at the glittering, faraway lights of Wisteria Park, lost in an Elvis Presley song, caught somewhere between a memory and the moment.

He had been happy. I had painted it.

45 | and then it all starts to happen very quickly

There's static—a new scene announcing itself, breaking the exhausted stalemate between Dom and Cooper—and then we're looking through the windshield of Cooper's car. It's the middle of the night—pitch-black save for the faint yellow of the car's overhead light and the bluish white of the dashboard, neither bright enough to illuminate the car's surroundings.

In the front row, Iris is leaning across the center console toward Cooper, dabbing makeup on a bruise that spans the bottom of his left cheek.

"You should see the other guy," Cooper says, and then, at Iris's look of deep skepticism: "No, I'm serious. I got him right in the ribs."

"And I can't believe it worked," Iris says.

"Of course it worked!" Cooper says. "I mean, I get that Dom is big and buff and scary—"

"—and right here," Dom interjects. He leans forward from the back seat, coming into view between Cooper and Iris.

"But I mean, I work out all the time. I'm very strong—"

"That's not what I meant," Iris says, rolling her eyes. "I meant, I can't believe the whole thing worked. The fighting. All this time I thought I could convince Jianyu to be a better friend by telling him about how his actions made me feel. Really, I should have just gone over and punched him in the face."

"Oh," Cooper says. "Well, in addition to being very strong, I'm also moderately clever, so."

"He actually did it," I murmur. "He actually changed Dom's mind."

Iris pats a few more drops of color onto Cooper's cheek and then caps the tube in her hand. "There, that should be fine," she says.

I recognize the foundation: It's mine. Cooper must have dug it out of a closet somewhere.

The three fall into silence, turn to face forward, and it's like they're all looking directly at me and Kenny, wearing identical expressions of determination.

"There's no need to be nervous," Cooper says, though he's visibly, obviously nervous.

"Let's all just stick to the talking points we discussed," Iris says. She *doesn't* look nervous. But Iris never really does, once she's made up her mind.

"I promise I won't hit anyone this time," Dom says.

And then the three of them get out of the car, and the shot widens, and a bunch of automatic lights come on at once, illuminating a three-car garage, a covered porch, a terraced stone staircase that winds through ferns and succulents and brightly colored flowers on its way from the base of the front yard to the door.

When they get to the top of the staircase, Iris steps forward and knocks on my family's front door.

46 | now we'll never be again

The door swings open.

"Hi, Mom," Cooper says, weakly.

"Hi, Amy," Dom says, grimly.

"Hi, Mrs. Davison," Iris says. She holds out her hand. "I'm Iris Mutisya. It's nice to meet you."

"Iris was one of Kenny Zhou's friends," Cooper says.

"Hello, Iris," my mom says. She's smiling a smile so polite it can only communicate great displeasure. "I'm not sure how much Cooper's told you—"

She spares Cooper a brief glance that communicates the promise of many long conversations to come.

"—But it's a bit of a busy night for us here, and so perhaps it'd be better if—"

"Oh, this won't take very long," Cooper says. "Mom, can we come in?"

I have to hand it to Cooper for having guts. I suppose surviving a punch in the face from Dom has emboldened him.

This time my mom's meaningful glance is longer—and perhaps more of a glare. But eventually she relents, and then ushers them down the hall and into the living room, where my dad is sitting on the couch, looking over a set of handwritten notes.

"What's all this?" my dad says.

"You're here?" Cooper says. "I thought you were at the apartment."

"As I said," my mother says. "It's a busy night. Your father and I are just finalizing our statements for tomorrow's hearing."

"Tomorrow," Kenny breathes. "We're running out of time."

The last time we were in the living room, Cooper had just smashed a vase. My mom had been sitting on the floor, alone in the resulting debris field, surrounded by shards of glass and the soft velvet of lily petals, crying.

Now, there's a new vase of flowers on the table. The floor is lustrous once again, dry of water and free of glass. I think of all the time that's elapsed between then and now, and everything that's changed—the passing seasons, the precarious alliances, grief in all its shape-shifting forms—and I wonder if this homecoming feels to Cooper like the crossroads that it feels to me. I wonder if he feels the heaviness of it.

"Mom," Cooper says. And then, almost as an afterthought: "And Dad. Iris and I were talking, and we think you should reconsider the statement you're making tomorrow at the hearing."

He takes a breath. It's a good thing that my parents only have eyes for Cooper, because next to him, Iris has started to mouth the words that he says a few seconds in advance, as if she's trying to will him into remembering his lines.

"I know you guys want justice for Caroline's death. But there is no version of this justice that gives you guys what you really want—what *we all* really want—which is for Caroline to still be alive. To still be with us today. To still be laughing in the kitchen while Dad cooks and making us listen to oldies in the car while Mom runs errands. There isn't a sentence in the world that puts Caroline back in the stands at my games, screaming her lungs out even when it's just preseason. A longer sentence doesn't make our lives better. In fact it doesn't make our lives any different at all. It just makes two other people's lives worse."

Cooper looks at Iris, who picks up where he left off.

"Mr. and Mrs. Davison," Iris says. "I know it may be hard to find sympathy for Kenny's parents—especially his mother. But you don't need to send Mrs. Zhou to jail to make her regret her actions, or to make her understand the pain you're feeling right now. She knows that pain already. She's going to know that pain every day for the rest of her life. She feels your love, and your sorrow, and your grief for Caroline—because she feels that love and that sorrow and that grief for Kenny."

Iris looks back at Cooper, who nods.

"I'm really sorry for your loss," Iris says. "I wish I'd gotten the opportunity to know her better."

One beat of silence stretches into another. Iris's words hang in the air, suspended between her expression of determination, my father's of surprise, and my mother's, which is unreadable. Then:

"Oh, Iris," my mom says. "I'm sympathetic. I really am. We met the Zhous, didn't we, Roy—after the state championship two years ago, when we went to the restaurant with Caroline's team to celebrate. They seem lovely, and I don't wish them harm. But because of Mrs. Zhou's actions, our daughter lost her life. We lost our daughter. Cooper lost his sister. And you're right, Cooper, that there's no sentence that could bring her back. But there is a fair sentence, a just sentence, that acknowledges what we've lost and provides us with the closure our family needs in order to heal. And I hope it's closure that helps Caroline rest a little easier above."

My mom looks at my dad, who's still staring into Iris's face even after the conclusion of her plea, searching for— searching for what, exactly?

"Amy," Dom says. "I know you think this is what Caroline deserves. What Caroline would have wanted. But Caroline—"

He pauses. Iris's face tightens; concerned, perhaps, that Dom is going to go off-script. But then he collects himself and continues, his voice now so soft Kenny and I can barely hear him:

"Caroline was the type of person who saw the best in everyone around her. She was the type of person who made you believe you could be happy, even if history said that you only knew how to be sad. She made you believe you could be kind, even if you'd only ever chosen to be cruel. She made you believe you could be whole, even if everyone else believed that some things are so broken it's impossible to repair them. Caroline believed so strongly in the better version of me that *I* started to believe in the better version of me—even in my worst moments. And I think she would have done the same for Kenny's parents."

My dad clears his throat, steps forward. He's teary, too, but it seems like he's perpetually teary these days— it's hard to know if it's Iris's speech or Dom's speech or something else entirely. "Thank you for saying that, Dominik. And Iris, thank you for . . ."

His eyes catch hers, and he seems to lose the rest of his thought.

"Thank you," he repeats. "We'll certainly give everything you three have said some serious thought. But it's late, and Amy and I have a lot to sort through tonight. So unless there's anything else you wanted to share . . . ?"

"No, that's all," Iris says. She's trying so hard to mask her disappointment that it almost looks more pronounced. "Thank you both for your time. We'll see you tomorrow morning, I guess."

"Cooper," my mom says. "Could you stay behind for a second?"

Cooper's face contorts into an expression somewhere between guilt and panic. "Totally," he says. He pulls his keys out of his back pocket and tosses them to Iris. "I'll meet you guys at the car."

Dom and Iris look at Cooper with twin expressions of sympathy as they leave.

"What's going on, Coop?" my mom says, after the sound of the front door closing has echoed down the hall. "What's this all about?"

And her voice—which was so guarded, so polished just a few minutes ago—goes soft, gentle, suffused with the easy tenderness of speaking to someone you love. Cooper doesn't stand a chance against that tenderness. He disintegrates.

"I just—I wanted to do the right thing," Cooper says. "I want us to do the right thing."

"Oh, Coop," my mom says. She puts one hand on each of Cooper's shoulders and pulls, very gently, so that he takes a few steps forward, a few steps toward her.

"This is what we wanted to protect you from—isn't it, Roy?" my mom says. "I know this has been hard on you. And I wish it didn't have to be. And all I can tell you is that it will be over very, very soon."

"I know, Mom," Cooper says, choked up. "I know it'll be over soon."

"I can tell you two things, actually," my mom says. She lets her hands slide down Cooper's arms so that his hands come apart behind his back, and then she holds on to them, lacing her slim fingers through Cooper's calloused ones; pressing the pale skin of her palms into his.

"The first thing is that this will all be over very, very soon," my mom says. "The second is that Caroline was incredibly lucky. Incredibly lucky. To have had you for a brother."

Cooper says, *"Mom"*—helpless, adoring, like a very young child. In the glow of the overhead lights, his hair looks blond, like it was when he was a kid, like I *remember* it being, abruptly, another repository of lost memories suddenly unearthed: Cooper at five, running around the house with a stuffed animal he'd stolen from my room; at four, knocking green beans off the dinner table because he hated them so much; at three, calling for my mother with that exact same helpless adoration.

"I was lucky to have her, too," Cooper says, and lifts his head up to look at our mom. His eyes are filled with tears. "And both of us were lucky to have you and Dad."

They're both right. I was lucky to have him, and we were lucky to have them, and they were lucky to have us— we were all lucky to have each other. We were that rare family that looked happy and *actually was*, and now—

Now we're not any of those things anymore.

"Mmm," my mom says. "You know, when we got pregnant with Caroline, everyone warned us that parenting would be the hardest thing in the world. And sometimes it was. But most of the time, it was easy. You two made it so easy."

Cooper makes a noise in the back of his throat, tries to turn away.

"Oh, honey," my mom says. "I'm sorry, I didn't mean—"

"No," Cooper says. He presses his fingers to the skin underneath his eyes so he can wipe the tears away before they track down his cheeks, before they wash away the makeup and leave his bruises exposed. "No, it's fine, it's— it's good, I'm sorry, I shouldn't be—"

My mom looks at him—full of sympathy, full of love. "Why don't stay in your bedroom here tonight, honey? I'll make you breakfast in the morning."

Then she smiles, a little rueful. "That's not a very good sell, is it?" she says. "We can order something. Your dad can join us, if he wishes. We can all head over to the courthouse together."

My mom pauses. She's more contained, now, the easy tenderness of a few minutes ago ebbing. And I love that about my mom—I always have: how poised she is, how impossible to ruffle, even after being accosted by my brother and my boyfriend and a complete stranger on the eve of a court appearance—but sometimes I wished I saw more of the side of her that only seemed to exist very late at night and very early in the morning, when drowsiness sometimes blurred her judgment, rendered her careless and unguarded.

"I can't," Cooper says. "I need to take Iris and Dom home. I drove them both here, and besides, I just—I need—"

"Cooper," my mom says, firmly, "I know you made a decision to move out with your father, and I respect that. But this is your home. This will always be your home. Whatever happens—"

"Mom, stop," Cooper says.

"—whatever happens tomorrow, whatever happens with the sentencing, whatever happens between me and your father," my mom continues, her voice rising, Cooper clearly growing closer and closer to tears, "this will always be your home. Do you understand that?"

Cooper presses his hands against his face, sniffling.

"I need to go," he says.

"Oh, Coop," my mom says. "I love you. You know that, of course. But I do."

"I love you, too," Cooper says, and then: "Good night, Mom," and then he leans forward and wraps my mother in a hug, tears falling freely from his eyes into her hair. My mom's arms come up around him; she presses her face into his shoulder.

"Good night, Cooper," my mom says.

Cooper nods, pulls back, wipes at his eyes.

"We'll see you tomorrow," my mom murmurs, and then she and my dad watch as Cooper walks away.

"What a night, huh?" my mom says. And then, when my father doesn't respond: "Roy. You can't tell me you're having second thoughts. I feel for Iris, I really do. And I'm so proud of Cooper for speaking up for what he believes in. But this—this is our daughter."

"Our daughter," my dad repeats.

I look from my mother's face, all grit, and my father's face, all sorrow. Equal in their determination.

I look over to the old desktop computer. One last chance to make a change, if I want it.

47 | it was never supposed to be this hard

In school and on the field, I learned that doing the right thing was supposed to be satisfying, was supposed to feel virtuous, and that even when it involved sacrifice, it was generally *self*-sacrifice, like skipping a party because a friend needed help with an art project or sitting on the bench so a teammate could play.

Sacrificing someone else—sacrificing someone you *loved*—that wasn't something you were ever supposed to have to do. The woman holding Cooper's hands so tenderly in her own wasn't supposed to be the same woman who would get dressed up the next morning to make a statement in court that could ruin someone's life, and she especially wasn't supposed to be doing all of that *for me*, in my name.

But that's what it is, isn't it? *Our daughter,* my mom had said. All of this for me.

"Kenny," I say, with such sudden seriousness that he looks alarmed. "I want to help."

Kenny stares at me. Unsure of what to do, of what to believe. Of *whether* to believe. And why wouldn't he be unsure? I had been furious, livid, cruel. *Selfish,* I had called him.

"What about what you deserve?" Kenny says.

"I still think it's wrong that I was killed," I say. "I can't lie about that, Kenny, and that—that's a hard feeling to have. And I still think that in a perfect world, there would be some kind of *proof*, some kind of *testimony*, to that fact, to the wrongness of it all. But it's not worth all this. It's not worth Cooper and Dom at each other's throats. It's not worth the two of *us* at each other's throats, fighting over a phone call. And your parents," I say, and I hope he hears the apology in my voice: "It's not worth what it would do to them."

"You seemed pretty comfortable with the collateral of what it would do to them before," Kenny says.

"I'm not sure I understood," I say. "What it looked like. How it would feel. To watch someone's life come apart in front of your eyes."

Kenny just keeps staring at me like he doesn't know what to say. And I want to give him the time and space he needs to process his emotions, but the fact of it is—*we're running out of time.*

On-screen, my mom is padding into the living room to collect Cooper's untouched glass of water, the documents and loose paper that have accumulated on the table, and then she returns to the kitchen.

We've always kept things relatively neat, but now it's so clean that it almost feels sterile, like a showroom that's been staged to suggest the possibility of life more than the actual reality of it. The countertops are finally free of the food and flowers that had accumulated after my death. My dad isn't there to cook, so the stovetop is clear and the sink empty. Cooper isn't there to track dirty footprints onto the floors and stain the surfaces with water rings, and I'm not there to leave my headphones lying around, which always drove my mother insane.

We're not going to buy you another pair when you lose them for the fifth time this year, she'd say, and I'd roll my eyes and respond, *You won't have to. I'll just steal Cooper's.*

I imagine my mom moving through the empty house, day after day, week after week, with no one to lecture and nothing even to clean, absorbing more and more of the white space until absence itself has settled into her bones, a sort of omnipresent loneliness.

This isn't a homecoming. This is barely a home.

"Let me help you," I say. "These are my parents, Kenny—I know how to get through to them."

"OK," Kenny says. "OK. She's getting out her laptop, so if there's a moment, it's probably now."

I get up off the couch and walk over to the desktop computer, punch random buttons on the monitor until the screen lights up. My mom is sitting at the kitchen table with her laptop in front of her, reviewing notes in such small font they're illegible to us. I click the Wi-Fi icon in the top right corner—more of a guess than anything else—but sure enough, there's our internet network: Davison-5G, full strength.

There are only two applications on my desktop. The first is Internet Explorer. The second is *Minesweeper.*

"*Minesweeper?*" I say, incredulous.

"It's actually pretty fun," Kenny says. "Don't knock it till you try it."

"Somehow this doesn't feel like quite the right time," I say, and open up Internet Explorer. When the browser loads, we're looking at a search engine named

Ask Jeeves, complete with an enormous illustration of a smiling butler.

My mom is still reading her notes.

"What should I do?" I say. "And who's Jeeves?"

"Search something," Kenny says.

I type HELLO, and then hit Enter.

On-screen, I watch as my mom gets a pop-up: an illustration of the word *hello* written in script, each letter a different color.

My mom looks confused, then closes the pop-up window.

"It's working," Kenny says. "OK, find a way to tell her who you are. Maybe you could use an alphanumeric code to communicate your birthday, or your social security number, or—"

"Sometimes I think you're too smart for your own good," I say. I type: IT'S CAROLINE.

Another pop-up. This time a photo of a woman I don't recognize, blond with curly hair. My mom frowns, no recognition in her eyes, and then closes that window, too.

"It's displaying the top search result for whatever you type in," Kenny says. "You have to search something she'll associate with you."

WHAT DO YOU WANT TO SAY? the room had asked, once upon a time.

"Is there—do you guys have a pet, or anything?" Kenny asks, even though he knows as well as I do by now that we don't. "Or maybe there's a place you two go together, or a song—"

A song. Instantly I can hear the notes: a trill of chimes; a timeless melody; Doris Day's voice, reaching out to her own lost child. My mother's favorite song. She used to say it was like if the Serenity Prayer were a song.

QUE SERA, SERA, I type.

Sure enough, an image of Doris Day pops up on my mom's computer. But she exes that out, too, to get back to her notes; doesn't even give it a moment's thought.

"I don't understand," I say. "It's literally the perfect clue. She used to make me listen to it every time I was angry about a game or a breakup or a fight with a friend. She should know. She should know it's me."

"Try something else," Kenny says.

"Why isn't she understanding?" I say, and the living room light starts flickering.

"Be careful, Caroline," Kenny says. "This is what I accidentally did at the restaurant that first time—when your emotional distress scatters through the mirror, it can short out the electronics on the other side."

I try something else: ROMAN HOLIDAY. A princess and a reporter sit shivering on the banks of the Tiber. Their time together drawing to a close. The only movie scene that ever made her cry. We had watched it together one Valentine's Day after a middle school breakup had left me devastated. Now I don't even remember what the boy's name was.

But all of this is just making my mother confused—perhaps even annoyed—rather than creating the wonder we had seen flood across Dom's face; the certainty set deep in Mrs. Zhou's.

"Roy," she calls out. "I think we need to reset the router."

"But that was our *movie*," I say. "How could she just—"

And I don't even care what message the scene sends her. I don't care how she interprets it or what she thinks it means. I just want her to know that it's me. I just want her to recognize that I'm here, that I'm with her, that I need her to be with me, too—

"Caroline," Kenny says. He puts one arm around my shoulders, which have started to shake with the effort of holding back tears. "It's OK. You tried. I appreciate it. I'm sure my parents would appreciate it, too, if they knew."

And I was so caught up in my own devastation I'd forgotten what all of this was for in the first place. I'd forgotten about the accident; I'd forgotten about the hearing; I'd forgotten about Kenny's parents, who were surely awake in their own home at this very moment, devastation settling just as hot and desperate in their own chests.

KENNY ZHOU WINTERTON HIGH SCHOOL, I type.

This time, when the pop-up appears, my mom simply presses the power button on her laptop. Her screen goes dark, and she presses the backs of her hands to her eyes in exhaustion.

I don't think she even recognized Kenny.

A note flutters to the ground.

TICKET #39,842,430, it says. CONDUIT 3 OF 3: CLOSED.

"No," I moan.

"It's not a big deal, Caroline," Kenny says. "She probably wouldn't have changed her mind, anyway."

But I wanted her to understand. I wanted her to hear me. I wanted her to know *him*.

"*No*," I say, and even as the desktop computer is dissolving in front of me: "There has to be something else. There has to be another way." I look up at the ceiling, suddenly furious. "You're literally a *sentient room*—this room is *chock-full of miracles*—you can't possibly tell me that you can't pull *one more miracle out of your invisible a—*"

And then the video tracks out of the living room, through the house and up the stairs, and then down the hall and through the second door on the left and then we're in—

My bedroom. We're in my bedroom.

I haven't seen it since getting here, and God, it takes the breath out of me. It's like traveling back in time; it's like traveling back *to* time, back to the version of my life that had rhythm, that had routine.

I used to wake up at 6:45 every morning. I used to shower and do my makeup while listening to whatever dumb rap album Dom was trying to foist upon me that week. I used to drive to school thinking about the homework I needed to do during free period and the awful drills Coach Navarro was going to put us through at practice that day. I used to spend every Thursday evening at Dom's house, learning how to cook a new dish, except we'd been stuck on Polish foldovers for the past month because I could never get the dough right.

I had a whole life there, in that time, in that universe, and as it reasserts itself in my mind I find that there's so much of it I've forgotten. What was the album I had been listening to the week of March 12? Had I worked on my history essay or my math homework in study hall that day?

I remember we had made blini before the foldovers, and ratatouille before the blini, but everything before that is a blur; an indistinct mélange of alliums and spices and loose flour.

My dad stands in the middle of the room, looking lost. Like this isn't a place he's been a thousand times before. That he himself decorated. He pulls on a corner of the comforter with trembling hands, smooths out the wrinkles. He kneels in front of my bedside table and uses his shirt sleeve to clear the dust off the lamp, off my journal, which I had been too busy to write in for several weeks. Then he kneels in front of the dresser and sifts through my jewelry stand—collecting a handful of earrings in one hand, a set of bangles I haven't worn since middle school in the other. Everything looks smaller in his palm than I remember it being—but maybe that's just perspective, a trick of the light, a trick of memory.

Then he stands.

"I miss you," he says, abruptly. And then:

"Caroline, it's your father. And I—I really miss you."

A ragged breath. He puts the bangles back on the jewelry stand.

"I'm trying to do the right thing for you, kiddo," he continues. "I'm trying to be the person you knew me as, the person you were proud to call your dad. But it turns out that it's harder than I thought it would be to remember who that person was."

And it's hard even for *me* to remember who that person was: a version of my father fully present in the moment, his eyes unclouded by grief, his voice smooth with easy happiness. It's hard to remember who any of my family members were—my mother, consumed by PTA bake sales and tiny, tiny sandwiches instead of by prison sentences and Breathalyzer results; Cooper, keeping time by playoff games instead of court dates.

I used to be able to picture them so clearly—the sound, the color, all the small details that comprised their joy. But those memories are harder now to recall than ever—desaturated with distance and displaced by newer, darker images. My father, flinching away from my mother. The raw knuckles of Cooper's left hand. Dom's bruised ribs.

And what of everyone else? I think of Iris, kneeling on the floor of Kenny's parents' house, her face contorted as if their grief was her own, or walking away from Jianyu's, knowing their grief was no longer his. I think of Kenny, saying my name like it's the name of a stranger, holding the portal to our home world hostage.

Kenny hadn't always been those things. Once, Kenny had been a cartoon green dinosaur in a game of *Mario Kart*. Kenny had been the uninhibited glee of a physics textbook; Kenny had been the quiet peace of a familiar meal. That's the version of Kenny I want to remember. The version that I want *all of them* to remember.

My dad walks over to the closet, one uneven step after another, and then pulls the door open. The closet is a mess, like it always is—it's the one part of the bedroom my mom doesn't regularly look at, and so it's the part of the bedroom where all the clutter gets thrown: old clothes, random art supplies, piles of notebooks. In the very back of the closet are dozens and dozens of paintings—pieces I never framed and projects I never finished.

The first one is a self-portrait. Half a self-portrait, actually, because after I couldn't get my chin right, I gave up and wrote the whole thing off.

My dad crawls to it, pushing aside a stack of ACT preparation books and the bottom of my dress from the sophomore year homecoming dance, whose layers and layers of tulle have swallowed up half the floor.

He traces my eyebrows, my eyelashes, the tops of my cheeks, my botched chin, which is too narrow at the point and not quite symmetrical. After a few seconds, tears begin to splatter onto the painting, banding into small domes and skimming the surface of the canvas in tiny rivulets, and then, after my dad has traced every line of my face, every contour of paint, he lets the portrait fall forward so he can look at the next one.

The next one is a still life of the fruit basket in my kitchen. It's dated December 12, two years ago. I had been on some insane fad diet, which my dad had patiently indulged: Half the basket is filled with grapefruits.

Behind the still life is a sketch of water lilies; behind the water lilies is a painting of the softball field. Then comes a set of abstract paintings, which I'd assumed would be easier than realism until I realized that the only thing harder than painting something that looked like something else was painting something that looked like nothing. And behind those—

My stomach bottoms out. It's like I've just hit the ground after a hard dive, and I've got the ball in my glove but my diaphragm is seizing, in shock from the force of the impact, unable to take in new air.

"Oh my God," I say, clutching Kenny's hand, making his whole arm shake.

"What?" Kenny says. He looks at me, concerned. "Are you OK? Are you having a panic attack? Remember to breathe, Caroline, remember—"

"That's my painting," I say.

Kenny blinks at me.

"Well, yes," he says. "They're all your paintings. And they're very good?" he adds, uncertainly. "I'm not much for art, but—"

"I wanted him to know," I say. "I wanted him—"

"You wanted him to know what?" Kenny says, baffled, and then, when it becomes apparent that I've exhausted my ability to form coherent sentences, he turns to the video for answers. There, my father is looking at a painting of a boy he's never met, but whose face he almost certainly knows.

The boy is sitting in a library. In his hand are a pair of chopsticks. In front of him is a plate of dumplings.

The library is small, and cluttered, and the dumplings are half gone. But there's something settled and proud in the boy's expression. Like he's presiding over a kingdom in miniature.

There's something bittersweet, too. Like he knows that the kingdom before him is only a facsimile of the one that once existed, and that now only exists in his memory.

Kenny does a double take. He looks from me to the screen, from me to the screen.

"But that's—that's me," Kenny says. "When I was—"

I nod. Barely a movement.

"I didn't even know you were working on it," Kenny says. And then the screen turns off.

"I wanted him to know you," I say.

"Reverse translocation of affect nonneutral objects," Kenny says, a little breathless himself. "But that must have taken an incredible amount of energy, Caroline. Those paintings would have been like letters—remember what the room said?"

Of course I don't remember what the room said, I want to say. But I don't even have to say it, because Kenny takes one look at my face and follows that up with:

"Never mind. The room said 'Letters are comprised of thoughts and feelings and subjective experiences, requiring a translocation of the socioemotional contexts in which they were formed by the sender, and in which they will be read by the receiver.' Letters have *affect*—they're not simply physical objects like a fancy couch or a random television booth. And paintings—I mean, it depends on the painting, I suppose, but I can't imagine those have less affect than letters. What were you feeling? What did it feel like?"

Every single thing Kenny has just said has gone over my head. All I can think of is my dad, kneeling on the floor of my bedroom closet, looking at the portraits of me and Kenny as if each one contained a few last breaths. Breaths that had remained hidden, secret, unspent, safe. Breaths that might harbor some measure of life.

"It felt like a miracle," I say.

48 | the event horizon

In the driveway, Iris wraps Cooper in a hug.

"Thank you," she says. "Thank you for trying."

Cooper shakes his head, wordless. He motions toward the car. "Let's go somewhere," he says, his voice hoarse, and then: "Can one of you guys drive?"

The three of them climb back into the car—Iris in the driver's seat, Cooper in shotgun, Dom in the back. They pull out of the driveway, and the motion-activated lights switch off behind them, leaving the house swathed in darkness once more.

We follow the car to Wisteria Park, the route an echo of Cooper's trip to Dom's house months ago. When they arrive, we pan down so that we're looking through the windshield again, to the front seats where Iris is behind the wheel, and Cooper is crying again.

Iris parks, then switches off the car headlights. Our video dims and goes grainy. She leaves the engine running, though, and the key in the ignition, and then she looks at Cooper and says: "Do you want to go back?"

"What?" Cooper says.

"Do you want to go back?" Iris repeats. "Either of you," Iris adds, and then Dom appears, his head looking eerily disembodied as he leans forward in the dim light.

"If you wanted," Iris says, "you could drop me off at Hummingbird Junction, and you guys could go back to your mom's. You could tell her you've changed your mind again, Dom, and you still want to speak at the hearing tomorrow. And you—you could tell her that you've realized she's right. She's—she's your mom. I would understand."

And then it's silent, Iris's offer suspended in the air between them, heavy with consequence.

"I think," Cooper says. "I think this is the right thing to do. I just wish it didn't have to feel like this."

Iris looks at Dom.

"I want to be here," Dom says. "With you guys."

He stares out the windshield—looking, I know, at the empty parking lot before them, and the park that lies dark and quiet beyond that. But it feels like he's looking at us.

"And with her," Dom says, so quietly the video barely picks it up.

"Subtitles," Caroline says. The conversation is being carried out in English, of course, but I understand: She wants to see the words.

And with her.

"So now what?" Cooper asks.

Iris reaches across the center console and takes his hand in hers. The pads of her fingers are still stained with makeup, the bones of his still trembling from earlier in the night. The two look out through the windshield, where the sky is starting to turn the soft, bleached gray of pre-dawn; where the two ancient elm trees at the entrance of the park stretch toward each other, their branches shadowed and still; where their gazes converge with Dom's at some far-off vanishing point in the distance, some point that may well be in this very room.

"Now we wait," Iris says. She cuts the engine. Undoes her seat belt. And the three of them wait for the sun to come up over Wisteria Park.

Caroline refills her mug of tea, her fingers shaking so badly that some of the liquid sloshes over the edge of the mug as she brings it to her lips.

Evaporate, I think, and it does.

"Thanks," Caroline says.

"Thank *you,*" I say. "You didn't have to do that. Any of that. It was "

"Pointless," Caroline says. "We didn't get through to my mom. Who knows what my dad made of the portrait. And now we're out of conduits."

When I was alive, I had figured that miracles would be clean, obvious affairs—blinding flashes of light, thunder echoing down from the mountaintops, certainty emerging triumphant from the shadows of doubt. But our miracles had been much less revelation and much more like lab work—experiments thrown in the direction of a hypothesis, feelings extended in sound and in color in hopes of catalysis. They had been convoluted and messy and fraught with unintended consequences. Quite often, they hadn't even been deliberate.

"I just wish we could see them," Caroline says. She chucks a softball at the darkened television screen in frustration, then vanishes it before it can shatter the glass. "I wish we could *know.*"

Then there's a whole flutter of error codes I don't even bother to read. We've never been able to control the mirror—not in that way, at least. We won't know what Caroline's father has decided until the morning.

But Caroline had sent the portrait.

It's striking, to me—the capacity of human beings to change, to grow, to heal. Caroline had been so furious at the revelation of my suicide, and even her dawning horror as we watched Cooper and Dom fight had seemed more about the impropriety of violence between two loved ones than about the conflicting opinions that had led to the violence in the first place. And yet—after all her fury, despite all the flashbacks, in the wake of all her inherited righteousness—Caroline had sent the portrait.

All these miracles. What was one more?

CAROLINE

50 | but I need to let go

"For what it's worth," Kenny says, "I think I understand her more now. Your mother, I mean. She clearly loves you both very—"

"Please," I say. "Don't. Not when we've just betrayed her like that."

"I'm sorry, Caroline," Kenny says, even though we both know that the forgiveness I'm searching for is forgiveness that isn't his right to grant.

"If it makes you feel any better," he says, "I know how you feel," and the sentiment—which is neither reassuring nor consoling—is at least morbid enough to make me laugh.

The last time I had been in my room alone, after learning how Dom's father had died, I had felt this odd flatness, this ambivalence. Kenny and I had been at a stalemate. There had been nothing left to rage against, and I had temporarily exhausted my supply of tears. I had called the feeling blankness at the time, because against the Richter scale tumult of our time in the room—the constant roar of anger and sorrow and fierce, fierce love—it had barely seemed a feeling at all. But I wonder now if it had been something else—something so small and quiet that I had registered it as a nonemotion rather than for what it really was.

I picture that feeling now less as a desert plain and

more as the long, flat bed of a garden trench, left behind, quiet and soft-soiled, as all those louder emotions eroded away into the dirt, into the compost from which new feelings of peace and forgiveness might one day grow. Was that healing? Would that one day be happiness?

"Kenny," I say.

"What? Is it starting?" he says, and whirls around to check the television screen even though there's been no static at all.

"What? No, it's—it's not about that."

I hesitate. I'd been waiting for the right moment to bring this up. But I don't think there's going to be a better moment than this.

"It's about how you died."

Kenny's expression shutters completely. "I don't want to talk about that, Caroline," he says. "I don't—"

"I'm sorry," I say, abruptly, and Kenny cuts off.

"I shouldn't have called you selfish," I say. "That was awful. I'm sorry."

"That's all right," Kenny says, warily. "I probably shouldn't have said some of the things I said either. Like about you treating Dom like a house. I know you really loved him."

"I loved Dom," I say. "But you were right. Dom spent so much time telling me about how sad and angry he used to feel all the time, and I thought the right thing to do was to convince him that those feelings were wrong, because I didn't want him to feel sad and angry. But maybe I should have spent more time just—just trying to understand. Just listening."

I think of Dom, his father, all those heart-wrenching conversations, vague allusions that I never picked up on, signs that I wasn't looking hard enough to see.

When he had given me that radio, three days into the new year, beating himself up over the fact that he hadn't managed to fix it in time for Christmas, he had said: "I just never want you to not know how much you mean to me. I could never live with that, Caroline, if you didn't know." And I had said, "Oh, Dom," and kissed him, because how typical of him to make something so wonderful and happy so utterly *morose*, and of course I knew how much I meant to him. He'd just spend a month fixing a radio he got out of a junkyard, for God's sake, just so he could make a joke about how much I loved oldies.

Kenny softens, a little, and then we lapse into silence, and I'm thinking about how much richness there was in life; how complex the webs of love and pride and joy and loyalty that wove us together, and that sometimes tore us apart. The room can give us furniture and coffee and music; the room can keep us ageless and immaculate, but it can't give us that richness. It can't give us life. And then, before I know it, I've gotten all teary again, and Kenny, for all that he looks sympathetic and understanding, also kind of looks like he wants to escape.

"OK," I say, sniffling a little bit. "I'm done. I know you hate talking about this kind of thing."

"I don't hate talking about this kind of thing," Kenny says. "I just—"

He pauses. "No, you're right. I hate talking about this kind of thing. I think that's the only reason why Jianyu and I stayed friends for so long. It was easier to drift forever in uncertainty than to have a definite conversation about where we stood."

"Physics only from here on out," I say.

"Right," Kenny says. "But, thanks, Caroline, for saying all that. It means a lot to me that you'd think about—tell me that—find a way—"

He flails around a bit, looking increasingly like he wishes he'd never started the thought in the first place.

"Physics only from here on out," I repeat, firmly.

All in all, it's a peaceful few hours up in the room. Kenny tells me some more about physics, and about time, and I resume work on the *Winterton, Evening Hours* portrait series, which is finally nearing completion.

And then, just as Kenny is halfway through an explanation of how much emotional energy is required to execute different types of IDEAs, the television turns on. And it's game day.

KENNY

51 | the sentencing hearing

The first thing I notice is my mother is wearing a new outfit. A simple gray blouse with a black blazer over it. No handcuffs.

I wonder if they ended up having to dip into my college fund to buy it. The thought makes the sight wrenching. It's wrenching enough as it is.

The second thing I notice is that Iris, Cooper, Dom, and Dom's mother are all sitting together. The hearing is closed to the public, so they're easy to find, clustered in the back of the courtroom, centered between the aisles like they didn't want to split up.

It's hard to believe that six months ago, Iris and Cooper didn't know each other. Iris and Dom didn't know each other either; Dom and Cooper were barely friends; Dom and his mother were barely speaking. It's hard to believe that six months ago, *Caroline* and I didn't even know each other, and now we're all here, having raced across time and space to a drab little room in the Winterton Courthouse.

The second thing I notice is Caroline's parents, seated together at the front of the room, dressed to the nines. Her father in a suit and tie. Her mother in a pretty blue dress.

"I bought that with her," Caroline whispers. "Mother's Day three years ago. We had a shopping date and then went to the spa together."

A beat. "She really does love me," Caroline says.

"At this time we will have our two victim impact statements," the judge says.

"The first victim will be publicly identified," another man says. Their lawyer, maybe. Kriminsky. "His name is Mr. Roy Davison. Mr. Davison, please come to the podium."

Then there's a little buzz of feedback—the microphone turning on—and everyone snaps to attention, watching as Caroline's father makes his way to the front of the room.

"Thank you, Judge Dvoretz," he says. "I'll be brief. If there's anything the past few months have taught me, it's that days like today should be spent outside, enjoying the sunshine, with the people we love."

He pauses, and it's dead silent in the courtroom. Our own room is filled only with the sound of Caroline's breathing, which is far too steady to be natural.

"I want to tell you a little bit about my daughter," Mr. Davison says. "Her name was Caroline Davison. I believe you, like most others in this town, knew her.

"Caroline was as much a part of Winterton as Winterton was part of her. She was in the town's streets, which she'd take to every night for her evening run. She was in our Christmas festivals and our town fairs, both of which she often helped organize. She was at the baseball stadium—as a sister, a friend, a teammate, and a player—always the first to hug a loved one after a victory, and equally quick to shake a rival's hand after a defeat. That was the kind of person Caroline was: gracious and humble, win or lose, a genuine smile on her face either way.

"I had the privilege of being on the receiving end of a few of Caroline's smiles over the years, although—

and you might know what I'm talking about here, as a father yourself—thirteen through seventeen was tough, I gotta say."

My dad smiles.

So does the judge.

"But when it happened—when she smiled at you—it made you feel lucky to be in the same room as her. It made you feel lucky to live in the world with someone who could experience life with such joy, and who, for some reason, had chosen to share that joy with you."

I sneak a look at Caroline, and her face is ablaze with adoration. Once, what feels like a very long time ago, Caroline had been embarrassed to talk about being in love with Dom. She had flushed halfway down to her collarbones; she had reached, almost instinctively, for the nearest pillow, and buried her face in it. But how could he not have known? How could anyone Caroline loved not have known? She wore her affection so easily, so wholeheartedly, so transparently: It would be like staring into the sun and mistaking the consequent blindness for a lack of light.

"In preparation for this hearing," Mr. Davison continues, "Amy and I struggled to find a way to express the magnitude of our loss. How could we capture the anguish of each final memory—her last smile, our last hug, the last day—which is rivaled only by the equal but opposite fear that we might forget? How could we capture the phantom pain of lost birthdays, graduations, anniversaries? And what of the community's loss? What of everyone else in Winterton who won't ever again hear Caroline's tireless encouragement, or feel her warmth, or see her artwork?

How could we possibly quantify those things? What recompense could possibly set it right?"

He pauses. Scattered sniffling throughout the courtroom. Dom's tough-guy façade melting in a pool of tears and snot.

I've sort of come to like Dom over the past couple of months. Then again, I suppose it would be difficult not to like the version of Dom I've experienced, which is a collage mostly assembled through the rose-colored glasses of his girlfriend's yearning.

"Eventually I came to the realization that perhaps Caroline would not have wanted us to talk about loss at all, and certainly not of recompense. Perhaps she would have wanted us to move forward rather than to litigate the past. To uplift our peers for their virtues rather than to condemn them for their mistakes. We were all lucky, here in Winterton, that we had Caroline to extend to us those acts of grace, even in our worst moments. And I think she would have wanted the same for the defendant who stands before us today."

Next to me, Caroline says, "That's exactly what Dom—" her voice so hoarse it's barely audible, and I say, "Caroline, he isn't—" and then both of us fall silent, this time not even daring to breathe, as her father finishes his statement.

"It is my request today, on behalf of—"

He falters, ever so slightly.

"It is my request today, on behalf of our family, that the defendant receive a probationary sentence in lieu of jail time."

I think I've stopped breathing. I think I might die all over again.

"My mom," Caroline says. And it doesn't take much more than a glance over in Caroline's mom's direction to see that her father has gone way, way off-script.

"I would like to make one last note, if you'll indulge me."

Caroline's father pauses. For the first time since the hearing started—perhaps for the first time ever—Caroline's father looks at my parents. My mother is crying freely. But my father is dry-eyed. He does his best to return Mr. Davison's gaze with poise; to be strong for the both of them.

One final lingering moment of unexpected connection between our two worlds.

"There is no loss like the loss of a child. There is no guilt like the guilt of thinking of all the ways I could have prevented her death. There is no regret like the regret of knowing I let her go to school that morning without telling her one last time that I loved her.

"But Amy and I are not the only parents who have suffered that loss, that guilt, that regret over the past few months. I would like to take a moment to extend my sincerest condolences to Mrs. Yining Ye and Mr. Jun Zhou, who lost their son late last year, and to the community as a whole, which lost a bright, talented, beloved young man. I hope you'll join me in a moment of silence for Kenny Zhou."

Thirty seconds, perhaps a minute, perhaps more tick by. Some far-off infinitessitude of space-time.

"Thank you for your statement," the judge says.

Mr. Davison nods and steps off the podium.

CAROLINE

52 | thirteen through seventeen was tough for me, too

There is the sentence itself: a year of probation, a suspended license, a five-thousand-dollar fine.

There is Kenny, wrapping me in a hug that mirrors the ones being exchanged on-screen: Iris and Cooper, Dom and his mother, Kenny's parents.

Mostly, though, there are my parents. My mom, who is so stunned after the sentence is announced that she simply walks out of the room, without a word to Kriminsky or my father. There is my dad, who leaves separately, taking longer and longer strides, moving faster and faster, as if he can leave his grief at the hearing if he just gets far enough away.

He pushes through the insignia'd double doors of the courthouse and into the blinding sunlight of the parking lot.

And then he stops short.

There's nowhere else to go. There's not a home to return to.

My dad sits down on the cement curb stop at the front of an empty parking spot, wiping his eyes, paying no mind to the other people around him. I'm not sure if any of them are paying attention to him either; I might be the only one who sees what comes next.

My dad slips his wedding ring off and slides it into his pocket.

I bury my face in Kenny's shoulder. When I pull back, his eyes are wet, too.

KENNY

53 | the future

Later—after the television has shut off, after Caroline and I have spent what feels like hours sitting on the couch crying, delirious with shock and relief—Caroline turns to me and asks:

"There's just one thing I can't figure out. If time is a fixed dimension, and everything that just happened had actually . . . already happened—then what was the point of doing all of that? The mission was always going to succeed, right?"

It's something I've been thinking about, too. Back in the winter, when the block universe was nothing more than a concept I'd encountered in passing in a textbook, things had already felt pretty pointless. Now, Caroline and I have been confronted with actual evidence that every decision either one of us has ever made may very well have been stitched into the fabric of the universe from the start, which makes it bizarre how much *less* pointless everything feels.

It's something about Iris, illuminated by the unsteady light of four wax candles, throwing herself at the mercy of an unknown God. Something about my mother, pulling an old photograph out of her purse as incense smoke curls into the air, defying science and logic and my father's good sense to chase down a connection that was not only unproven, but *unprovable*. It might even be something about Caroline's mother, standing single-minded in purpose and principle even when she was standing alone.

In life I would have found all of it foolish—embarrassing, even, how everyone was so willing to prostrate themselves before unknowable forces to chase after uncertain outcomes. But now I wonder if it's not about the outcome; if it's never been about the outcome, not *really*—not for Iris or my mother or Caroline's mother. I wonder if it's about the prostration—the release of it, the liberation. You could never control the outcome. Nobody could. You just bowed your head and hoped that you stood for something on your way there.

"The thing about the block universe is," I say, "the success or failure of the mission—that wasn't really within our control. Either the universe was one in which it succeeded, or the universe was one in which it failed."

"Then why—" Caroline starts, but I already know what she's going to say. And I already have an answer.

"Either the universe was one in which it succeeded, or the universe was one in which it failed," I repeat. "But I wanted to be in a universe in which I tried. In which I was always destined to try."

"Well, I wanted to try, too," Caroline says. "Not because I wanted the universe to be *this* or *that*. I wanted to try because it was the right thing to do."

That makes me smile, because doesn't she see the irony? But stripping Caroline of her free will feels like a conversation better saved for another day, so instead I just say: "Well then, that's the point. You have a system of morality that compelled you to act in a certain way. Just because that feeling of being compelled was preordained doesn't mean it was any less real."

"Questions of ontology are difficult to answer," Caroline says, modestly.

"Where did you—" I start, as her straight face dissolves into a laugh.

"You're not the only one who reads, you know," she says.

"Where was this attitude when I was going through five-hundred-page physics textbooks by myself?"

"You *wanted* those textbooks to yourself, don't lie," Caroline says, and then I start laughing, too, because maybe I did. I turn toward the library, wondering if I could summon some light reading about the philosophy of physics, except—

The library is gone. There's no desk anymore. No chair, no whiteboard, no bookshelf.

Then I turn back around and do a second double take, because the bedrooms are gone, too. And even as I scramble up and off the couch in alarm, even as principles and properties start flying through my head, arranging themselves into hypotheses and experiments, objects around us continue to disappear, the room emptying before our eyes. Pillows, blankets, rugs—all gone without explanation.

"What's going on?" Caroline says. The laughter has died on her face, replaced with fear.

A note flutters down from the ceiling and lands on my shoulder. I open it, and read:

TICKET #39,842,430: CLOSED.

"But that's not—we're not *done*," Caroline says. "Sure, we've helped Kenny's parents, but what about my parents? We've got to keep them from getting divorced, and I have to convince Dom to go to college, and what if Cooper decides—"

Another note.

I MUST APOLOGIZE, it says. Now the plants disappear in two waves: first the small succulents and bonsais, then the larger floor plants in their big clay pots. THE TWO OF YOU HAVE USED THE MIRROR WELL. I ASSURE YOU THAT NOT EVERYONE IS SO FORTUNATE. BUT NOW THE TICKET IS CLOSED, AND THE MIRROR WILL SOON EXPIRE.

"But that's not *fair!*" Caroline says. "There's so much that we haven't figured out, there's so much that hasn't happened yet—"

She cuts off as the coffee table in front of us vanishes, sending two mugs careening toward the floor. Then they, too, disappear, popping out of existence while still in midfall.

I spin in a slow circle. The walls are colorless again, the floor cold and bare beneath my feet. All the things that gave the room character—all the parts of *our* character that *we* gave to the room—the old records and physics textbooks, the coffee mugs and the video game console—all of it just gone.

MY DEAR, the room says. THERE ISN'T ANYTHING THAT HASN'T HAPPENED YET. EVERYTHING HAPPENS AT THE SAME TIME, WHICH IS TO SAY, IN NO TIME AT ALL.

"But then," Caroline says. "But then—"

"But then we should be able to see it," I say, finishing her thought. "It's already out there, isn't it? It's already happening? We should be able to see it—to see *them*—my parents and her parents and everyone else, just so we know that they're OK, that they're happy—"

One more note flutters down from the ceiling, settling softly in Caroline's hair. She unfolds it, her fingers shaking, and reads:

THERE ISN'T A FORCE IN THE WORLD THAT CAN GIVE YOU THAT KIND OF CERTAINTY—THAT KIND OF UNCOMPLICATED CLOSURE. BUT I SUPPOSE—WHAT I CAN GIVE YOU—

And then the television buzzes to life, and I'm looking at my parents for what I know will be the very last time.

They're inside my house. My mom is sitting at the kitchen table—still frail, but brighter behind the eyes—and my dad is standing over the stove, ladling freshly steamed dumplings onto a platter.

The doorbell rings.

"That'll be them," my dad says, as my mom calls: "It's unlocked!"

There's the sound of the front door opening, people tramping down the hallway, and then the house seems to shrink in size as Iris, Dom, and Mrs. Novak pile into the kitchen, all wrapped in several layers of winter clothing. Iris crouches down to the ground, and Princess Moonlight comes shooting out of her hands, a quick blur of jet-black fur.

"So cute!" my mom says, and goes after the cat.

"She wanted to say goodbye," Iris says.

Goodbye? I think, baffled—but then I look past the kitchen, into the living room behind it, and see stacks and stacks of cardboard boxes.

They're moving.

After all the interventions, the fundraiser, the hearing—after all that, my parents are leaving Winterton. The town where they first landed two decades ago, jet-lagged from a sixteen-hour plane flight, awash in a language neither of them spoke, knowing no one, and started over. The town where they had me. The town where they built everything.

"Iris bring cat," Mrs. Novak says. "Cute, but not edible. I bring golabki—only way I can get Domek to eat vegetables."

"I eat vegetables," Dom says. "I love a good potato."

Mrs. Novak sets a large dish wrapped in tinfoil onto the counter and then walks over to my dad. "Oh!" she exclaims. "But these are just Chinese pierogi!"

"Chinese pierogi," my dad repeats. "I do not know the pierogi, but surely they are just Polish jiaozi."

Dom drops into a seat at the kitchen table, next to Iris. "How are you doing?" he says.

"I'm going to miss them," Iris replies, and Dom says, "Me, too," and pulls her into a sideways hug. "But the sun will be good for them, I think. Sure could use some more of that around here."

Then my mom comes back into the kitchen, having finally captured Princess Moonlight. "Hurry!" she says, while the cat wriggles furiously in an ongoing bid for freedom: "Take photo!"

Dom and Iris exchange fond, indulgent looks, and then they both pull out their phones. "Smile, Mrs. Ye," Iris says, even though my mom is always smiling when Princess Moonlight is around, and then—

And then that's it.

The screen goes dark.

CAROLINE

54 | the end

My mother is at a dinner party.

It's a sight so familiar that for a moment I think I'm watching something out of the past, rather than in the future. A couple dozen adults that I recognize—and a few I'm surprised to find that I don't—are gathered in the parlor room of Maddie's mother's house, where trays of hors d'oeuvres and hot food have been lined up against the back wall.

It must be after the dinner hour, because the guests have broken up into smaller groups—some standing by the windows, silhouetted against the indigo of twilight, and others by the bar, deep in conversation, swirling glasses of whiskey or gin while they talk.

Now and then, one of the kids will come into the room to pile some more food onto their plate. Then they'll leave again—headed back to the den, where all the younger kids are watching a movie, or the basement, where all the older kids are playing *Smash* or some dumb drinking game.

Maddie's mother and my mom are sitting by themselves on one of the couches by the fireplace, each with a drink in her hand.

"Paul and I have finally accepted the fact that it's rather serious between them," Mrs. Rhys is saying. "But, you know, it's not all bad. He's incredibly smart; Maddie tells us that he aced all his classes last semester and still had time to help her with her essays. And his parents are lovely—his father and I actually used to work together, years and years ago, at the hospital. Can you believe it? Anyway, here I go again, prattling on and on about Maddie. How's Cooper?"

"Cooper's doing well," my mom says. And I should be looking at her face—I should be memorizing every line, every detail, because this may be the last chance I get. But I can't take my eyes off her left hand—the one that's resting in her lap, the one that should be wearing a ring. "He's decided that he wants to study psychology now, which Roy and I have told him we're happy to support, as long as we can get a family discount when he starts taking patients."

I flinch, the darkness of the joke making my heart thud—but Mrs. Rhys just laughs, and my mom herself is smiling, pleased that the quip has landed.

"And Roy?" Mrs. Rhys asks.

"Roy . . ." my mom says, and pauses, her smile fading into a complicated expression. "Roy asked if we could do Christmas as a family this year—all together, for the first time since—well. You know. And part of me wants to, but—"

My mother sighs.

"I just don't know if I'm ready," she says.

Then the two look up, where one of the women I don't recognize has just walked up to them.

"So sorry to interrupt," she says. "But we've got to get going, Lucia, and I just wanted to say thank you again for hosting."

"Of course!" Mrs. Rhys says. She smiles with the effortless brightness of the perfect party host. "We're so glad you could make it. And I'm so glad I could finally meet that son of yours—so charming; you and Peter weren't exaggerating."

"If only he were half as charming with his own parents," the woman says, and then a young man who must be her son appears at her side, as if summoned, except that young man—

—is Jianyu. Looking a few years older, but—yes, that's definitely Jianyu: a dark red peacoat draped over his arm and a scarf draped over the coat.

"Dad went to go warm up the car," he says to his mom, and then he turns to Mrs. Rhys. "Thank you for hosting. It was lovely."

"It was our pleasure," Mrs. Rhys says. "I'm so glad you could finally make it to one of our dinners. Remind me again where you're going to school . . . ?"

"Georgetown," Jianyu says.

"Oh, that's a great school!" Mrs. Rhys says. "Maddie was never academic enough to get into a school like that—so focused on athletics, you know, and she just could never sit still for long enough to study—but our son, Luke, is a real brain. He's only a sophomore, but Paul and I always tell him it's never too early to start thinking about colleges. Especially these days, with everything so competitive . . ."

"Well, if he's ever curious about Georgetown, I'm happy to chat with him," Jianyu says. He shrugs his coat on, loops the scarf around his neck and ties it in a neat knot. "I can have my mom pass along my cell phone number."

"Oh, that'd be great!" Mrs. Rhys says, happily, and then the adults exchange one more round of goodbyes before Jianyu and his mother head out.

"It's so funny, isn't it?" my mom says. "How life just goes on. After Caroline died, I thought things would never go back to normal. Dinner parties, college planning, holidays. All of it seemed—offensive almost, like it'd be an insult to Caroline's memory. And then there was the divorce, the mess of it, the heartache. But now—everything's just gone on."

She smiles, but it's a funny smile, the corner of her mouth quirking downward instead of up—a little brittle, a little sad. But I had been brittle, too, hadn't I? I had been brittle, and then I had been resentful, and then despairing, and then flat, and out of the flatness had sprung something else, something soft and quiet and sweet.

I look at my mom's face—every line, every detail. She's not quite there yet, I don't think. But time is real for her, even if it's not real for us, even if it's not real for real, and these things always take time.

And then it's over, the screen dark and lifeless.

I look around. More of the room has disappeared: It's just the television screen now, and Kenny's smiley recliner, and my portrait series, the space around them so empty and white that it almost feels like they're on exhibition in a gallery.

And then they, too, vanish.

"No," I say. "No, I wasn't done with those, give them back, *those weren't yours to take—*"

And then I'm crying—shaking—hysterical. "Caroline," Kenny says. He pulls me into his arms. "Caroline. Breathe through it, I know you can do this. One, two, three . . ."

And he counts me through my breaths, one final time.

"Thank you," I say. The words jumbled by tears and snot. "I don't know what I would have done without you, all this time."

"Well, you'd—you'd still be alive, I suppose," Kenny says.

"Shut up," I say. I pull back so I can look at him, press through the sentences even though I can hear my voice growing shakier and shakier. "You know—Mrs. Macmillan always told us that in order to paint a scene, you need to understand the scene, and to understand the scene, you really need to *see* the scene. And I feel like, after all of this, after all this time, after everything we've been through, the person I've learned to see the clearest is—is you."

"Thank you," Kenny says. "Really—thank you." And then his eyes unfocus a little, and his expression goes worried.

"What?" I murmur.

"Caroline, I—I think we're being evicted."

I follow Kenny's gaze to the front of the room, where the television screen has always been but is no longer. Instead, there's a door.

It's dark blue. There's a brass knocker on it shaped like an eagle.

"I won't go," I say, a whole new wave of devastation hitting me, and this time, it *is* tinged with panic. "I won't go, I won't go, *I won't go*—"

"I don't think it's a good idea for us to stay," Kenny says, and even as he says the words, I can see that the room itself is starting to disappear—the walls going oddly translucent, the glass of the skylights blurring so it's hard to tell what's inside and what's not.

"I've already lost everyone once," I say, miserably. "I don't want to lose them again."

Kenny's chest hitches against mine, and he pulls me tighter against him.

"I don't want this to be the end," I say.

There's a loud, rumbling noise, like that of a distant train. When I look up, scanning for the source of the noise, I can barely see the ceiling anymore; and then when I look back down, the walls seem very, very far away.

"This isn't the end," Kenny says. He pulls himself out of my arms but takes my hand in his, and then we both turn to face the door, which has started to glow around the edges.

"How can you say that?" I say. "How can you be so sure?"

"Of course I'm not sure," Kenny says. He takes a few steps toward the door, and I follow, stumbling after him instinctively, without thought. "But I have faith."

Even Kenny is starting to look a little fuzzy now: His features, which have become more familiar to me than my own, are strangely indistinct. It's weird. I feel like I'm forgetting what I'm looking at as I'm looking at it; like with every passing moment I have to work a little bit harder to remember where I am, and how I got here, and where I'm going—

But there's that door. There's *only* that door—there's nothing else left.

"You're not scared at all?" I say.

"I'm not," he says. The boy next to me. I know him like a brother. His name— his name—

He pulls me another step forward, and then reaches out to touch the doorknob.

"Here—we can go through at the same time," he says. "On my count, OK? One, two, thr—"

epilogue

It's ten minutes before closing when the couple walks into the restaurant, the jingle of the bell on the front door barely audible over the roar of the storm outside.

He sent his cook home half an hour ago, when the snow started sticking, and ordinarily, he'd put on his best apologetic face and send the couple the same way—*Sorry, but the kitchen is closed; would you like some fortune cookies to go?* But then he sees that they're Chinese, and he reconsiders. The restaurant doesn't see a lot of Chinese customers in the winter, after the tourist traffic slows for the year, and sometimes it's nice just to speak the language, to feel the easy glide of his mother tongue.

He seats them. He used to cook all the time, back when the restaurant was basically a one-person operation, and he doesn't think they'll order anything overly complex, anyway. The man sinks into the booth, looking like he's just pleased to be out of the cold; the woman follows, sitting next to instead of across from him, the side of her body never leaving his.

"On the road?" he asks them.

"Headed to California," the man responds. "A friend of ours used to live there, recommended some neighborhoods that aren't too expensive. But the storm has set us back on our driving schedule, and now we have three more hours before we reach our hotel . . ."

The man sighs. The restaurant owner wonders what is bringing the couple across the country in such a rush, at this time of the year, no less. But such things aren't his business, so he just pulls his notepad out of his apron pocket and asks: "Are you ready to order?"

"Oh," the man says. "Please—whatever you have left over from today's business—whatever you can heat up from the fridge—that'll be fine."

It's an unorthodox request. The restaurant owner protests three times, twice because it's the minimum number of protests mandated by politeness, and the third out of genuine chagrin. This is his restaurant; he's not going to let guests eat leftover food.

But the man insists. "Please," he says. "It's not a matter of politeness. It's only a matter of time."

So the restaurant owner goes into the back, and looks in the fridge.

There's the eggplant Bing had made for lunch, even though lunch was the busiest time of the day and they never had time to eat. There's a large container full of spicy shredded potato, which had turned out so spicy it was only suitable for Asian customers. There's a large gallon bag of ugly dumplings—the ones where they got careless while rolling the wrappers, which inevitably led to lopsided, uneven folds; or where they got careless during the steaming, which inevitably led to clusters that were impossible to separate without tearing the skin.

The restaurant owner takes the eggplant out of the fridge, because it's the freshest, and heats it in a wok with some red peppers and day-old rice. It's unconventional, but soon the steam is rising up from the pan, rich and aromatic, and he knows the dish will be good, feels the warm pride that accompanies a meal well-made. *Perhaps I should spend more time in the kitchen,* he thinks. That is, after all, why he started the business in the first place.

He brings the eggplant out, and the man begins to eat with relish, the sauce climbing higher and higher up his chopsticks. It's a sight that's familiar to a part of him that's foreign. It's a sight that makes him feel suddenly homesick, as if the perpetual tug of his motherland has been awakened by the presence of another expatriate.

The woman eats more slowly. He wonders again what is waiting for the couple in California—or what they are leaving behind where they came from. But now they're both busy eating—mouths full, not even speaking to each other—so he stifles his curiosity once more.

The restaurant owner goes into the back again and takes some of the dumplings out of the fridge. He tries to pick out the ones that aren't too ugly and then fries them in a skillet with some cornstarch, flour, and vinegar. He brings those out in a to-go container with the lid on the side, just in case the couple is ready to resume their drive.

The man takes one look at the dumplings and an expression of indescribable nostalgia crosses his face. The restaurant owner knows the expression, because oftentimes it is the same expression he sees in the mirror after talking to his parents, who are growing old with no one to take care of them, or to his wife, who is beginning to wonder if she'll ever be able to join him here, on the other side of an ocean that feels larger now than ever.

The man picks one of the dumplings up with his chopsticks and starts talking to his wife in their regional dialect, which the restaurant owner can't understand. *Something from the south of the country*, he thinks, though of course there are so many dialects he can never be sure.

"Sorry," the restaurant owner says, feeling self conscious. "I can get you something else, too, we have some shredded potato—"

The man's gaze snaps to the restaurant owner, as if he is surprised he's still with them.

"Oh, no," the woman says, switching back to Mandarin. It's the first time that he's heard her speak, and her voice is steady. "Please—you've been too polite already, keeping the restaurant open for us when it's so late. Thank you."

"The eggplant was very flavorful," the man adds. "And the dumplings—the dumplings—" the man has to stop, his eyes welling with tears.

"Lao Zhou," his wife says. A term of endearment. She takes his hand into her own under the table and looks at him so tenderly the restaurant owner feels embarrassed, all of a sudden, like he's intruding on a private moment. He wants to call his wife. He wants to fly back home, across the Pacific and its dark, fathomless waters; he wants to climb up the cement steps of his family's apartment building; he wants to go back to the place and the time where he, too, had people who looked at him in that way.

"I was just telling my wife," the man says. "They remind me of our son."

Acknowledgments

I wrote this book in a series of very beautiful places and am endlessly grateful to those who shared their homes with me to make that possible.

Thanks to the Prestons—Bonnie, Roger, Gaz, and Lauren, the best wrangler anyone could ask for. I may never have picked this project back up after my LA lull were it not for the long afternoons I spent sitting at the table ledge, or on the front porch, of the old saloon. And to the rest of the Bedford crew—Natasha, who endures my wistfulness to this day; Julia, who introduced me to Shakey Graves; Helen, who told me to pray; and Cullen. Cullen, I miss you dearly.

Thanks to Doug and Shannon Weaver, who allowed me to sit in their beautiful log cabin living room at 5:30 every morning to watch the sun come up, listen to the song "Blood Bank" by Bon Iver on repeat, and write. Shannon, let us never speak of the spider incident ever again. And thank you to Emma, my partner in huckleberry picking, jam making, cabin chinking, and real sad-ass songs to road trip to.

Thanks to Jeff and JoAnn Michelsen for sharing the Bunkhouse with me—and the Bunkhouse library, where I often wrote while Patches the cat circled my feet, meowing for attention. Jeff, without your guided tour, I would still be wandering the Wave, dehydrated and confused, to this day. And thanks to Kylie, Chris, and Daniel for being the best desert hiking buddies I could ask for.

Thanks to Tori and Adina, who read the first draft of this novel in serial installments as I wrote it and who cheerleaded faithfully the entire way through. To Tori doubly over, for drawing the room's floor plans and thus fulfilling our middle school dreams (simpler days!). To Christina and Shinri, who read the early complete draft and shared their feedback and encouragement. To Diane Aronson, whose thorough line edit came with surprise personal notes and affirmations that helped push me over the final, rather grueling, revision. And finally, to my agent, Elana Roth Parker, and my editor, Maggie Lehrman, for shepherding the book through countless iterations and deadlines, none of which I met.

JENNIFER YU is the author of *Four Weeks, Five People*; and *Imagine Us Happy*. When not writing, you can find her weeping intermittently about the Boston Celtics, photos of the Earth from outer space, and the etymology of the word "disaster." She has lived in Kansas, Boston, and Los Angeles, though these days she is mostly living out of her 2018 Toyota Corolla LE as she hikes her way across the Mountain West.